LONDON LARGE

Bloody Liberties

Garry and Roy Robson

London Large: Bloody Liberties

ISBN 978-0-9934338-4-9 Paperback

ISBN 978-0-9934338-5-6 eBook-Kindle

Published by London Large Publishing

For more copies of this book, please email: info@londonlarge.com

Cover Designed by Spiffing Covers: http://spiffingcovers.com/

LONDON LARGE

Bloody Liberties

Prologue

1

April 2014

'They just want to meet you, guv. I've told them so much about you. They're intrigued, and they want to see who it is I'm spending all my time with, who gets me out of bed in the small hours to go look at yet another dead body in some seedy part of London.'

'They're not harbouring any wrong impressions, are they?' said H. 'It's a bit unusual Ames. I've never gone to meet the parents of anyone I've worked with in all my years on the force.'

Amisha laughed. 'No guv, they haven't got the wrong idea. They're just really concerned about me, about what I do. They want to know I'm in good hands, and you'll like them – they're very old-fashioned.'

H smiled. 'What will we have for dinner?'

'Just a mild chicken curry and some chapattis, which is a type of bread.'

H winced. He was one of the few Englishmen not yet seduced by the smell and flavour of the new national dish.

'You have told them I've never had a curry before? What if I don't like it?'

'Trust me guv, you'll love it. It goes very well with a few pints of cold lager. If you don't like it just fake it and don't forget to tell my mum she's a terrific cook.'

Amisha was gorgeous and full of life, no doubt about that, and if he was a younger man and if things were different – if he wasn't with Olivia, the great love of his life – he'd have had a pop at her by now. But he was her superior, her guvnor, and his job was to show her the ropes and try and turn her into a decent detective. Harry Hawkins knew

3

where the boundaries were; it had been his life's work to try and protect the ones that really mattered. H had become determined to teach Amisha everything he knew.

***

They'd been partners for six months. When she was first assigned to him he'd had real doubts; baby-sitting a scrawny little Indian girl on the toughest streets in Britain was not his idea of fun, and he'd tried to palm her off on one of the other murder squad detectives; but his boss, Chief Inspector Hilary Stone, had been adamant.

'Detective Inspector Hawkins,' she said, 'H, do this for me. The top brass thinks she has huge potential. She stands head and shoulders above all the other fast-track recruits in every test she's done.'

'Tests, tests! Don't talk to me about tests. How's she going to handle herself on the street? There's nothing of her – I've seen more fat on a chip. What'll she do when it comes on top and some eighteen-stone growler comes at her? I'm not a wet-nurse Hilary; if she's so clever put her behind a computer or something.'

'She's already done all that H, but she wants to get out on the street now. The high and mighty upstairs have agreed; she ticks all their boxes. She's the dream ticket, a brilliant female all-rounder with tons of potential. When they look at her they think all their Christmases have come at once.'

'But what…'

Hilary Stone knew H of old, and could see he was starting to work himself up into a lather; she pulled rank and shut him down.

'This is not a request, Detective Inspector Hawkins, it's an order. You will take her under your wing, you will show her the ropes while at the same time protecting her like the

4

Crown Jewels. This has come down to us from on high. Am I making myself clear?'

H believed in the chain of command – except when he didn't – and on this occasion, he did as he was commanded. In the early days Amisha had found it difficult to get on with her abrasive, coarse and do-whatever-it-takes superior, but she came to understand he was the kind of man you had to earn respect from. She kept her head down and got on with the job, and quickly began to prove her worth. She was hard working, sharp, used her analytical skills to make connections between things H had missed, and was highly proficient at gaining information from databases and online sources H didn't even know existed. They quickly proved to be a formidable partnership: the Met's homicide clear-up rate began to take a distinct turn for the better, and everyone who mattered was happy.

✳✳✳

H now sat in the car outside Amisha's parents' house close to Wembley stadium in north-west London, and prepared himself for the occasion. Steaming into a gang of armed thugs was one thing – but meeting the parents of his young, beautiful and still somewhat enigmatic partner was a whole new experience. He had no idea what the form was in an Indian house and felt the butterflies flap their wings in the pit of his stomach.

He took out the flask of scotch from his inside pocket and downed a quick swig of the golden nectar before jumping out of the car, walking directly to the front door and giving a confident rat-a-tat-tat with the knocker. Not so loud as to appear arrogant, not so soft as to appear timid. Just about right, he thought. He was clearing his throat, preparing himself for the introductions, when a stunningly beautiful woman in her mid-forties opened the door. She was dressed modestly, wearing a red *salwar kameez* which, in H's terms, was loose trousers and a long tunic, and a multi-coloured *dupatta*, which was a length of material arranged in two folds over the chest and thrown back around the shoulders. Minimal light makeup and large gold chandelier earrings added to her allure: she was beautiful, poised and exuded class – real class.

Fuck me, it must run in the family with this lot.

'Hello, I'm Harry. H to my friends.'

Amisha appeared at the door alongside the apparition who'd opened it. 'This is auntie Zaida,' she said. H's heart rate went up a notch or two as he shook the woman's hand, and he thought the night might not be so bad after all as the trio made their way into the front room.

Amisha introduced her mother, who wore similar attire to Zaida and was almost as beautiful. Older and more worn, to be sure, but no doubt an absolute cracker in her day. The old man was next up: Mr. Ratish Bhanushali gave a firm handshake and held H's stare for a few moments during the introductions, as the two men sized each other up. If there was one thing in this world H couldn't stand it was a man with a weak handshake who didn't look him in the eye.

'Delighted to meet you, Detective Inspector Hawkins – I trust you are taking good care of my daughter out there?'

H sensed the serious concern behind the semi-jocular tone. He had no problem being put on the spot and he'd always liked people who came straight to the point.

Seems like an alright geezer.

'Yeah, of course I am Mr B. Don't worry, I keep a close eye on her. She's doing great. She'll be doing my job soon if I'm not careful.'

2

Amisha, once again, had been right. The food was delicious. As well as the chicken curry, there was vegetable curry for Zaida and a plethora of side dishes that H helped himself to liberal portions of. One or two of the dishes made him sweat a little but the sweats were easily put to bed by the ice-cold Indian beer. H was soon three pints in, feeling merry and bright. Just the way he liked it.

Mr Bhanushali talked generally about his life, about his belief in marriage, and family, and strong values. H found himself agreeing with most of what Ratish had to say, though he felt the regret he always did when the subject of solid parenting came up. They talked about each other's backgrounds – H's life on the street and his background growing up in south-east London, and the Bhanushali's life in India and experience in England.

H heard how Amisha's grandfather had seen active service in the British Army during the Second World War and how Mr Bhanushali himself had been a police officer for a time back in Gujarat. The family had been attracted by adverts promising the chance of a better life if they moved to the UK, an opportunity they'd embraced with relish and made the most of by setting up their own successful clothing businesses.

This was all good stuff as far as it went; but H, mesmerised by Zaida, was hungry for more information and enquired further about her background. She was fifteen years older than Amisha, and her branch of the family – she was the daughter of Amisha's paternal uncle – had arrived in Britain ten years before Amisha's parents. A bright pupil at primary school, she'd won a scholarship to Bluedown, one of the most prestigious independent girl's schools in the country. After that, a first-class Honours degree in Political Science at Cambridge.

Well that accounts for the class, the poise and the cut-glass accent then.

Zaida continued to give H the outline version of the story of selected aspects of her life since leaving university; he saw the sadness in her eyes when she told him her husband had been killed in a car crash several years earlier, and changed the subject.

'So what do you do for a living then,' he asked with a smile, 'I mean with your first class Honours degree in Political Science and all that?'

'Well, I'm just a Civil Service girl,' said Zaida, 'nothing very exciting or glamorous I'm afraid. I joined straight after Cambridge, so I suppose I'll be a lifer.'

'Well, there are worse things to be,' said H. 'What branch are you in…what do you deal with?'

'Oh, a bit of this and a bit of that. You know, they shift us around a fair bit these days,' she said with a bored sigh.

H sensed he was losing her interest; he changed tack, and poured on the charm for Amisha's mother:

'This is absolutely delicious Mrs B. Your family are lucky to have such a fantastic cook in the house.' The compliment went down a treat and there were smiles and laughter all round, followed by tales of Mrs Bhanushali's legendary culinary prowess.

H was now on firm ground and the company was getting on famously, until the topic turned to religious beliefs. Zaida explained that she, like many Hindus, was a vegetarian for religious reasons, because it minimised the hurt one caused to other life forms, especially cows.

'Have you ever thought of becoming a vegetarian, Detective Inspector?' she asked.

For H, cows performed two functions in life: to make milk for his tea and provide a decent Sunday roast.

'Er, no,' he said. He understood that there may be a health case for being a vegetarian, if meat upset the stomach or something, but he thought the moral case was misguided. He'd never come across the religious case this directly before – it was too far outside his own experience for him to even have an opinion on it, so all he could muster was '…well, if that's your religion who am I to argue?' Like most Englishmen H had been taught to avoid religion and politics in general social discourse, so he moved the conversation on again, to a subject in which he had real expertise.

'Those bottles Mr B, over there in the cabinet – what's in them?'

Lined up together were several small dark bottles that, thought H, must contain an exotic alcoholic beverage of some sort.

'Ah, Detective Inspector, I see you have a keen eye. That is Royal Mawalin.'

'Which is what?'

H got a quick history lesson about the many small kingdoms that existed in India before independence, all with their own recipes for liqueurs based on various herbs, and that this one was made with dates and a few other spices H had never heard of. There were still thousands of small distilleries that made local liqueurs – although the drinks rarely got out of their states, let alone the country. Mr Bhanushali, however, had his sources, and they ensured a regular supply of his favourite tipple. H was intrigued.

'Would you care for a drop, Detective Inspector?'

H had always thought of Indians as mostly teetotal. He seldom saw them in the pubs he drank in, unless they were Sikhs. If he'd ever checked the World Health Organisation stats he would have found out that Indians in India are rather fond of a snifter, and binge just about as frequently as the Russians. He was feeling very comfortable, and didn't need to be asked twice. The social inhibitions he'd felt at the beginning of the night had long gone.

'Are buses red?' he said with a grin.

Mr Bhanushali had never heard the expression but, given the tone of H's reply, and knowing that buses in London were indeed red, took it as a yes. He fetched a bottle and two glasses while the ladies cleared the dishes. Mr Bhanushali poured the drinks and gave what was his best English toast.

'Down the hatch, Detective Inspector.'

H gulped his back in one. The drink had a bitter flavour that evaporated cleanly from the tongue.

'Hmm…not bad. Not bad at all. A man could get the flavour for this.'

The men were onto their third shot when the women appeared with ice-cream for the desert. H gulped it back and then sank another beer.

'Can we assume you're not driving home tonight guv?' said Amisha, when it was time to leave.

'Absolutely. Call me a cab please Ames. I'll pick the car up tomorrow.'

'No problem guv, I'll give you a lift.'

'No, no need for that. It's a long way.'

'I insist.'

H had enjoyed his evening greatly; he said his goodbyes, and held his hug with Zaida just a little longer than he should have, but he was too far gone to care. He clambered into the car clutching the bottle of Royal Mawalin his host had gifted him, and which he'd accepted with relish.

'Well, that went well,' said Amisha in the car, 'I think they really like you.'

H laughed. 'You make it sound like I had to pass the boyfriend test. Tell me about Zaida, what's her story? Why's she so shy about what she does for a living?'

'Well I could tell you guv… but then I'd have to kill you. Family joke. It's all a bit hush-hush – she's never really even told me what she does.'

H stretched out as best he could in the passenger seat and drifted into a state of blissful semi-consciousness as the London night sped by. The streets were quiet, the trip from north-west to south-east London went by without a hitch, and Amisha pulled the car up outside H's house in Eltham in what seemed like no time.

'Thanks for a great night Ames, absolutely blinding, see you tomorrow.'

He gave her a kiss on the cheek – first time he's done that, thought Amisha – forced himself out of the car and went into his house. He downed a couple of shots of the Indian Royal by way of a nightcap and slid up to bed. Olivia was already asleep. She hadn't been best pleased that he was going to Amisha's parents and decided not to go along herself, although she was invited. She wasn't exactly over the moon with the idea that her H had a beautiful, accomplished young woman as his partner.

H gave her a kiss on the forehead and settled down to his slumbers. It was not Olivia or Amisha or blood-spattered crime scenes that occupied his subconscious mind while he slept, but dreams of Zaida – the most beautiful and enigmatic woman he'd ever met.

PART ONE

1

Andrew felt Cressida grip his hand tightly as they emerged from the station and joined the surging crowd on Olympic Way. The stadium, lit up ahead of them like a gigantic spaceship preparing for take-off, filled her with awe. Andrew could sense it. She'd never been to a football match before, and this was a big one: England v. Russia, in a game that would decide which of them would go to the next European Championships.

Through the turnstiles and in: up, up, up, they went, to their seats in the highest part of the stadium. The brightly-lit pitch looked very small, like a postage stamp, and a long way down; but it would be the centrepiece, Andrew knew, of what was going to be an evening of great drama, and he was glad to have such a commanding view of the event.

The national anthems were sung. Andrew was surprised to see that there were so many away fans all around the stadium, in among their hosts. They were not all corralled into a single section in the usual manner. He put this down to the sheer numbers of eastern Europeans living in London these days, to the new situation: Russians, and Poles, and Croatians, and Slovakians, and Czechs, and many more, all embedded within the everyday life of the city. Eastern Europe was 'here' and the distinction, at a game like this, between 'home' and 'away' supporters, had broken down. They were all Londoners now.

The first half, despite all the noise and clamour around the stadium, was dull and scrappy, with neither team able to put anything much together. This was effectively a knockout game; there was too much at stake and the players were afraid of making mistakes. Andrew groaned and, with five minutes to go before half-time, assured Cressida that it wasn't always this boring, and went to get the beers.

He was gone for twenty minutes, and finally managed to trek his way back to his seat just as the second-half was about to begin. He surveyed the scene...and noticed something, something he couldn't quite put his finger on. The atmosphere had changed, and it seemed to him that the air was pregnant with something. He sat, and watched for a minute, and waited, and scanned the crowd, and then he realized what it was - and he put a name to what he was feeling: menace.

His skin began to crawl, his senses becoming alert to a kind of invisible current running around the stadium. He knew something was coming, and exactly ten minutes into the second-half it came. The ground erupted. Everywhere there was a new kind of movement, with violent confrontations bursting out simultaneously across his field of vision, like bubbles finally bursting to the surface of a pot of slowly boiling water.

People were being attacked; everywhere he looked, people were being attacked, with gaps in the crowd opening as people tried to get clear of scores of minor conflagrations, from the most expensive seats to the cheapest. People were being wrestled, battered to the ground, chased up and down stairs, and in a couple of places being heaved over barriers into the sections below them.

Panic set in. In Andrew's section, as in most of the others, people abandoned their seats and headed for the exits en masse, while chaos reigned as songs and chants swirled around the stadium. Andrew knew better than to join the panicking herd - little good ever came of that - and remained in his seat with his arm wrapped tightly around Cressida's shoulder, assuring her that everything was going to be OK. But he'd spent enough time around his guvnor, Detective

Inspector Amisha Bhanushali, to know that when your gut - your copper's instinct - told you something was wrong you should listen to it. And his gut was speaking to him now, loud and clear; something bad, something very bad, was beginning to happen.

2

Andrew gave it five minutes more – thankfully there was nothing going off in their immediate vicinity – and led them down to the stadium's surveillance and operations room, which he knew was built to provide a perfect overview of the stadium and the area surrounding it. He showed his warrant card, gained entrance, took up a position with Cressida at the window and watched what was happening, referring occasionally to the bank of screens along the wall behind them.

He could hardly believe what he was seeing. Olympic Way was like a CGI battle scene in a Hollywood sword-and-sorcery epic. A huge, panicking crowd was heaving, scattering, moving back and forth in waves; in places there was hand-to-hand fighting, as some English fans pushed back, but more often non-combatants were being attacked and forced to run, and then chased down and beaten.

The aggressors were ruthless, armed with bats, staves and knives and were, Andrew thought, extremely well organized. They appeared to be working in small squads of 8-10 men, and to a plan. They seemed intent not on forcing a clear confrontation with those England fans who might form up and fight them as a group, but on terrorizing individuals.

The noise – screams, threats, pleas – was incredible, and blood-curdling, and hit Andrew deep inside, in his chest and belly, to the point that he found it hard to process and understand clearly what was happening. He drew on his training, calmed himself, ordered his thoughts and began making notes.

The police were having a hard time bringing the situation under control. The away fans were operating in scores of small groups, refusing to cohere into the kind of mass that the police knew how to contain and neutralize. They were also leaving so many casualties on the ground that much of the police effort was concentrated on retrieving the wounded from the teeth of the melee and escorting them to safety.

Andrew focused in again, away from the big picture towards details; he saw a group of men force a teenager in an England shirt to the ground and jump repeatedly on his head when he was down; he saw an elderly man struck full in the face with a baseball bat, and wondered how the assailant had managed to bring a bat into a high-security environment. He saw a burly, middle-aged man trying to fight back but heaved with main force over the edge of a walkway onto the concrete fifteen feet below. He saw all this and more, and his mind began to reel.

What is this? Why is it happening? What point is being made?

And then things quietened, suddenly. As quickly as they had flared up inside the stadium, things died down. The noise and movement abated, and the thugs seemed all at once to melt away. He could still see the odd scuffle here and there, but the air was now more a hubbub of conversational voices and groans than a maelstrom of fury and panic. Able to think better now, Andrew began to see clearly the pattern of events; the whole thing had been planned and synchronized, and expertly conducted.

It was a quarter to eleven; there was still time to catch the tube. There would be no cabs anyway. He checked that Cressida was ready and they moved down, through empty stairways and concourses and into the scene of the carnage. They moved slowly up towards the tube station through what looked like the aftermath of a natural disaster. A fleet of ambulances had arrived, and more were on their way judging by the sirens filling the night air. In the blue light they cast, Andrew saw dozens of people still down, some of them looking to be in a very bad way, others being helped to their feet by friends, passers-by, paramedics and police officers. The occasional shout and scuffle could still be heard in the distance, but overall an eerie calm prevailed.

As they approached the station through a small crowd of stragglers they heard a commotion behind them; a group of men, jogging in formation at a good pace but not shouting or chanting. Andrew realized, too late, that they were exiting the scene and simply knocking people over like ninepins as they went. As he turned to face them he felt Cressida's hand slip from his. She hit the ground face-first – no fuss, no drama, no sound.

He picked her up and carried her onto the station concourse. Her face was a mess, her nose especially, but she was conscious and felt around to the back of her head with her hand. It came back covered in blood, from the wound made by whatever had been used to knock her down. He moved back out of the station again, to one of the waiting ambulances. A paramedic was just closing its back doors.

'Room for one more?' asked Andrew.

' 'fraid not mate,' said the paramedic 'you'll have to try one of the others. We've got a dead one here.'

3

Detective Inspector Amisha Bhanushali was awoken just before midnight by a call from Chief Superintendent Hilary Stone and brought up to speed on the events at Wembley; confusion reigned, and nobody yet had any clear idea of what had happened, but at least two people had been killed.

'Get up there Amisha, quick as you can, you and Andrew. It'll be an absolute dog's dinner at the moment; we need to calm things down and let whoever's in charge there understand that the Murder Squad is running this one. I'll find out who's running the show on the ground and troubleshoot for you, but I want you and the others to start setting it up as a murder scene, OK?'

'Yes ma'am, on my way.'

Fifteen minutes later Amisha was in her car, rushing out of her Greenwich flat and headed for north-west London. Andrew wasn't answering his phone, which wasn't like him. She listened to the radio for a bit – just long enough to satisfy herself that, like her, they had no clue what had happened – and set her phone up on hands-free so she could check Twitter and Periscope as she drove. Nothing on show there except blurry scenes of people running, shouting, fighting. All sorts of wildly varying accounts of what had happened.

She phoned Andrew again; this time he picked up.

'Where the hell have you been?' she said, beginning to work her way up onto her high-horse.

'At the hospital…me and Cressida were at the game – I told you we were going, remember? She's injured, someone cracked her round the back of the head with a brick or something and she fell on her face.'

'My God, how is she?'

'Well she's in one piece, but her face is in a bad way. Broken nose. I suppose we should be thankful for small mercies. People have been killed.'

'You saw the whole thing?'

'Yes, all of it.'

'And?'

'Well, it was absolute chaos, most violent thing I've ever seen. Looked to me like a planned attack.'

'On whose part?'

'The Russians. They were going nuts, just attacking everything that moved. You remember that game in Marseille not long ago, when they attacked English fans?'

'Yes.'

'Well, it was like that, but on a much bigger scale.'

'Yes, but why, what's behind it all?' asked Amisha, exasperated.

'I suppose they just wanted to show the English who's boss, like they did in Marseille. This, however, was way over the top, and it seemed so organised. Mind you, that's not what the media and the Russians are saying. I've just been on Twitter. Some Russian minister is claiming their people were attacked by English nationalists – payback for Marseilles, that sort of thing. The BBC, CNN, ITV, Russia Today, they've all running the interview.'

'And what are our guys saying?'

'The usual…too soon to say, review of evidence, full investigation, etc., etc., etc. Nothing, basically.'

'Terrific. Damage wise, Hilary Stone tells me two dead.'

'I'll be surprised if it doesn't turn out to be more. Hundreds injured, dozens seriously. The whole thing was off the charts. Before I left I was in the control room. I told the Wembley people to start collating the CCTV coverage.'

'Alright then, good. Keep me posted on Cressida, and let me know when you'll be able to join us – I'm going to need analytics, Andrew. I'm nearly there now, I need to sort the Keystone Kops out before they ruin the crime scenes.'

4

It had already been a long night, and there was still a long way to go. It was 2.30am when Hilary and Amisha called the team to order. The Commissioner had held an impromptu press conference in an effort to reassure the public that the police had control of London's streets; privately he'd been hauled over the coals by the Home Secretary and was spitting blood, and had given the order that a full Murder Squad investigation team was to be put in place before he had to deal with yet another early morning press conference.

The chaos at the Met was reminiscent of the chaos at Wembley earlier that evening – headless chickens running around the Yard in search of understanding. Detectives had been called off other investigations and were pouring in en masse. Scores of them were milling around the major incident room with smartphones and tablets in hand looking at the images and the news clips and listening to the talking heads on the TV streams. The rumour mill was working overtime but eyeing the truth, at this stage, was like trying to see your real reflection in a hall of distorted mirrors at a fairground.

'Bring this rabble to order for me Ames, now please!'

Hilary Stone didn't usually get directly involved during the setup of a murder team but this was not a usual event and the Assistant Commissioner, Jane McPherson, had called her directly, and told her to ensure her best people were on the case.

'Guys, everyone. All phones off and in pockets please. Eyes front. This meeting is now in progress.'

Amisha had a slight and diminutive frame but her keen intelligence and relentless dedication meant she was one of the most formidable Inspectors at the Yard; her words carried authority. The assembly did as told, and calm enveloped the room. Hilary noted Amisha's command presence with satisfaction, feeling vindicated in her decision to push for her promotion to Inspector – one of the youngest in the history of the Met. She spoke to the room:

'OK people, I've just come off the phone with the Assistant Commissioner. She informs me that the Commissioner is on his way to Downing Street to discuss tonight's events with the Prime Minister in person. I don't need to tell you any more than that about the pressure we're going to be under on this one.'

A rustle of anticipation, laced with anxiety, moved across the room.

'For us assembled here this is, first and foremost, a murder investigation. Detective Inspector Bhanushali has just returned from the scene and will update you on her findings and progress. We need to move swiftly but efficiently. There is so much going on it will be easy to let standards slip, in pursuit of a quick result. Resist that temptation – attention to the detail of what happened will be vital in carrying this investigation forward. We'll be working round the clock. There will be no budgetary restrictions. Get them rolling, DI Bhanushali.'

Amisha took her cue and began the debrief.

'So far we have four murders on our hands. The whole area around Wembley stadium has been sealed off. People fled quickly amid all the chaos so we have only secured the names and addresses of a small handful of eye witnesses.'

Amisha moved crisply through the essential information: the CCTV coverage of Wembley stadium and surrounding areas was nearly ready for analysis. Luckily, if that was the right word, DS Glass had been at the game and was on his way back from hospital – his girlfriend had been injured in the violence but was not in a serious condition.

'We know the identity of two of the victims, but the other two had no identification on them.'

She then broke the group into sub-teams: one for coordinating and reviewing the CCTV data and small working teams to attend each of the individual murder scenes – all of which she would co-ordinate personally.

'Emergency call numbers?' said Inspector James Marsh, a pan-faced and ageing Inspector of the old school, who was looking forward to his retirement after almost forty years of solid, if not spectacular, service.

'Yes. We are setting up one phone number for concerned family and friends to call. That should help us find out who the other victims are, and another number for witnesses to call.'

Amisha continued her master class in delegation. Detectives were appointed to organize and co-ordinate the calls that would shortly start flooding in. There would be information overload on this, so others were appointed to make sure the systems were in place to log and verify all calls and witness statements.

***

Andrew arrived, looking dishevelled and worn. There was a perfunctory exchange of niceties and an update on Cressida before Amisha got down to brass tacks.

'Tell us all what happened Andrew. Just what you saw. Facts. No speculation,' she said. This had been drilled into her, remorselessly, by Harry 'H' Hawkins, her one-time boss: 'Get the facts first, Ames. Always get the facts before you try and understand the why.'

Andrew gave his update and Amisha moved him onto his thoughts on reasons, causes, motives.

'Well,' said Andrew, 'before it all went off I sensed the atmosphere change. Like people were getting ready for something. There was an energy in the air, a menace. I could just feel it.'

'So you don't think it was a spontaneous eruption? Like one fight sets of another and feeds through to the primal instincts of a crowd, and everyone gets on board?'

'Absolutely not,' insisted Andrew. 'This was premeditated, well-planned for a specific time.'

Amisha moved the conversation on to potential suspects.

'Assuming DS Glass is right, who could have coordinated such an attack? What do we know about Russian football hooligans? Are they organised enough to pull something like this off?'

The question was aimed at Sergeant Bob Peters, who'd been drafted into the investigation due to his expertise on the identities and movements of football hooligans across Europe.

He began speculating and pontificating. Amisha quickly realised he was as clueless as the rest of them, and was about to stop him in his tracks when a young Detective Constable burst through the door. He was extremely agitated, and staring directly at Hilary Stone.

'Ma'am, scores of calls are coming into the emergency room. Riots breaking out all over east London, centred around Tower Hamlets.'

5

The assembled sleuths reached for their smartphones as one, and switched them on; #whitechapelriots was already trending above #wembleyriots on Twitter. Hilary was holding her head in her hands as the room again descended into chaos. What on earth was going on? She took a deep breath, gathered herself and prepared for the coming storm.

'Detectives! You have been assigned jobs to do. Go and do them; give them your undivided attention. Now! Amisha, with me.'

The two women retired to the sanctuary of Hilary's office – Amisha already absorbed in the glow of her screen. Twitter. Periscope. Facebook. Instagram. YouTube. The images and the theories were flooding in. Hilary tried to make a call to the Assistant Commissioner but couldn't get through. Amisha concentrated on her social media. After a few minutes of concerted screen engagement, she was ready to update her superior.

'You're not going to like this much, ma'am.'

'Just give me the worst, DI Bhanushali. Before the Assistant Commissioner calls back.'

Amisha looked up. The stress lines on the face of her boss always deepened at times of extreme pressure. She hadn't seen her this bad since the mass murders at Bedgebury Forest the previous year, a case that had been solved, in an unorthodox manner, by the now retired Inspector Hawkins.

'There are pictures posted all over the internet, of an armed uniformed policeman gunning down Imam Usama Sethi, one of the local community leaders. The shooting appears to be completely unwarranted. It seems to have set

28

off riots all over the borough, and they appear to be spreading across London.'

'What? What? What?'

Hilary could not process this one. She didn't speak for several moments.

'Ma'am, you alright?'

'Ames, what are we going to do? We'll need every copper in London on the streets. The dust hasn't even settled on the Wembley thing yet. What on God's green earth are we going to do?'

'It seems to have happened just over an hour ago, as far as I can make out. With the speed it's moving at it's completely colonised social media. I'm looking for a picture of the officer's face,' she continued, 'someone here should know him – we need to get him into custody immediately, get the community leaders together, then a press conference expressing utter condemnation and a plea for calm.'

Amisha continued to look hard for the best image.

'Guv, something's not right about this. In the best video I can find, the first one that was posted, the image of the police uniform is crystal clear. There are shots zooming in and out showing close-ups of the uniform, but there's no clear image of the face. It's grainy, indistinct. Like the video has been doctored to hide the shooter's identity before being put out. I can't be sure, but I do know a lot about this kind of thing…something's not right.'

'You mean it's a put-up job? 'Who? What? Why? I…'

The sickening feeling in her stomach was crushing the Chief Inspector. She was lost for words.

'Maybe a right-wing nut job, something like that?' speculated Amisha. 'And ma'am, it's getting worse.'

'Worse? Worse! How can it get any worse?'

'The riots, ma'am. There's livestreams and footage coming in of riots starting beyond London. This is going national.'

The same DC that brought the last glad tidings knocked and burst into Hilary's office again.

'What now?!'

'Ma'am, it's the Assistant Commissioner, on the phone.'

'Put her through.'

The desk phone rang. Hilary picked up.

'Ma'am.'

'Have you heard…?'

'Yes.'

'We've lost control. I've just had the Commissioner calling from Downing Street and I'm on my way to the Yard. I'll be with you in ten. The Commissioner has asked me to get all our senior people together now and provide him with an update and advice in an hour; the Prime Minister has called for a meeting of COBRA, the national crisis response committee, for 3.30am.'

'What ma'am,' said Hilary, 'the full thing – ministers, civil servants, intelligence services, army?'

'Correct,' said the Deputy Commissioner, 'and us. Us taking the lead, to start with, with a chance the army will be called in to take control of the streets, the way things are shaping up. Get your head round this fast Hilary, no flapping. All our heads are on the block for this one.'

'Fucking hell,' said Hilary, as she put down the phone.

6

Jack Bell finished polishing his sleek black shoes and started to dress for his evening's entertainment. In the background, the TV was informing the populace about riots in progress in Wembley, but there was no way he was going to let that get in the way of a good night out. Anyway, London was a world away. The Geordies of Newcastle knew how to have a laugh and, as far as they were concerned, lived in the most handsome city in Britain.

A few ponces throwing bottles at the Old Bill down south barely registered as he prepared himself for a night on the town in Britain's party capital. He pulled his stomach in and held his breath as he pulled up the zip on his new Levi's and then buttoned up his slim-fit, non-iron black and white checked shirt, confident that if he held his stomach in the buttons wouldn't pop.

He put some styling gel on his hands and ran it through his jet-black hair, ensuring just the correct amount of spike, before double-checking he had removed all the visible hairs from his nostrils. He was in the habit of getting himself dressed to go out, prior to a quick snack, the purpose of which was to line his body, prepare it for the stunning volumes of beer that would soon be coming its way. He bowled downstairs, strolled into the kitchen and spoke to his mother.

'Mam, where's me scran? I'm clamming.'

His request for food was met with an indifferent look, but his mother had already baked some singin' hinnies, which he feasted on with relish. Jack's mother was a patient soul and had waited years for her son to find the right girl and settle down, but at the tender age of 31 Jack was still more into boozing with his mates in Newcastle city centre. He washed down his scones with a glass of milk before heading out.

'Mam, gannin the toon the meet ta git mortal.'

'OK pet.'

Having informed his mother he was going to town for a drink where he would then get smashed out of his head, Jack walked out of the modest three-bedroom terraced house into a freezing north-eastern night and headed for the Tyne Bridge, that symbol of Newcastle that sweeps majestically across the river of the same name. He strolled confidently towards the city centre, the buttons on his shirt straining under the pressure of his stomach, but holding firm nonetheless. He was heading for Georgian Grey Street in the heart of the city, and would soon be knocking back a decent pint of Newcastle Brown Ale and eyeing up the ladies – who, occasionally, he had some success with.

***

Amelia Grainger was twenty-five years old. An after-work session at the sunbed centre followed up with a liberal application of fake tan had given her a lively orange glow. She adjusted her mini skirt and tight-fitting top as she admired herself in the full-length bedroom mirror. This was traditional winter plumage for the Geordie lass – the lower the thermometer plunged the less they were expected to wear. She looked like she would be more at home on a beach in Tenerife in the middle of summer. Possibly, some had speculated, it was a survival-of-the-fittest strategy designed to prevent weaklings – locally known as southerners – from settling in the area.

Amelia was looking forward to her night out, to getting wrecked with her mates at one of her favourite night-spots – and to the rest of the evening's entertainment around the back of the nightclub. Maybe even a kebab on the way home, if she was lucky. Her excitement rose as a bevy of scantily clad beauties knocked at her door. It wasn't long before Amelia and her mates were heading into town towards Georgian Grey Street. There was a long queue at the club but the lasses were in no mood to wait outside. They sweet-talked the bouncer and were let straight in.

Inside it was already rocking. A few quick shots of vodka and the lasses were strutting their stuff on the dancefloor. At the bar Jack Bell was downing the pints with his mates. He was supping his fourth Newcastle Brown when he became captivated by the peculiar orange glow emanating from the dancefloor, and watched with admiration as Amelia downed a glass of vodka whilst simultaneously twirling her body and twerking for all she was worth. Nice, he thought to himself, as he supped up his ale and wiped his mouth.

Jack tapped on the shoulder of one of his mates and pointed to the orange one strutting her stuff on the dancefloor.

'Reight gud sooart,' he said.

'Yer, a reight bobby dazzle,' agreed the friend.

The night wore on. Six pints in, and with the mercury rising, the boys made their way onto the dancefloor and started to perform movements akin to dancing. An onlooker would have been hard pressed to see any synchronization between their movements and the music playing on the sound system.

The atmosphere, at this stage of the evening, was jovial but filled with an underlying sexual energy. Jack and Amelia danced round each other for several minutes – smiling, laughing, singing along to the tunes. Then Jack moved in with his favourite chat up line.

'Fancy gan outside wi me?'

Amelia was considering the proposition and was in the mood to accept. Jack would never know if his charm was going to work its usual magic as at the very same moment Amelia opened her mouth the bomb went off; the bomb that had been planted days before beneath the floorboards of the club. Jack and Amelia and all their mates were scattered into tiny parts across Georgian Grey Street on a freezing Newcastle evening.

7

When news arrived of a second bomb, this time in Birmingham, Hilary Stone was practically in pieces herself. This was all way above her paygrade. She sat alone in her office, disconsolately sipping ginseng tea; waiting, quietly, while all hell broke loose around her, for news on COBRA's position and strategy.

Assistant Commissioner McPherson called her again at 4.30am. A State of Emergency was being declared; all leave for both army and police personnel had been cancelled. The decision to deploy the army had been made, to London and Birmingham first and thereafter to other hotspots as they emerged; and emerging they were, like dominoes going down in a line, as night turned to day and a watery dawn light crept through the window of Hilary's office – extensive rioting, hand-to-hand fighting and widespread arson in Bristol, Glasgow, Swansea, Manchester, Nottingham, Leeds and across London; bombs, one after another, in all these places and more.

It was down to the army to take control of the streets; the police response and investigation into the bombings would be led by local forces; but shortly, McPherson conjectured, the Yard would be asked to co-ordinate a national police response. For now, Hilary was told, her own priority was to concentrate on getting the response to the Wembley murders right. The calls were pouring in and Amisha was doing a sterling job, multitasking like an android, coordinating the detectives and forensics staff at the Wembley murder scenes and reviewing various social media livestreams on assorted devices, as if she had two brains. Everything, it seemed, was being streamed, and there was way too much to follow in real time. Hilary joined her in her office. It was Pandemonium, everywhere.

'What are you seeing Amisha?... Big picture. Any thoughts?'

'Well…look at this ma'am,' said Amisha, turning the laptop towards Hilary so that she could see the screen. 'Another bomb's just gone off in the midlands, Wolverhampton. These are livestreams, on Facebook and Periscope.'

Hilary nodded.

'The thing is…these images are not all being put out by random passers-by. A lot of the pages seem to have been pre-built with the express intention of showing the bombings and riots as they happen. Someone with a smartphone was on the spot here, in Wolverhampton, before the bomb went off, as if waiting for it to happen.'

'Jesus wept,' said Hilary.

And then Watford. Watford shopping centre. When was it going to stop? Britain had seen nothing like this since the Blitz. Cities and towns in flames. Hilary could bear the scenes no more. She had to be professional, her and Amisha to concentrate on the Wembley investigation, as she'd been told. Own and focus on her own thing, like a soldier ant who knows it has only a single role to play and lets nothing get in its way. She left Amisha's office and emerged back into the scene of bedlam that was the New Scotland Yard Murder Squad headquarters.

'Watford!?' she heard someone shout, 'what is the fucking point of putting a bomb in Watford?'

8

At seven in the morning Amisha sent half her team home to get some rest; she'd need them fully alert and switched-on for what was coming and she was well-versed in the science of sleep. Andrew made it to bed at eight; he lay motionless for a time, working to put the events of the previous evening into some kind of shape, to recall and organize the timeline in his head. This was not as easy as it should have been – what with hospitals and debriefs and emergency meetings, and Hilary Stone and Amisha Bhanushali breathing down his neck.

He was due back on duty at midday but couldn't stop himself from switching on the TV. Cities in flames across the country; rioting and hand-to-hand fighting, bombs and gunfire; the police and emergency services overwhelmed; COBRA deciding to put the army on the streets.

He switched off and threw the remote across the room – no one on the TV had any idea what was going on. All was speculation, dodgy 'facts', unsubstantiated theories. He picked up his tablet and scanned a few of his usual YouTube channels, Tweeters and blogs, hoping to find useful information or serious analysis, and landed on the site of the infamous blogger Joey Jupiter.

YOU WERE WARNED, PEOPLE

Well, boys, girls, and others, here we are. The time for joking, for sarcasm and irony, is over. The situation I have been predicting these last eight years or so is now upon us. We are on the verge of collapse as a society, and it gives me no pleasure to say I told you so. It was all so predictable.

Over the years I have discussed on this blog a wide range of issues, and have been even-handedly scathing and contemptuous across the board, as I neither trust nor respect any of the fools and manipulators who infest our public life. Look back and you will see that three themes in particular have attracted my ire: an elite and governing class so incompetent that it seems at times to be almost purposely dysfunctional; a disintegrating and increasingly chaotic society that has not, by any stretch of the imagination, been adequately policed; and the rapid decline of the 'legacy' media, which has been spinning the 'news' and misinforming the public for so long that it has now lost all authority.

So how are we to understand the events of the recent hours – the killings, the bombings, the rioting, the murderous police officers, the near-collapse of law and order? Who is to blame? What are we looking at? A massive right-wing conspiracy? An Islamist revolution? Both? A random series of unfortunate events? Are we facing the collapse of the social order, whether accidental or planned, and who at the moment can even say?

Not me. I have no answers. The media has no answers. The 'experts' have no answers. The police have no answers. The 'authorities' in general have no answers – and even if they did I suspect they wouldn't let us have them. Look to yourselves, people, and to the people you know you can trust. The wolf is at the door; we will not be able to send him away without good information and analysis and the old Dunkirk spirit. We must know our enemy before we can defeat him. Find out what is going on. Figure out who you can trust. Don't be fooled again.

9

Little Harry Hawkins, an eighteen-month old ball of fizzing energy and mischief, woke up at 6.30am, leapt out of bed, wobbled at some speed along the corridor between his room and his parents' and launched himself up onto their bed at full steam. He wormed his way in between them and turned his attention to his dad, pulling his eyelids up and shouting into his ear. 'Pop! Pop! Breakfast, breakfast.'

The big man groaned. 'Alright boy, alright. Give me five minutes.'

'Breakfast, breakfast, monster box. I hungry. Pop!'

'Alright boy, I'm coming. Go and put your slippers on.'

Harry 'H' Hawkins, formerly of New Scotland Yard and scourge of the criminal classes, smoothly eased his ageing bulk out of bed. He was spending a bit of time in the gym these days, working to stay in shape, and he was doing well. Even so, he reflected, as he yawned and stretched, early morning starts with a sprog was a young man's game.

But his spirits were high, as they usually were these days, and he padded cheerfully along to his son's room, scooped him up with one arm, slung him, belly down, over his shoulder and carried him downstairs to the kitchen.

Boy into high chair. Bowl from dresser. Cereal flakes from the box with the monster on. Kettle on. Cup of tea. Sit down.

The morning routine was invariable, and that was the way H liked it. Since his 'retirement' from the Metropolitan Police he had slowly but surely become de-stressed and semi-domesticated and was now comfortable in his own skin, as a father, a husband, a potterer-about and park dweller. Swings, roundabouts, football with the boy; that was his thing now.

He had never known such ease of life. The pension he received upon his forced retirement at fifty-eight was generous – designed as it was to shut him up and get him out of the way – but he'd set himself up as a Private Investigator anyway, to give him something to do if he felt the need for it.

Harry Hawkins, the uncompromising, scotch-gargling and occasionally wayward London legend, had become a homebody. He was loving every minute of it, the house in Eltham now a refuge from the chaos of the world and the ordeals of police work and criminal chaos. Olivia had taken his phone away – he did not put up much resistance – and was doing all she could to protect him from the world, and himself. She loved him more than ever, and wanted him to survive long enough to be a father to Little Harry.

'Alright boy, you sit there in your chair and I'll make your mum's coffee. I need to get this done sharpish, I've got to drive up to Birmingham this morning.'

He moved around the kitchen, singing as he went – he was teaching the boy songs he thought he should know: 'And did those feet, in ancient times, walk upon England's mountains green, and…'

The kettle boiled. H made the tea, poured Olivia a cup, scooped the boy up out of his high chair and over his shoulder with his free hand and headed upstairs.

10

Olivia was awake, propped up in bed with her tablet on her lap, looking aghast at the screen.

'What is it babes, you look like you've seen a ghost; what the fuck's happened?'

'Language, H.'

'Alright, sorry Liv. What's happened?'

'I don't know where to start…all hell's broken loose.'

'What? Where?'

'See for yourself, there's a sort of infographic thing here.'

H swapped the boy for the tablet, got into bed beside Olivia, and stared quietly at the screen for half a minute, grinding his teeth before saying anything.

'Jesus, they throw me off the firm and a year later the whole country is going to bits. What did I tell you? No one's got a grip on things.'

This was intended as a joke, but Olivia wasn't laughing; and neither, inside, was H.

'Find out what's happening, H. Christ, what sort of a world have we brought this boy into?'

H took Olivia's phone and went back down into the kitchen; he was going to have to get in touch with his old muckers at the Yard. But who? He couldn't phone Amisha – he couldn't remember the last time they spoke, and she wouldn't give him the time of day anyway. She still blamed him for the death of her boyfriend Graham, who had gone off radar with the big man to help him save his oldest boy, Ronnie, from the clutches of an international drug ring. It hadn't gone well – four dead, including Graham. She'd probably never forgive him.

He tried Hilary Stone: no joy. Voicemail. She must have her hands full.

He punched in Andrew Glass' number – he always knew what was going on, H recalled. The phone rang and rang, but never went to voicemail, so H assumed he just hadn't heard it – not like him – and hung on the line.

Andrew answered eventually, sounding confused: 'Hello, Mrs Hawkins? I…'

'No, it's me Andrew, H – how are you son?'

'Um, hard to say guv, just trying to deal with what's going on.'

'No need for the "guv" Andrew, I'm not your boss anymore. Just call me "H"'.

'OK H. I…'

'Have you got a minute for me Andrew?'

'Of course, H.'

'Good. Can you tell me, in a nutshell, what's going on and who the key players are? I've not been paying attention – I know you're busy, can you just give me the executive summary?'

Andrew took a breath deep, enough to be audible at H's end of the line, and started.

'OK, I think it's best if I give you a timeline of main events, insofar as we know what they are – it's a very fluid situation. Then I'll tell you what we know about who's involved, which is very little. I'll be honest with you H, things are happening too fast, new things are coming in all the time, we're having trouble figuring out what's going on. It's crisis management.'

'Alright son, let me have it,' said H, and he listened hard while Andrew laid it out: the chaos and the killings in Wembley; the apparent police execution of Usama Sethi in Tower Hamlets, and the continuing rioting and street fighting; the bomb blasts and their death tolls and the fighting in the cities; the reports of shots being fired in various locations. It was a picture of murderous violence and

43

chaos spreading in waves across the country, in some places sustained, in others popping up and dying down before anyone could really get a handle on it.

Andrew paused for breath.

'OK, got it,' said H. 'And what about the culprits…who do we think they might be?'

'Well the main problem is figuring out who's who – it's all claim and counter-claim, and our hands are too full to do any proper investigating. We're just putting out fires. The media are talking about a right-wing nationalist conspiracy, the Muslims, the Jews, the Russians – all the usual stuff. The Russians are claiming their people were targeted and killed at Wembley, but I was there H, the Russian fans were the aggressors.'

'Have any of them been picked up?'

'No.'

'Then we cannot be sure who they really are?'

'True.'

'Go on.'

'Well, others are talking about a full-on Islamist revolution, others about an international criminal conspiracy, others still are going on about bankers and murky hedge-fund globalists orchestrating everything to crash stocks to rock bottom. The conspiracy nuts of all stripes are having a field day. The main thing is this: there are people bombing and shooting at each other all over, and fighting hand-to-hand, and we're having a hard time figuring who's fighting who. I…'

'Alright Andrew, thanks. Got it. I'll let you get back to work. I'll buy you a pint when this is all over. Keep up the good work son.' H ended the call and sat down to collect his thoughts.

He sat for a minute or two and then Olivia spoke: 'H, is the phone working OK?'

'Why, what's the matter babes, why are you asking about the phone?'

'Just wanted to know if it's working. The tablet's gone dead, I can't get a connection. It looks like the wi-fi, or the Internet or whatever, is down.'

He and Olivia looked at one another without speaking; they didn't need to, because the situation was clear. Their blissful domestic idyll was about to come to an end.

11

The government was determined to keep the motorways open and demonstrate to the country that normal life was continuing, after a fashion; in any case, no amount of trouble was going to stop H missing visiting hours with his son, Little Ronnie, who was banged up in Winson Green prison in Birmingham.

H recalled, as he travelled up the M1, the events of the previous year in which his son had been brainwashed, and forced to escape from Durham prison with the Albanian gang overlord Basim Dragusha. He recalled the chase to Harwich to prevent his boy being taken out of the country, or worse, and grimaced as he remembered the fight – the clawing, gouging, biting, blood-spattered death match – he'd had there with Dragusha. It had taken him several months to recover from the treatment he received at Dragusha's hands. A smile of pride, and love, filled his heart as he remembered how Little Ronnie had saved him.

Nevertheless, he was in a pensive mood as he left the M1 and eased into the traffic on the M6. The country was on its way to meltdown and he was doing his level best to convince himself it was no longer his job to take care of business. He'd done his bit, and then some, over the years. He was concentrating on his family now. He'd lost one boy to the prison system, but he'd been given a second shot. He knew he was no longer a spring chicken, and he'd convinced himself that for the rest of his life his time and energy would be spent with Little Harry and Olivia, and Little Ronnie, whenever he regained his freedom. He owed it to them, and to himself – and he was making efforts to get back in touch with his estranged daughter, Grace, who had emigrated to New Zealand several years earlier.

46

Thought's about Little Ronnie's situation circled his mind as he made his way through the snarling Brum traffic. The army had taken control of the streets, and he had to navigate some roadblocks. Progress was slow but eventually he pulled into the prison car park. The sound of distant gunfire and wailing of numerous sirens reached him when he cut Sinatra off mid-song. He stepped out of the car and crunched over the gravel towards the reception area.

Fuck me, the boy's probably safer in than out with all this lot going on.

Little Ronnie was waiting at a small table in the middle of the visiting area. They'd had several visits since his arrest – or re-arrest, considering the stretch he'd been doing for drug-smuggling before Dragusha busted them out of Durham. Oddly, by killing the country's most wanted criminal, Ronnie had become something of a mini-celebrity. He'd been part of Dragusha's inner circle it its final days, before the organisation had started to unravel, and had learned secrets and come across information that had been useful to the authorities. Now the system was looking after its asset, making sure he stayed safe while it tried to figure out what to do with him.

'Hello son.'

'Hello Pop. How was the drive? Roadblocks slow you down?'

'Nah, it was a piece of cake…absolute doddle.'

Ronnie had been subjected to some severe brainwashing techniques when he was in Durham, techniques that Dragusha had used to turn him against his father. Yet at the end of the day, with a gun and the power of life and death in his hands, under the most extreme pressure imaginable, instinct had led him to spare his father and take the life of Dragusha. He'd since spent several months with a group of

47

anti-extremist specialists who had helped him recover his real identity.

The two men hugged each other tight; a wave of unspoken love surged between them.

'Still treating you OK in here are they son?'

'Not too bad Pop. I've still got my own cell, and I keep myself busy in the gym, and I've been reading a bit.'

'Reading? Reading what?'

'Oh, just some of the old classics. Stuff they try to get you to read at school, but I never did.'

H laughed. He'd never done much reading either, apart from some military history, but was pleased his son was making the effort.

The visits to date had concentrated, mostly, on small talk, but Ronnie was recovering now and he wanted to get to the real issues on his mind.

'What do you think's going to happen to me, Pop, in the long run?'

Thoughts of the events at Harwich were still flashing through H's mind. He recalled how Ronnie had not only killed Dragusha but also Graham Millar-Marchant – H's own partner – and Paul Walsh, an old time armed villain who was in the wrong place at the wrong time. After Ronnie killed the Albanian he'd had the presence of mind to make sure Dragusha's prints were also on the gun he'd used, and, schooled by his father and a good lawyer, he'd shifted the blame for the other killings onto the dead gangster. H had lied to the investigation team and told them Graham's final words were to say he'd been shot by Dragusha, who also shot Walsh. If Amisha ever found out the truth God only knew what would happen.

There was also Ronnie's gruesome murder of Jack Butcher, another old school villain, to consider – a crime he'd committed, in a confused and brainwashed state, under the express orders of Dragusha. This one remained under investigation. Dragusha's firm had done a good job of tidying up the crime scene and there were no eye-witnesses. Nor were there ever likely to be. Any one of Dragusha's men could have done it.

The upshot was Little Ronnie was only in the frame for a single murder, a murder the system would have to ensure he was held accountable for, despite it being of the country's most wanted gangster.

'Well son, there's the original drug offence, the escape and the killing of Dragusha to atone for. With all the extenuating circumstances, and bearing in mind that everyone wanted that mass-murdering bastard brought down for what he did to all those migrants, I'd say you won't be in here too much longer. Maybe another couple of years, so the public can see you didn't get away scot-free. I'd say you'll still be a young man with plenty of lead left in your pencil when you get out, and if some busy little toerag starts taking liberties and tries to throw a spanner in the works, I'll take care of him myself and come and get you anyway.'

H winked at his boy and gave him a wicked smile.

Little Ronnie smiled back. His dad had a way of making him feel better, giving him confidence in his future. It was a train of thought that made him think about his little brother, and then about his little brother's safety.

'Pop, what happened to that Russian geezer, the one you said turned up out of the blue and gave Little Harry a toy? Agapov, wasn't it, Vladimir Agapov?'

'I rooted about for a bit looking for him, but as far as I know he went back to Russia. The trail's gone cold, stone cold. I'm sure he's not in the country anymore. I've talked to everyone I know, told them to keep their eyes and ears open. If he ever surfaces again I'll know about it.'

49

Again, feelings of reassurance. Like his dad would do anything to keep them all safe. Little Ronnie moved on. They talked about the trouble in the country and H told him what he knew and that Ronnie didn't need to worry about it.

'Just keep your head down son. Screw your nut. Keep doing your gym and your reading and you'll soon be out. Trust me.'

Little Ronnie sighed. Advice from his dad was nearly always spot on. The men continued with their chat. H told him how his little brother and Olivia were getting on, and that he'd even been to see Ronnie's mum Julie and her soppy boyfriend Justin, and buried the hatchet. They'd told him that his estranged daughter Grace was still in New Zealand, but she wasn't answering his emails. Yet things in the family were about as good as they could be, considering what they'd all been through. The two men hugged again as visiting time came to an end. Little Ronnie lowered his voice for one last question.

'Dad, after the system has dealt with me… those other people I killed, how do I deal with that?'

'You just do son. It'll be with you every day of your life. Lock it in deep and learn to live with it.'

His dad was right; of course he was, but back in his cell, fidgeting on his bunk, he thought that learning to live with what he'd done was going to be a long journey, the hardest part of which was still to come.

12

Ronnie Ruddock had been doing OK. He'd settled into prison life and accepted that he was in for a long, long stretch. Maybe he'd get out when he was an old man, maybe the grim reaper would come for him first. There was no way of knowing. He consoled himself with the knowledge he'd lived a full life.

His kids visited on a regular basis. He was a grandfather now. Maybe he'd never be able to play with and enjoy the company of his grandchildren, and he'd see them grow up from afar – but at least he'd see them. They would know who he was and, when the time was right, he or his own children would tell them why he'd done what he'd done. They'd learn, one day, about how their grandmother had been murdered and how he and his best friend, Harry Hawkins, had delivered uncompromising justice to the guilty parties. If he got the chance he'd even tell them, when it was too late in the day for anyone to care anymore, why he'd held his hands up for the whole lot and ensured H had stayed out of prison.

He'd found his niche inside. His keen intelligence and business background set him apart from most of the other inmates, who came to him for all types of advice about legal matters, or just about their lives. His counsel was highly respected. He stayed clear of those who hated him because of his friendship with H and bided his time either helping others or simply reading and reflecting.

***

Lights out would be soon. Ronnie jumped up onto his bunk and settled himself down with the Financial Times to check on his investments. He still had a huge net worth on the outside – he knew everything there was to know about tucking money away – and liked to ensure he kept abreast of what was happening in the business world, making sure his fortune stayed well invested to guarantee his grandchildren's future. At least he could still do that for them.

The chaos raging across the country had knocked investor confidence and stocks were down everywhere – so there was not a lot he could do about moving his money around from one collapsing stock to another. They'd bounce back, they always did in stable countries with low levels of corruption and proper institutions. He'd always kept most of his investments in the UK; it was rock solid, at the end of the day. He'd lived through the bombs of the IRA in the seventies and the more recent bombs of the Islamists. If this latest outbreak proved to be either of those, or perhaps a new group of right-wing nutters, like the media was saying, it didn't matter much in the long run. The system would sort it, sooner or later. No chance, he thought, as he read about the prospects of the latest technology company to announce a listing on the London stock exchange, of *this* country descending into permanent chaos.

The Queen will have no fucking soldiers before this country goes belly-up.

He was turning the paper to the detailed listings section and its information about hundreds of companies and statistics and yields and rates of return, the page that only a tiny section of the population understood.

Then his world went belly-up. First, he heard an explosion in the distance. Then the alarm went off. Then he heard the gunshots. It was the gunshots that clinched it – this wasn't a couple of hotheads kicking off after a disagreement over a game of snooker. His heart rate rocketed; he jumped down from his bunk bed and rushed outside his cell.

All the cell doors were open. Someone had got into the security system. Masked gunmen, dozens of them, were swarming all over the prison. There were no screws to be seen. Prisoners were being shot at random. Some were fighting back, most were making a beeline for the exit.

Ronnie and his cellmate, Johnny Reeves, looked at each other, perplexed, dumbfounded.

'What the fuck is going on?' said Ronnie.

Johnny Reeves began to shrug just as a bullet went clean through the centre of his forehead. He went down like a sack of spanners, dead before he hit the ground. Ronnie stood transfixed, in a state of utter confusion. Masked men made their way up the stairs and swarmed all over him. Him in particular. A leather cosh smashed into his face and he fell to his knees. One of the men grabbed him by the collar and dragged him back into his cell.

The man removed his mask and gave a relaxed smile, as malign and confident as the devil in his lair. Ronnie had never met him face to face, but he recognized his picture from the papers, and he knew the grim reaper had come for him, and that he would never see his grandchildren again.

'Mr. Ruddock, just the person I wanted to see,' said the devil, as he pulled out a pair of pliers and unsheathed a long, long knife.

13

Amisha and Andrew parked up in Heneage Street and hit the ground running. The plan was to go door-to-door and shop-to-shop along Brick Lane and the cluster of side streets in which the trouble – the unwarranted shooting by a still-unidentified policeman of Imam Usama Sethi, of the East London Mosque – was thought to have started. This was on Brick Lane itself, not far from the market.

Hilary Stone had pulled Amisha and Andrew off the Wembley murders and brought them into the investigation of the Sethi case. She said that this case took priority due to the violent unrest, which could be expected to continue until the police satisfied the community with an arrest, so she wanted her best team on the job. Amisha suspected that it was more probably a case of Hilary thinking she'd somehow be able to 'relate' to the locals – senior Murder Squad detectives with a South Asian background were as rare as chicken's teeth. Amisha herself doubted the wisdom of this move; being a Hindu was not going to be much of an advantage around here, and she couldn't recall ever having so much as met a Bangladeshi.

They set off on foot through morning drizzle, still-smoking cars and an atmosphere of menace and suppressed rage you could cut with a knife, as if Jack the Ripper was still lurking around a corner somewhere. Then down towards the market and Fournier, Princelet, Hanbury and Woodseer Streets; this would be their patch for the next few days.

'Let me do the talking Andrew,' Amisha said, 'we don't want you antagonising these people with your butter-wouldn't-melt-in-his-mouth golden boy routine.'

'I didn't know I had one, ma'am.'

***

They went door-to-door; Amisha flashed the grainy photo of the mystery policeman-shooter that they'd captured from the CCTV to all and sundry; but nobody had seen him, and all they got were second hand accounts of something that had already become an urban legend, and angry contempt from people who clearly saw the two of them as part of the problem. Nobody had anything to say about the hand-to-hand fighting that had apparently continued into the early hours of that morning. One thing was clear: this was a community that felt itself to be under siege.

They plodded on, and turned into Woodseer Street. As they prepared to enter a block of flats they heard a commotion, behind them on Brick Lane: shouting and running, the kind of electricity in the air that always indicated violent confrontation.

They arrived at the scene to see three Bangladeshi men prone on the ground, and a group of half-a-dozen or so white men, their faces uncovered, running back towards and disappearing into Hanbury Street. Amisha did not call it in – there would not be the resources to deal with it, this sort of thing was happening all the time – but attended to the wounded herself. They were not in great shape, all of them seeming to have been clubbed about the head with blunt instruments, but they would survive. Amisha and Andrew helped them to their feet, showed them their warrant cards and started asking questions. Nothing: getting information from these boys was like trying to squeeze blood out of a stone.

The two detectives looked about them. It was midday, and they took stock together, in silence. A slate-grey sky, getting lower by the minute, pressing down on them, a perma-drizzle soaking them through, dark grimy buildings all around them, closing them in. More sounds of scuffling, running; a gunshot ringing out in the distance.

14

The street itself was buzzing, and filling now with just about the strangest assortment of people Amisha had ever seen. Banglatown locals, hipsters, journalists, police officers, tourists and small groups of thuggish-looking men mingled uneasily together. Later in the day, Amisha knew, the area would be closed off to non-residents, when reinforcements arrived.

But for now, things were as they were, and it was not looking good. An Imam appeared and began to address the crowd, many of whom were clearly of a mind to set out in search of someone to bear the brunt of their anger and frustration. Things were on the verge of turning ugly again; the hipsters moved along quietly with their heads down, the tourists retreated into the coffee shops, the police stood ready for whatever was coming next.

The crowd scattered in panic. A small drone appeared, buzzing down low overhead, just above the line of the buildings, and moved on. It didn't look like much – just the sort of thing anyone could buy online – but it spooked the crowd and turned up the heat. Riot police arrived and formed a line across the street; Amisha strained her head back to get a better line of sight, down towards the far end of the street, and saw another line of police already in place. The crowd, now perhaps two-hundred strong, was being kettled.

Another drone appeared, even lower than the first, and buzzed directly over the head of the crowd, spraying onto them a misty substance of some kind. People clutched their scarves and hoods to their faces, trying to protect their lungs, not knowing what the hell was going on. In the middle-distance more shots rang out, and a unit of police officers detached themselves from the kettling-cordon and went in search of its source.

'Well, the tourists are getting more than they bargained for today,' said Andrew. 'But what the hell is going on?'

'What's going on is that someone is messing with these people's heads. Consider what's happened this morning, and what we already know: a white motorcycle policeman, who nobody can identify, turns up out of the blue and shoots an Imam, apparently for no reason. The neighbourhood, predictably enough, goes up in flames.'

'Yes,' said Andrew.

'Next, interlopers arrive and start agitating – the usual suspects: various Muslim groups, Antifa, Class War etc., and ramp up the chaos. The whole thing escalates, and we have reports of mobs attacking police, hand-to-hand fighting. But consider: who's doing the fighting? Surely not these political activists – they're here to throw their weight behind the locals and cause political chaos, not fight with them.'

'Go on.'

'Then there's another element involved. The guys we saw this morning, the guerrilla-style attack. What if they're connected to the killing, to the mystery policeman, and the policeman was not a policeman at all, but a provocateur?'

'Where are you going with this, ma'am?'

'Here, Andrew, right here: I think the media may have got it right. I think we could be looking at a planned, concerted, nationalist attempt to start a civil war.'

'It all fits with what I read on Jupiter's blog: the fog of war, misinformation, fake news. Cause chaos, make the authorities look ridiculous, get everyone close to the edge…and then tell your story, offer your solution.'

They heard the buzz of another drone, again coming in low. This one stalled in mid-air above the kettled-up mob, and stopped. It fell silently from the sky directly onto the heads of the people below. They were penned in by the riot police, and had nowhere to run. The drone was a small thing, and probably not very heavy, but it came down directly onto them, and they were already expecting the worst.

The mob surged, like a giant wave cresting a defensive sea wall, broke through the police lines and moved, at speed, up towards Whitechapel, cracking the heads of policemen, hipsters and tourists as it went.

'Fuck,' said Andrew, 'someone's putting on a master class here, on how to drive an already ramped-up mob over the edge. What are we going to do, ma'am?'

'What we are going to do is get back to the Yard. We need to tell the team what we've seen, and our analysis of the situation, and get that fed up the chain to the strategy people, the big thinkers at COBRA.'

'But surely, they will be thinking about all this stuff, ma'am.'

'Maybe Andrew, maybe not.'

15

Hilary and the rest of the team at the debrief were impressed by the presentation and analysis given by Amisha and Andrew when they got back from Brick Lane, and agreed to feed their analysis up the chain. After the meeting Andrew headed to the hospital to collect Cressida, and Amisha went home – or tried to. The traffic lights were out between the south side of Westminster Bridge and the Elephant and Castle; it took her two and a half hours through snarled up traffic and a cacophony of horns to get back to Greenwich. She picked up a bottle of red from the shop on the corner of her street, fell into the house and then onto the sofa.

She was still asleep when the grey dawn crept into the room. Forcing herself awake through a slightly fuzzy head she reached out instinctively for her phone and found it on the coffee table. First things first – she would shower and eat something after she'd reviewed whatever chaos had been unleashed throughout the night.

There was too much to get a handle on; things seemed to be getting worse, wherever you looked, and she had a painfully anxious feeling in the pit of her stomach when she realized that this wasn't going to go away, not yet; there was going to be no return to normality in the foreseeable future.

The rain was battering her window as she checked the emails in her personal folder and was surprised to find one from her auntie Zaida, as she hadn't seen her in ages. She was even more surprised when she read it:

> *"Dear Friends. The time is at hand – stay calm and be patient. The BPF will quell the chaos and restore order to our great country. The call will come soon. Be ready."*

She dropped the phone and put her head in her hands, as if to stabilize it, give it a chance to work. This was the strangest thing she'd seen yet. Her auntie Zaida, of all the people in the world, throwing her weight behind the British Patriotic Front?

Amisha quickly thought it through and lined up the three most plausible possibilities. Her aunt had either a) gone completely off her head, b) undergone some kind of road-to-Damascus conversion, in the stress of the deepening crisis, and was now a full-on right-wing British nationalist, or 3) her email account had been hacked.

The Occam's Razor test suggested that the third option, being the simplest, was most likely. Amisha nodded sagely to herself, feeling more composed. Before writing to her aunt she checked her work folder – she'd have to be up and out the door quickly if she was going to be there on time, and she was always on time – and saw that there was a message from Hilary Stone. She clicked, and read:

"Dear Friends. The time is at hand – stay calm and be patient. The BPF will quell the chaos and restore order to our great country. The call will come soon. Be ready."

16

'Morning Andrew. How's Cressida?' said Amisha, bearing down on the Detective Sergeant's cubicle holding coffees.

'Not too bad…her face is starting to settle down and the wound in the back of her head is healing nicely. She's in very low spirits though.'

'Aren't we all?'

As usual, the two of them were the first in the office; the others would be along soon for the 8.30am meeting.

'Anyway,' said Amisha, 'listen: have you had a chance to look at any of your emails yet this morning?'

'Yep.'

'And?'

'Looks like the BPF have had a busy night hacking into most of the main servers. Powerful piece of work. They may not be quite as stupid as they look.'

'Correct. Other thoughts?'

'Well, I'm surprised they have the capacity for a thing like this, it has to be one of the most extensive things of its kind ever pulled off, in this country at least.'

'OK,' said Amisha. 'Let's take a step back. Who, as far as we know, does have the capacity and know-how to pull something like this off?'

'Well, the big American security and intelligence agencies, obviously. Our people, if they kept it very quiet and put it all through GCHQ. The Chinese and the Russians, again obviously. Not sure about who else is up to it. Maybe one or two of the major independent hacking groups, like Anonymous. Maybe a very sharp criminal group, like the one that's been locking systems down everywhere with ransomware. Or an Islamist group – some of those are developing fast.'

Amisha took a slug of coffee and sighed. 'This is all making my head spin Andrew. We have so many dots to try and join up.'

'Does this relate to our specific case?'

'I don't know, but everything seems connected, somehow.'

Andrew stood up, stretched, began to walk the floor in circles. Amisha saw that he was getting into a state of creative agitation. His brain was starting to boil, in a good way.

'OK, ma'am, let's look at it from another angle. You know what Joey Jupiter says: trust nobody you can't vouch for, only accept what you can confirm for yourself.'

'OK. And?'

'Well, things are either what they seem, or they are not what they seem. In the current circumstances, if we assume the latter, what if it wasn't the BPF, but someone seeking to put them in the frame?'

'For what?'

'For being behind what's been happening; or, to try and make them seem bigger and more important than they really are. What if it's a smokescreen, an attempt to keep the focus off whoever's running the show?'

'Or is it equally likely that this is just...shit starting to go wrong, like H always said it would? Too much social fragmentation and tension, not enough real law and order, too many nutters with different agendas running about? Maybe the social order is just beginning to collapse?'

'Jesus, ma'am,' said Andrew. 'That is so scary.'

'What is?'

'What you just said.'

'What did I say?'

'That maybe the "social order is just beginning to collapse" – it just sounded weird, put like that – like something that may actually be happening.'

'Well, Andrew,' said Amisha, rising from her chair and heading towards the meeting room, 'in that case we'd better pray that it is a conspiracy. That we might be able to deal with.'

17

His visit to Little Ronnie had done H the power of good. Birmingham had been locked down after his visit so he'd had to stay the night in a hotel. As he drove home he remained positive and quietly content – regardless of what was happening at the big-picture level – and as he turned the key to the door and heard Little Harry padding along the corridor to greet him he was in good spirits. There was still the matter of Grace to deal with, but she still refused to give him the time of day, and he would have to wait until she was ready. Piece by piece, H was making himself and his family whole again.

The boy launched himself up at his dad and H caught him, pulling him up so that Little Harry could wrap his arms around his neck. 'Evening babes,' he shouted to Olivia, as he walked towards the kitchen, 'any danger of a cup of tea?'

She gave him a peck on the cheek. 'How was it?'

'Blinding, he's looking well, fit and well. We had a good talk. He's really starting to open up to me now, tell me what's going on. It was a good trip – or I should say "visit"; the trip itself was a pain in the arse. Nice to be home though.'

'OK, take the boy into the living room. Sit yourself down and I'll bring your tea. Hungry?'

'Starving.'

'Pie and mash? I brought some back from the place in Bexleyheath. I can warm it up.'

'Quality. I'll have some of that, how many pies have we got?'

'Well, *you've* got two, tiger. Settle yourself down in front of the telly.'

'Yes, your ladyship. Come on boy, let's go and see what's on. We better have a look at the news, see what's going on in the world.'

***

The news offered the same sorry stuff as it had for days, and went through the litany of woe, but now a new element: prison riots. Prison riots in Brixton, Wandsworth, Belmarsh and others. Nothing about Winson Green; H breathed a deep sigh of relief.

Olivia arrived with dinner, on a tray, and sat down next to him on the sofa.

'What now, H?'

'Riots, in half a dozen nicks. Seemed to have started yesterday and now spreading. There's no way this is a fucking coincidence.'

'What about where Little Ronnie is, where you've just come from?'

'Nothing about Winson Green so far.'

'Thank God for that. Eat your dinner babes, I'll cut the boy's up.'

H dug in, his eyes fixed on the screen. He'd lost some of his appetite, and things got worse when a bar appeared at the bottom of the screen: 'Latest…rioting at Durham prison. Many injured, fatalities feared.'

'Fuck it!' said H, slamming his tray down onto the floor. Look Liv, Durham. It's gone off in Durham. That's where Ronnie is now. Ronnie Ruddock.'

18

H and Ronnie Ruddock went back a long way – just about all the way. Their fathers were good friends, and though Ronnie was a few years younger than H he'd always been around, first as a kind of cousin, later as a brother. A blood brother. They'd fought side by side on the football terraces of the 1970s and later in the Falklands, where Ronnie had literally taken a bullet for his friend; they had been utterly loyal to one another all their lives.

Ronnie was doing thirty years for the murder of Timothy Skyhill, a peer of the House of Lords, who had ordered Ronnie's wife Tara to be killed as part of an attempt to cover up a paedophile conspiracy that went all the way to the top. A few years back he and H had gone on a mission to avenge Tara, on Ronnie's part, and find and save H's then police partner, Amisha Bhanushali, who'd been kidnapped by some very bad actors.

Along with the two people in the room with him now, and the son he'd visited earlier, Ronnie Ruddock was the person H was closest to. Ronnie had arranged to have the full weight of the law come down on him, and him alone, so that H could go free following the death of Skyhill and the rest. Not a day went by when H didn't think about what Ronnie had done for him, with a mixture of deep guilt and eternal gratitude.

He's in Durham, in the middle of fuck-knows-what. I should be there with him.

'Is that it?' shouted H. 'Useless media…many injured, they said. Are they just going to leave it like that?'

Olivia left the room and came back with her tablet.

'Amisha must have told you a hundred times H,' said Olivia, 'it's no good waiting for the legacy media to tell you what's going on. Did you never listen to what she told you about social media? Try and stay calm, I'm sure Ronnie's OK.'

She got busy opening tabs – Twitter, Facebook, Periscope.

H, looking over her shoulder, said 'Periscope? What the fuck is Periscope?'

'Language, H.'

'He's got his face in his pie-mash – have a look at him. He's not listening.'

'Not the point.'

'No? Not the point? I'll tell you what the point is – Ronnie's in the middle of a major prison riot, and they're talking about "many injured". He's got plenty of enemies up there, because every fucker knows he's my friend. Are you going to try and help me with this Liv, or what?'

Olivia realised it wasn't the time or place to go schoolmarm on him. She rolled her eyes, got down to business.

'OK babes, we'll start with Twitter and take it from there.'

It was wall-to-wall footage, some of it surprisingly professional looking, of fires, people fighting. She looked in the trending and scrolled down until she found #prisonriots. She went in.

H's legs were twitching and he was chewing the inside of his own mouth away. He looked and felt like a man seconds away from an epileptic fit.

Olivia scrolled and swiped and jabbed on, her strained, intent face made almost spectral by the light coming off the screen.

'What are we looking at babes? Speak to me.'

'I'm just going through the #prisonriots stuff. If there's anything about Durham we'll see it in a minute,' said Olivia.

H sat on his hands and waited, like a hungry schoolboy who can't work the cooker, waiting for his mum to knock up the beans on toast.

'OK, here it is. Durham. Someone's put up some footage – maybe a prisoner with a phone. The riot was last night.' Olivia tapped the link and went in.

H inched closer and they studied the screen together. Scenes of chaos. Fires had been set, and to begin with the images were largely concealed by the smoke, though they could hear sounds of shooting and scuffling.

Whoever had been holding the phone was moving, at will, around the prison. There was a lot of chaotic movement, and wild sounds off-camera. A number of men were lying on the ground amid the debris, and there was running and shouting – it was feral, unrestrained. The camera closed in on one of the bodies and showed the man's face; it was badly swollen about the eyes, and his throat had been cut. A crimson gash ran the entire width of it.

Olivia retched, dropped the tablet, stood up, scooped up the boy and hurried from the room.

19

H picked up the tablet and looked again as the film continued. He noted that there were no prison officers to be seen and came to a swift conclusion: this had been planned, God alone knew by whom.

It was a bloodbath. People often used the word like they knew what it meant. But H had been in bloodbaths for real – situations in which every trace of civilized and restrained behaviour had disappeared, and in which men simply ran amok, hurting and slaughtering whoever they could lay their hands on in fulfilment of some primeval need.

H's heart sank, all the way down, to the point he knew of old: to the place where there was no hope, only fear and dread, and the sense that human life was pointless and humans had been put on the earth by an insane god who wanted only to expose them to never-ending cosmic anguish.

He felt sick – not because of the blood and guts, but because he knew his dearest, oldest friend was in the middle of all this somewhere. In the middle of hell.

He refocused on the screen in time to see the clip end. He jabbed and swiped around frantically, until he came to 'Durham riot – Facebook video.' He ran with the tablet to the kitchen, to Olivia; she was sitting down, sobbing quietly to herself and holding onto Little Harry for dear life, as if letting go of him would spin her off, alone, into the heart of darkness.

'Liv, look. Can you snap out of it for a minute, love? Please. It says here there's a feed on Facebook of the Durham riots. Posted yesterday. Can you get me in there…please?'

She took the tablet from him, head still down, tapped at it and passed it back. H took it and returned to the living room.

This feed had been made by a different director than the previous one. They were using an HD camera held steady, as if they were making a documentary. The camera was moving slowly around a landing, going in and out of cells as it went, while alarms rang, men ran around hollering and hooting and objects crashed onto the landing from the floor above – which suggested to H that the wire meshing designed to stop this happening was no longer in place.

Once inside a cell the camera panned around and displayed the wreckage; if there was a dead or injured man inside the camera zoomed in, slow, steady and professional, and treated the viewer to a close-up of his injuries, ending with a close-up of his face.

The camera operator was walking around the place at his leisure, in no hurry at all.

Whoever was behind all this had taken control of the prison. The prison system's authority and control had been targeted; had been taken down. H realised that many of the pathologically violent lunatics he saw haring up and down would soon be at large, making their contribution to the ascending national chaos.

It's not random. It's planned. It's connected to the bigger picture…whatever the fuck that is!

H watched on, watched and waited for what he somehow knew, in his heart, was coming. The camera continued its unhurried passage from cell to cell, displaying torn, mangled, cut-up and bullet-smashed bodies, sending the viewer a simple, clear and frighteningly powerful message: *look what we're doing – if you can. No one is stopping us. We're in charge now.*

Another cell. A man was spread out on the floor in an unholy mess; he was a picture of mangled physical distortion, his shoulders were broken with his arms laid out horizontally, as if he'd been trying to fly away. They were the wrong way around. The camera panned up slowly towards the face – H knew it would be Ronnie's before they got there. He fought hard to resist the look-away reflex, pulling his head back around straight and his hands from over his eyes.

It *was* Ronnie. His eyes had been gouged out, but it was Ronnie.

H froze; he sat motionless, processing in slow motion what he was seeing. The camera panned back and a gloved hand laid a sheet of A4 paper sideways on Ronnie's chest, just below the chin. There was a message on it:

This one's for you, Hawkins. I took care of it myself. See you soon.

***

Olivia, calmer now and with the boy asleep in her lap, was startled by the sound of glass shattering, coming from the living room. This was followed by a stomach-churning sound, which she could not put a name to but knew it must have emanated from somewhere in H's chest.

Ronnie. Oh dear God. It's Ronnie.

She arrived in the living room to find H pulling himself up from the floor, his forehead streaming with blood, getting ready to shape up to what was left of the bay windows. He smashed his fist into one of the side panels. He was sobbing uncontrollably, coughing and spluttering, choking on the tears. He moved along to the wall mirror and hammered at it with his head, his face, his hands. He picked up the TV and hurled it through the gap in the window.

Olivia stood back and left him to do what he needed to do – breaking ornaments, laying into the glass coffee table – until he fell to his knees clutching at his left arm, and knelt there shaking, screaming among the blood and shattered glass.

Olivia raced back to the kitchen and phoned the emergency services.

'It's my husband...please be quick. He's lost a lot of blood – and I think he may be having a heart attack.'

20

The lights went out, and across Winson Green nick prisoners commenced to do what prisoners do in the dark: sleep, smoke, befuddle themselves with Spice, read by torchlight, gorge themselves on smartphone pornography. The group of masked men massing in a nearby park knew the score, knew that they would be dealing with men who were sleepy and switched-off. They also knew that when you have the codes to electronic doors, distant colleagues hacking into surveillance cameras, hand grenades, smoke bombs and automatic rifles at your disposal, British prison guards tended to melt away – quickly. Like others up and down the country those at Winson Green were not prepared for the assault. Why would they be? Nothing like it had ever happened in British prisons before the current chaos began. There had been riots and some riots had resulted in the death of some prison guards, but takeovers from the outside? This happened in Mexico and Brazil and Venezuela. In these places prison takeovers culminating in mass murder were not uncommon – but it didn't happen in Britain. The prison officers were not prepared when the first bomb went off and the outer steel doors of the prison were breached. They were not prepared when the attackers breezed through the security doors of the inner sanctum, or had keys to open the doors within.

Those officers not shot in the initial phase melted away like snow in a desert, relieved beyond measure to have got out with their lives. The prisoners would have to look after themselves.

It was the same pattern that had been seen in the other attacks. Gain entry, open the doors, kill a few prisoners to set the tone, let the rest scatter to the outside world. Thousands of prisoners on the loose, many of whom would create havoc, occupy and overwhelm police forces the length and breadth of the land and make their own contributions to the tidal wave of violent chaos sweeping the country.

One inmate sprang from his bed and dashed out of his cell, which was now open like all the rest. As the shots and barked commands rang out he kept low, taking in the scene, assessing what was going on. He was smart enough to grasp that the attack was planned, well organized. This was no riot, this was an invasion. He merged with the chaos, using other prisoners as shields, as the shots echoed around the prison. The interlopers didn't want everyone dead, he came to understand, they wanted them gone. They were clearing out the prison. He had no choice but to comply. Resistance was futile.

As the crowds swarmed back and forth in confusion he held his nerve, kept his head low, looked no one in the eye and made his way to the exit. He was soon outside, fully garbed in prison clothes. The easiest thing now, and it would be the course of action undertaken by those prisoners who didn't want to escape, would be to present himself to the nearest police station and give himself up. It would look good on his record, once all the anarchy was brought under control and the country stabilised. It would be the correct thing to do.

But he didn't want to do the correct thing. This prisoner wanted to do the right thing.

Middle of Birmingham in the middle of the fucking night. How the fuck am I going to get to London?

He didn't know yet, but he knew he had to find a way. Get to London. Get to his dad. He had seen how the invasions took place, useful information, and he knew that his dad would know the best course of action when he got there. Little Ronnie didn't want to break into a house, terrify and steal an old man's clothes and car keys. He didn't want to…but he did. He didn't have a choice.

21

It had been another long day, and getting home made it longer still. Taking a different route home than usual to avoid the now routine chaos on the roads, she came down through Camberwell and into Peckham, heading for Greenwich via New Cross and Blackheath.

The morning meeting had been a waste of time, and she'd been irritated about the direction received from Jane McPherson, who'd seemed rambling and unfocused. Amisha thought her insistence on ensuring demarcation lines on the various cases stay in place was misguided.

'Just focus on the cases in front of you. No 'big thinking' – this is a case of ensuring we stick with the details of each murder, concentrate on the fine details of each case,' she'd said.

'Bloody lot of good that will do,' thought Amisha.

She parked up on the corner of her street, bought a bottle of red from the corner shop and took it home, registering on the way the gunshots coming from the direction of Deptford. She shuddered for a second, composed herself, wondered how the civilians, the normal people, were coping with all this. If she, steeped and seasoned in the Harry Hawkins school of hard knocks, was becoming jittery, how must they be feeling?

She got in the door and went to the kitchen, dropped her bag and coat on the table, grabbed corkscrew, glass and bottle, moved into the living room, collapsed onto the sofa and picked up the remote.

It was a strange irony; the more Amisha became convinced that the mainstream TV news was concealing as much as it was revealing, the more of it she watched; or, more accurately, analysed: the mind-spinning dog's dinner of fake news and disinformation being served up on a daily basis needed careful scrutiny.

She started out with an early-evening Question Time special on the troubles. There was nothing much happening there except for the silver-tongued Lord Peter Lambert pontificating as only he could on the situation, arguing colourfully that they were in the early stages of a full-blown nationalist coup. She then watched the Channel Four news, the main BBC news and the ITV News in succession, making careful mental notes. In the last few days a consensus had emerged, and the finger was being pointed firmly towards the BPF, and an attempt to start a civil war. In fact, everything pointed to the BPF: its email hack; the countless sightings of groups of white men fighting with all-comers, all across the country. The BPF had form on all these counts.

But something was gnawing away at her, telling her that this was all too pat, too obvious. She remembered what Andrew had said about discounting the obvious, and the Joey Jupiter doctrine.

She clicked the TV off and sat back with her eyes closed, replaying and reviewing everything she'd seen so far.

She picked up her phone and punched Andrew's number into it.

'Evening ma'am.'

'Evening Andrew. Have you got a minute?'

'Yep, I've just put the rice on, I'm knocking up something for Cressida.'

'OK. Tell me something: why do we never hear their voices? All these white guys running around, attacking everything that moves. In all the footage we've reviewed, when we were in Brick Lane…they don't make any noise. Guys like these usually scream, sing, chant, and shout abuse when they're in action…in fact they always do. But with these guys – nothing. Why do you suppose that is?'

'Well I suppose, ma'am, that they are ...'

'Refusing to use their voices, Andrew – they are refusing to use their voices. Because it would give them away. They've got everyone believing they're BPF and, they don't want to say anything because their accents would give them away. They're not Brits.'

22

It was late evening when the cab from the hospital dropped H, Olivia and Little Harry home. It had been a long session in the casualty department, the highlight being that H had not, in fact, suffered a heart attack. His wounds were cleaned and stitched and, though he looked like he'd just done ten rounds with Marvin Hagler, he was fine.

In body. His spirits were another matter. Just as they were preparing to leave the hospital news of the trouble at Winson Green prison appeared on a TV screen. H sat in the waiting room with Olivia and the sleeping boy, reviewing on her tablet the streaming from Birmingham, desperate for a glimpse of Little Ronnie.

Nothing – just the usual bloody murder and chaos. The anguish and agitation he'd felt on seeing Ronnie Ruddock's mangled face surged back, cutting straight through the sedative he'd been given.

Now back home, sitting in their kitchen, H was as close as he'd ever been to the end of his tether.

'I can't fucking stand this anymore Liv. You saw that message they pinned on Ronnie's body. If they went for Ronnie to get at me they'll go for Little Ronnie. I'm going up there now.'

'H, stay calm. What good will that do? They're saying most of the prisoners have escaped. If Ronnie managed to get out he'll make his way here. He'll have nowhere else to go. And if he didn't get out...' Olivia didn't finish the sentence.

H nursed his right hand and adjusted the bandage wrapped around his head. The stress of the evening had sent his blood pressure rocketing and the wound on his head had opened up. The bandage had soaked up what blood it could before it had started to trickle down his head and over his eyes. He looked now like an old-school England football defender, bloodied and bandaged but unbowed against the onslaught as he headed away the incoming long balls in the final minute of a heroic defence of a 1-0 lead.

He knew Olivia was right – that was the worst of it. Staying put was the only option. But staying put wasn't in his nature.

The minutes crawled by, and they turned into hours. It would soon be breakfast time. H had made call after call to anyone who might have information, pacing up and down in his living room all night, like a rat in a cage. The calls had been useless; nobody had a clue about what was going on. Olivia thought a full-scale English fry up might help the situation; she knocked it up and called H to the kitchen. Not the sight of it, not even the smell of the fried bacon and sausages, enticed him. He nodded 'no'.

'Fucking hell Olivia, I'm going off my nut here.'

He turned on his heels and paced, once again, along the corridor and into the living room. Olivia followed him in. She'd cleared up the broken glass and general wreckage as best she could. She'd called the window repair company – a few days, they said – they'd never been busier. H pulled on his coat and announced he was going for a walk, that he needed to be on the move for a bit, and that he'd be back in ten minutes.

'H, be careful out there.'

'Nah, we're all right here babes. Who's going to put a bomb in Eltham?'

23

H powered to the end of his street and turned right into another one just the same; long rows of well-appointed terraced houses with tidy little front gardens.

He was on fire; the cold morning air bit at his cuts and made them sting, and his senses were reeling – reeling but sharp. As he surged along the pavement – looking, listening, sniffing the air – he noticed in his peripheral vision a figure lurking in the shadows of an alleyway between two houses he passed.

Whoever that is he's not very good at keeping out of sight.

H assumed it likely that it was some young tearaway having a late one, still working his way through his cans of super-strength cider or suchlike, taking the edge off while his parents slept. It didn't unduly bother him, but he tensed up anyway, as he always did in the presence of potential danger, and when the figure stepped out of the shadows and spoke he turned with such speed that the man had barely got his first syllable out before H had him pinned to the wall by the throat.

'Alright Pop, take it easy, it's me.'

There had been moments in H's life when a sheer sense of relief had overwhelmed him. When he was told Ronnie Ruddock had survived the sniper's bullet he took to save H's own life in the Falklands. When he'd found and rescued the kidnapped Amisha alive – if not well – after being taken and tortured by a ruthless pervert. But the sense of relief, of happiness, of sheer exhilaration he felt now went beyond anything he'd ever experienced. Not only was Little Ronnie magically in front of him, he'd had the sense and inner resources to keep out of harm's way and find his way home, amid all the carnage. The tears H found welling up in his eyes were tears of pride, as well as joy.

'Son,' was the only word he could muster as he held his boy close, all but crushing him. They embraced for several moments, neither man saying anything.

'Son. How the fuck did you manage to get here?'

'I got hold of a motor after the nick got busted open. It's worse than I thought out here – old bill and soldiers all over the place, people kicking off everywhere you turn. And what the fuck's happened to you? I take my eyes off you for a few hours and you show up looking like Terry Butcher. Been in the wars yourself, have you?'

'Long story son, long story. Your uncle Ronnie's dead,' H said with a sigh. 'I'll tell you all about it at home. Olivia's been knocking up some grub. How does a full English with all the trimmings sound?'

24

They all said their hellos and settled themselves around the kitchen table, overseen from his highchair perch by a gurglingly happy Little Harry.

They tucked into their breakfasts, while Little Ronnie breathlessly told them about the riot in Winson Green and how he'd made his way back down to London, and what he'd seen en route: the rioting, the helicopters whirring, the roadblocks.

'It's absolute fucking pandemonium out there, I could hardly believe what I was seeing,' he concluded, shaking his head, pushing his empty plate away and leaning back on his chair.

'Language,' said Olivia, nodding towards Little Harry. 'We're not using language like that in this house anymore Ron. Not when the boy's about, anyway.'

'Fair enough Liv. Fair enough. Sorry.'

H said nothing, but pressed Little Ronnie for more details of what exactly had happened during the riot.

'Well, it wasn't a "riot" Pop, I can tell you that for nothing. It was more like an invasion of the prison by an army, or a militia, something like that. They came in, a bunch of well-organized blokes in masks, did what they wanted, there were no screws fronting them up or anything. They basically opened the whole place up, punished a few people and emptied the place out.'

'What else did you notice? Anything unusual?' said H.

'What, more unusual than a tooled-up army coming into a British nick, taking it over, blowing a few people's heads off and letting everyone else go, with no cunt offering them any resistance at any stage? That not unusual enough for you, Pop?'

'Fuck!' said Little Harry in his cutest sing-song voice.

Olivia took a breath and got ready to start up; H gave her an imploring look – not now, please, not now.

'I want details son, details. You're just giving me the headlines. Think...what did you notice that you haven't mentioned yet? Close your eyes and go through it from the beginning. Pick out details.'

'OK...well, they were all wired up – you know, with earpieces and all that. Like they were being moved about by someone with an overview of proceedings. There was an explosion out the front when they first came in, but once they got inside everything just seemed to open up for them – all the electronic doors and that.'

'Good, that's more like it son. What else?'

'They shot a few people at random – that's what it looked like – then went around wing by wing barking at people to get out. They sounded like Eastern Europeans, maybe Russian. A couple of them were walking around filming everything, nice and easy, like they had all the time in the world. As I got nearer the exits I could hear screaming behind me, like someone was having it put on them. Badly.'

H nodded but said nothing, thinking quietly to himself for a minute.

'Right,' he said eventually, snapping out of his reverie. 'You'll have to stay here son, while we figure out what's what. I daresay you'll come in handy. It's the first really solid thing I've heard so far about who might actually be behind all this bollocks...or at least some of it.'

Olivia's blood froze; this was the first reference H had made to becoming actively involved in what was happening, and the churning in her guts told her where it was likely to lead.

'But won't they come looking for Ronnie, H? He's a high-profile prisoner.'

'I doubt it babes. It looks like there's untold villains on the loose now, thousands of them. Ronnie's high-profile, yes, but he doesn't represent a threat to the public, and most people like what he did to Dragusha anyway. They might be able to spare a few people to go looking for some of the dangerous Category A nutters but that'll be about it. With all this lot roaming the streets, on top of everything else, there'll be even more fun and games to contend with. I think we're only just getting started. Things are going to get worse before they get better. A lot worse.'

25

Amisha had drifted off, again, on the sofa – it hardly seemed worth the trouble of going to bed now – and was awoken by the pinging of her phone just as dawn broke. A text message from auntie Zaida:

Hello Darling, need to talk to you. Most urgent. Can you meet me on The Bridge at Seven-thirty?

'The Bridge' – the bridge across the lake in St. James' Park. It was where they always used to meet when Amisha was younger and her auntie was in town. Auntie's choice. It was all very *Tinker, Tailor, Soldier, Spy*, all very Graham Greene, in Amisha's imagination. She'd grown up around rumours that her aunt was some sort of spy at GCHQ, so it was always a thrill for the teenager, and later the student, to navigate her way through the park and onto the bridge, to find her aunt waiting there – always first, no matter how hard Amisha tried to beat her to it.

***

It was no surprise to Amisha, therefore, to arrive at 7.20am to find Zaida already in place, bundled up against the morning cold, looking down and staring hard at the ducks, deep in thought.

They embraced – quietly but strongly – and Zaida pushed Amisha back, holding her at arm's length, to inspect the little niece who was now a grown young woman, as aunts do. She smirked and nodded her head in appreciation but nothing; she looked far from her usual, composed self.

'What is it then auntie?' Amisha said. 'Have you come to extoll the virtues of the BPF, to try and bring me on board?'

For a second her aunt said nothing but stared ahead blankly as if she didn't know what Amisha was referring to. Then she shook her head and said, 'Oh no…sorry about that. What I want to talk to you about may be connected though, in some way.'

'Sounds heavy, auntie.'

'It is. Let's go and sit on a bench.'

***

They sat under a tree with a view of a section of the park that Amisha knew well. Extremely well. A few years before, when she was still a sleek and thrusting young DC with big ambitions, she'd worked on the murder of a pair of aristocratic women who'd been butchered in broad daylight at a time when law and order seemed to be breaking down and panic was sweeping the city.

It had been a small foretaste of what they were getting now. She recalled how she'd entered the park with H to take control of the scene, and how'd he'd tried to protect her from the worst of it even as he was beginning to fall apart himself.

'I want to talk to you, darling, for three reasons,' said Zaida. 'One, because I have something to tell you that you need to know in your professional capacity; two, because there's nobody else I can talk to or trust; and three, because…I'm scared.'

'OK auntie, I'm listening. Why don't you start at the beginning?'

They both jumped out of their seats: a volley of automatic gunfire rang out, from somewhere in the West End; sirens began to wail. The ducks on the lake headed for cover.

'Fuck me! As H would say,' Amisha said, laughing gently.

They both smiled, and sat in silence for a short time, relaxed, despite the growing noise of the sirens hurtling along The Mall, down towards Admiralty Arch and Trafalgar Square.

'Do you miss him?' asked Zaida.

Amisha shrugged, and at length said 'I don't know.'

'You should get back in touch with him.'

'Why?'

'Because after you've heard what I'm going to say you're going to need someone's help – someone you can trust completely. Someone you'd trust with your life. Who else have you got?'

Amisha, her eyes fixed on the spot where H had broken down under the weight of his own obsession with protecting innocent people from evil, said nothing.

26

'Things are even worse than you think,' said Zaida. 'What we're seeing around us now – all this chaos and violence – is on the surface. I've been working on things that have shown me that something very bad has been happening beneath it.'

'Worse than all of this?'

'Yes, and probably even more serious, in the long run. Of course, it may be that everything's connected somehow – what's going on out here and what's going on behind the scenes…but I have no idea how to begin to join up the dots.'

'What the hell have you been working on auntie?'

'Well, money flows. International money flows. You know – laundering, washing, masking, channelling, off-shoring. Anti-terrorism work, I've been on it for years, looking every which way for patterns, circuits, trends, things like that.'

'OK. And?'

Zaida took a long deep breath, exhaled, and said, 'I recently found something I wasn't looking for; I haven't told anyone yet. I'm not sure what to do with it, it's very near-the-knuckle.'

Amisha urged her to go on with a nod of the head.

'I suspect that significant people in the higher echelons of our institutions have been compromised.'

'In what way?'

'The old way. Massive sums of money. I'm talking about the political system, the civil service, the judiciary, the military…your people as well, I'm afraid. And people in the media, education, it's staggering.'

'Jesus, auntie. What do you mean when you say "compromised"?'

'I mean that these people have been in receipt of huge sums of money from a super-clandestine source, and that there's a pattern to it. I have no idea what the money is for, or what strings are attached to it, but I'm convinced there's a pattern, a common source. Or, I should say, a common method.'

'What does that mean?'

'That the techniques and channels being used are tried and trusted…and that we've seen them before.'

'Auntie, this is driving me nuts. Can you tell me something definite, something I can get my teeth into?'

'OK – try this: what I've found looks very similar to the system used by the Russian oligarchs to get their money out of country and into the places they like it. I've spent a lot of time on this recently – my own time, under the radar, once I realized where the money was going – and I'm convinced. To put it simply, though it's a far from simple matter, Russian actors – your old friend Kyril Kuznetsov's name has come up, for instance – have been funnelling money to people in high places. It's therefore logical to assume that many powerful and influential Brits have been bought and paid for. Don't ask me to what end, but they've been bought and paid for. I'm sure of it.'

***

The café by the lake opened at eight o'clock and they began to drift towards it, arm in arm. The park was still almost empty; the sirens had faded away. A moment of calm, on the surface of things, but Amisha was in turmoil.

'What am I supposed to do with all this, auntie?'

'It's need-to-know stuff for you Amisha, don't you see that? You're involved in investigating some of this insanity. How do you know you can trust your superiors, or your colleagues, or the information you're getting? The fact is that whether you work for the Metropolitan Police, or GCHQ, or London Zoo, for all I know, you have to assume that your institution has been compromised.'

She left this to sink in. They walked on in silence for a while.

'So,' Amisha finally said, 'how are things with your chums at the British Patriotic Front – any of your top guys been got at, do you know?'

They both laughed, but without mirth.

'Well, that brings us to the most important point. I need you to help me – there's nobody else I can trust now. We need to work out what's connected, and how. Is there a connection between what I've just told you and the things you're investigating, and all these other things? We need to find out – we need to find out because something big is going to happen. I mean something bigger and more serious than all the riots and the bombs we've seen so far.'

'What do you mean?'

'I'm saying I think the riots and the bombs are a sideshow. The amount of money I've seen moved has occurred over a period of years, and it buys much more than a few rioters and some bombs. There's some kind of deeper plan unfolding, I just don't know what it is.'

'Zaida, you need to take your findings to your superiors. This is too much for us.'

'I can't. I told you. Some of them are compromised.'

'What then? What can I do?'

'We need to build a team, a team made up of people we know we can trust.'

'That's what Joey Jupiter says. What exactly are you proposing? It all just sounds just so crazy…so big.'

'I'm proposing that you think about it, and that you contact H. People like us can go deep inside the system and look around, we can cover our tracks. But someone also has to be out here, amidst all the chaos, someone who can really confront what's happening.'

'Fucking hell, auntie, this is a lot to take on board. I don't know.'

'I do. Listen to me. A problem halved is a problem shared, and we need to find people who can help us try and fight this, or our country is in serious, serious trouble. Maybe the most trouble it's been in since 1941. Reach out to H. Forget everything else – get over your issues with him. Reach out to H.'

PART TWO

27

The first of the flying beer bottles to reach its target bounced harmlessly off the low fencing, and the second and third did the same. The throwers got their eye in and the follow-up bottles spun in low and hard, smashing into the gap between the bottom of the outdoor café's large umbrella and the low barrier separating the patrons' chairs from the street. Half a dozen or so of the dark brown missiles smashed and skidded onto the table tops, upsetting and smashing glasses and sending a tide of beer and broken glass up into the faces of the men at the table.

A group of large, toned-up thugs with scarves covering their faces – the infantry coming on after the artillery barrage – arrived seconds later, launching themselves with fists and bellowed curses into the befuddled and slow-reacting group of men only now rising from their chairs. Their flag of St George bearing the legend 'Nottingham Loyal' – a homage to the place they called home – ripped from its place and flapping in the wind.

They hadn't slept or washed for two days and were not geared up to defend themselves against an onslaught like this, but once roused they did their best and the usual calm of Krakow's Market Square was shattered as the melee spilled out into the road, scattering the tourists and frightening the plumed horses lined up waiting to take people on carriage tours of the Old Town.

The trumpet man high up in the tower of St Mary's Cathedral marked two o'clock as the crowd below egged him on, their necks craning upward; a bright, sharp Sunday afternoon in January in one of the jewels of Central-Eastern Europe. At this time of year, the usual crowds of tourists and British stag weekenders – a mixed blessing for the city's bar owners at the best of times – were joined by a fair number of Russians celebrating their New Year.

The fighting petered out as the police arrived; they took control of the situation and began shovelling the culprits into the backs of three meat wagons. Shouts and curses in English and Russian filled the square; a number of the men resisted arrest and were dealt with on crisp, no-nonsense terms. The sound of their cries was augmented by the sirens of ambulances, arriving in the corner of the square where Szczepanski Place meets Slawkowska Street, to take care of the fallen. Three men were down; one of them was not moving at all, except for a violently twitching left leg.

The meat wagons and ambulances pulled out; the atmospheric buzz faded away; the 'Nottingham Loyal' flag, swept along the ground by the wind like tumbleweed in a Western movie, disappeared into Jana Street; the people around the square resumed their gentle festivities.

28

Kuba Bukowski groaned, returned his phone to his pocket, and tried to catch his wife Magda's eye at the far end of the table. This was going to be awkward. He'd promised to keep the day clear, to be present and give his full attention to the party they were throwing for his mother-in-law's name day. He'd been as good as his word, eating, drinking and being merry with the company at large. A murder detective's lot, however, is a murder detective's lot, and with a sigh and a very slight nod of the head he indicated to Magda that she should meet him in the hallway.

Her face – in the normal course of events a source of never-ending delight to him – had curdled into a disappointed scowl. Her arms were crossed, her gaze unforgiving.

'What? What now?' she said.

'Someone's been killed, murdered, in town, in the Market Square.'

'What?' said Magda, her more normal face once again taking shape. 'Murdered? In the Market Square? When?'

'Not sure. Some fighting between two groups of guys earlier this afternoon. One of them has just died in hospital. You know I…'

'Yes go, Kuba, go. Come and say goodbye, keep me posted. I can't believe it… killed, just like that, in the middle of the afternoon?'

***

Kuba had been a Krakow policeman for twenty years, a murder detective for twelve of them; he'd seen everything the city could show him, and dealt with everything it had

99

thrown at him. But the situation in front of him now made him mad as hell – never had someone been killed, in broad daylight in the very centre of his town, its beating heart and tourist magnet. The Market Square was known as a beautiful, benign and civilized place, where people came to enjoy themselves and look around in a safe environment.

Sure, like everywhere else they'd had their fair share of trouble with late-night drunks, the odd scuffle or mugging; but the Krakow authorities prided themselves in having at their disposal one of the more secure and attractive urban tourist zones in the whole of Europe.

Kuba had put his fair share of vodka away earlier at the party and now, an hour or so since he'd downed the last one, the hangover was beginning to kick in. He was tired, irritable and angry as he burst into the Lubicz Street station a little after six.

They were having a busy evening and demand for holding-cell space was exceeding supply. Only two cells had been available when the participants in the fun and games on the Market Square were brought in and now they were crammed into adjacent cells in the basement – nine Englishmen in one, six Russians in the other.

Kuba walked slowly down the stairs, and observed proceedings quietly from the bottom of them for a minute or two before making his presence felt.

The activity in the two cells – they had bars at the front, with a concrete wall between them – provided a sharp contrast. The Englishmen were relatively quiet – sitting on the bunk and hunkered down on the floor, looking heartbroken, tired and hungover as hungover could be. Their friend was dead, and this was a hard fact to process. The Russians next door, on the other hand, were acting up – laughing, issuing threats, casting aspersions on English masculinity, making jokes about what had happened at

100

Wembley Stadium and singing, Kuba heard with a tired, bored ache in his heart, the usual Russian songs: *Kalinka, Czarne Ocho, Katyusha*. They resonated, like curses, around his head; how he hated the sound of them.

He stepped forward, out of the shadows, to the front of the Russians' cell and motioned to a serious looking individual sitting quietly on the bunk. He was a little less bulked-out than his friends, with the same cropped head as the others but with a cunning rather than bovine look emanating from his dark eyes. Kuba had picked him out as the ringleader, the driving force; with his finger he motioned the man to come forward, towards the bars. He spread his hands out and made a backward motion with them to indicate to the others that they should take a few steps back. They sized him up, looked him in the eye, and did as they were told.

The man came forward.

'Name?' Kuba asked in Russian.

'Konstantin Aleksandrovich Yuran.'

'Where are you from?'

'St Petersburg.'

'All of you?'

'Yes.'

The police had confiscated all mobiles before placing the prisoners in cells. Kuba wanted to view what was on them.

'OK. Listen – I don't have time for your bullshit. I just want permission to look at your phone. I'd like to see your home movies.'

'Get a warrant.'

'If you give me permission I can look at it now. I have a form upstairs, for you to sign. Then I won't have to wait until tomorrow or the day after for a warrant – I can get started now.'

'What the fuck do I care when you start?'

Kuba leaned in closer, bending his long, lean frame down low, and reduced his voice almost to a whisper:

'Because if you don't cooperate with me now, Konstantin Aleksandrovich Yuran, you will go home – if you ever go home at all – in a wheelchair. I will break your hip on the right side, and your ankle on the left side, your ribs on both sides and your jaw everywhere.'

29

Kuba's interest in the Russians' phones had been piqued upon his arrival at the station. Chatting to the arresting officers before going down to the cells, he'd been told that the Russians were almost hysterical on the ride in. Everyone had been piled in the back of the vans together, and the Russians had been shouting, threatening and trying to get at the English guys, and had to be clattered with night sticks to slow them down.

Most interestingly, before they were confiscated, a couple of the Russians had fished their phones out of their pockets and tried to show the Englishmen clips of something.

***

Kuba took the trays containing the Russians' personal effects – Yuran had decided, upon reflection, to comply with his request – into his office. He selected Yuran's phone and went into it with the code and password he'd also been kindly supplied with. His grasp of Russian was not sufficient for him to read too much, but was good enough for him to navigate the sections. Someone else would do the analytics later.

Kuba was more interested in the flesh and blood stuff, and it didn't take him long to find it. The thousands of photos and video clips housed on the device indicated that the delightful Mr Yuran pursued two broad areas of interest: violent pornography and violent violence.

He sighed heavily and began to scroll and swipe his way through the inside of Yuran's mind. The porn he left behind quickly, shuddering at the thought of the girls or women who'd found themselves at the mercy of this little bastard, and thinking also about his two daughters, Zosia and Kasia, and the filthy gadget-powered cesspit of a world they were growing up in.

His mind was drifting; the downward pull of the hangover and the need for sleep were making him blunt and fuzzy. He left his office, walked around for five minutes and came back with strong coffee – black, heavily sugared, with the spoon practically standing up in it.

Right, you horrible little fucker, let's see what you've got.

What he had, Kuba found quickly and with mounting excitement, was a collection of clips of the carnage at Wembley – the stadium itself could be seen in some of them, and Kuba knew his football stadiums, especially the big London ones. He'd spent six months there, working in liason with the Met a couple of years after Poland joined the EU, and he never missed an opportunity to go to a game: Chelsea, Arsenal, West Ham, Spurs – all the big London clubs. Someone had even taken him to a place called Millwall, one bitterly cold Tuesday night.

He isolated the Wembley clips from the rest and focused in. The first thing he noticed was the quality of the images – they were using a GoPro camera, as they had in Marseillle during the fighting at the Euro 2016 championship, so that there were long, continuous passages of film as whoever was wearing the camera captured everything they ran towards, into and through.

There were clips taken on the way to the game and inside the stadium during it but things really began to get interesting as the camera guy and his friends left the stadium. To begin with, they quietened down; the general babbling stopped.

And then all hell broke loose. Surging out onto Olympic Way, the camera captured one violent assault after another, the perpetrators moving with purpose through the crowds, beating people about the head, knocking them over, kicking them when they were down. Yet still no audible excitement, no war cries or roars of triumph, just a business-like dispatching of innocents. Their victims made plenty of noise, but their attackers remained silent except for the effort of breathing as they ran and attacked.

There was something almost agricultural about it, like a crop being mown down by dedicated reapers. Kuba's skin began to crawl, and he took a sharp intake of breath – a face appeared that he recognized. He couldn't place it, but he knew he'd seen it before.

A bulky, England-shirt wearing middle aged man with multiple chins and a black moustache was giving as good as he got, firing off a volley of abuse, in what sounded to Kuba like a northern English accent, confronting his attackers. They redoubled their efforts, and eventually three men – one of them Konstantin Aleksandrovich Yuran – surrounded him and forced him to the ground, like jackals bringing down a springbok, and stamped on his head until he stopped moving. The camera lingered for a second or two on the man's shattered features before moving on.

Kuba moved the file back, to the point at which the man was still standing. Olympic Way was very well lit, and the image was clearly visible. Kuba never forgot a face. He now sat, in quiet concentration, and waited until his previous encounter with this one came to him. And it did. He sighed heavily, turned towards the keyboard on the desktop and Googled 'England v. Russia murder victims.'

A second's wait, and there it was; he had his man: 'Terry Parkinson, 52, of Sheffield.' He read on: 'Died in the back of an ambulance en route to the Brent Urgent Care Centre. Cause of death severe brain damage.'

Jesus, Mary and Joseph…The poor bastard didn't stand a chance.

105

Filled with anger Kuba pulled out his phone and began to trawl through it for a number he hadn't used in a while. It came up and he hit it.

It went straight to voicemail.

'H, my old friend, it's Kuba. Kuba Bukowski. How are you? Where are you? Sleeping one off, I suppose, you old bastard?'

30

H, his head and hands throbbing from the stitches and his head a little woozy from the mighty painkillers they'd given him at the hospital, heard the letterbox go just before dawn. He was too distraught to sleep; the sight of Ronnie Ruddock's corpse had overwhelmed him, and he was still desperately agitated. At least Little Ronnie was at home, and safe. Thank God for that, he thought, as he released himself from Olivia's grip, eased himself out of bed and padded downstairs.

There was an envelope on the mat; he recognized Amisha's handwriting, and opened it on the spot.

> *Hi H. We need to talk. Extremely important. No phones or suchlike. I'll be waiting for you at the old bandstand in Greenwich Park at 9 in the morning. Also at 9 tomorrow if you're not there today. Please come. Don't tell anyone – not a soul.*

It was starting to get light. H had no idea what Amisha might want, but he knew immediately that he'd go. He could sense, through the all-level hurt he was feeling, that something important was beginning: the murder of his best friend, the late-night call he'd received from Kuba, the return of the prodigal son, and now this. The small number of people he trusted and cared for were either dying or coming back into his orbit. The accelerating and incomprehensible strangeness of things in the world at large was becoming personal, closing in on him.

He stood in the hallway, thinking. There was no way on earth he'd sleep now, and he had a couple of hours to kill. He crept upstairs, tiptoed into the bedroom, pulled some clothes from his wardrobe, and went back downstairs to get dressed in the kitchen while the kettle boiled.

He took his tea to the living room, cradling it carefully in his bandaged hand, and sat down with it on the sofa. Olivia had cleared up as best she could, and the room had a clean but broken look. There was no TV – he'd planned to watch an old film on TCM or one of his James Stewart videos but had forgotten what he'd done with the damn thing.

He couldn't think clearly; the cuts on his forehead and face throbbed, and his hand ached – but these were as nothing compared to the searing pain in his heart and the sickening, low-down feeling in his stomach. He couldn't sit still – he needed to be on the move, needed to do something, something that would take him closer, even if only by an inch, to whoever had killed Ronnie. He thought of waking his son for a chat but decided against it – it was early and they'd gone to bed late – best to let him have some shuteye.

He would drive. He would drive until it was time to meet Amisha. He pulled on his coat and picked up his keys. There was a frost on the ground, and the cold made his cuts sting, livening him up. He clambered into the driver's seat, punched Frank's *Blues in the Night* into the sound system and pulled off in the direction of Greenwich.

31

'Jesus Christ, H, what happened to you?' said Amisha, steam rising from her breath into the grey morning air as H approached her through the mist.

'I had a row with a glass table, after Ronnie got killed,' said H, as if it was natural the two events should be connected. 'I lost it for a bit, went a bit potty. They stitched me up at the hospital. It's not as bad as it looks.'

'Ronnie who, not...?'

'Not the boy, no. Ronnie Ruddock. You remember Ronnie. He was killed yesterday at that riot in Durham. Someone tucked him up like a fucking kipper. I need to find out who.'

'Oh H, I'm so sorry. I didn't know...there's so much going on, it's impossible to keep up.'

'You can say that again Ames,' said H, making Amisha feel like the last couple of years had never happened, making her feel for a second that everything just might be OK. 'What the fuck is going on? I've spoken to young Andrew and a few others and they've told me what they know, but it's hard to put it all together.'

'That's what I want to talk to you about, as it happens. I'm starting to form some sort of idea of what's what...shall we sit in my car?'

***

They got straight down to it; this was no time to catch up on personal things, not the time for Amisha to air all the grief and resentment she'd felt towards H since he'd got her man Graham killed in Harwich during the drama with Dragusha. Maybe that would come later. For now, it sat between them like a black hole, too dense to get close to. Amisha absolved him of the need to confront it now – she could see that H was tired, and not in the best of order, so she took the lead.

She swore him to silence and filled him in on everything Zaida – she saw his eyes sparkle a little at the mention of her aunt's name – had told her: the compromising of key players in the system; her certainty that nobody could be trusted and that something big was in the offing; her feeling that all the apparent chaos was being orchestrated from above; her suggestion that there was high-level Russian involvement in what was happening.

'Funny you should mention that lot,' said H. 'My boy Ronnie made it back to London last night after the riot at Winson Green. He thinks the Russians pulled all that off, and last night I got a call from an old mate in Poland – a copper – who's saying he's found film of one of the murders at Wembley on some nutter's phone. He's certain it was all planned, like a military thing. He's got one of the killers bang-to-rights. Says he'll process them through the proper channels.

'Great,' said Amisha, 'Andrew and I have just come to the conclusion that all these white "nationalist" guys running about attacking everyone are probably not Brits. You never hear them speak, or sing. We saw them in action in Brick Lane the other day, up close – very well organized, but not shouting like you might expect. So…'

'The Russians are the favourite,' said H. 'Makes sense. But where does it take us?'

'It's a start H, if we connect it to what Zaida says about all these vast sums of oligarch money sloshing around in the obscure offshore accounts of the great and the good.'

'OK, it's a start, I'll give you that. What else does Zaida say?'

'That she thinks some sort of info war is going on – you know, misinformation, fake news, all of that, and that it's being waged by someone who really knows what they're doing. She thinks that's key – that whoever is behind all this is making it very hard for anyone to get an overview of what's going on. Partly because the system's overloaded, and we're just dealing with crises as they come up, without having time to do proper investigations, and partly because the media is so weird now it's hard to know who's telling the truth.'

'Give me an example,' said H, 'something I can get my teeth into.'

'Well…how much do you trust the BBC and the rest of the mainstream media?'

'Don't get me started on that fucking lot Ames, you know what I think of them. It's normally just a lot of old bollocks. They make things up, or spin things that do happen their way. Everyone knows that.'

'Exactly…that's my point. Half the population thinks the way you do now and Zaida says this is being exploited by someone very clever, all this mistrust of the media. Joey Jupiter says the same.'

'What's that little fucking mongrel's opinion got to do with anything?'

'Read his blog, look at his YouTube channel. I think he may be one of the few people who's got a handle on what's going on – he's saying exactly what Zaida is.'

'I find that very difficult to believe, Ames.'

'No, seriously. He's sort of…more grown up now. Like all this is bringing the best out of him. He's much more serious than he was, and he's been helping people understand at least something about what's going on.'

H sighed, heavily, thinking back to the times when Jupiter had hounded him, made him a laughing stock before the

111

entire British public, and nearly tipped him over the edge. There were still times when he filled an idle moment with daydreams of holding the little bastard by the scruff of the neck, getting ready to bring the hammer down.

'H, we haven't got time for all that old stuff now. Trust me – Jupiter's independent, he's trying to see through the propaganda, the fog of war. Get over it…we might need him.'

'We?'

'Well we can't just sit on our hands and watch London, the whole country, go up in flames, can we? I thought you of all people…'

'Alright Ames, slow down, for fuck's sake. What have you and Zaida got in mind?'

32

'Basically,' said Amisha, winding down the car window to let in a gust of cold air for the flagging big man, 'we have three things to consider. First, all hell is breaking loose and we have only the faintest of theories to work on as to who's behind it. No doubt the spooks are working like crazy, but Zaida say's there's an inertia that goes all the way to the top. Second, it seems that with so many people compromised we don't know who, further up the chain than us, can be trusted. Third, it's not random – it's heading somewhere, its building up to something big, and we need to understand what it is and how to stop it, because it can't be good. Any thoughts?'

'I think you and your aunt have been watching too many spy films.'

'H, seriously. We need help. Who else do we have? I'm at the Yard with Andrew, Zaida is at GCHQ...we're basically all just desk-wallahs. Sure, I can do a little bit of hands-on, and we know how to go deep to look for information, and cover our tracks, and all that sort of thing, but we...'

'Haven't got a fucking clue about who's running things out here, on the street, or how to track them down and stop them. Am I getting warm?'

'H, where's all your patriotic zeal gone? All your "no one fucks with my city" stuff? Don't you care?' said Amisha.

'I don't need any speeches from the likes of you, young lady. Number one: whoever killed Ronnie Ruddock is going to die, and die hard, and my ugly, leering mug looking down at him is going to be the last thing he ever sees. Number two: no, we can't just sit on our hands, we've got to get weaving. Number three: who else you got on board? And don't talk to me about people like Joey fucking Jupiter.'

'Well, we were hoping you'd have an idea about who to bring in, people you would trust your life with, but they can't be "official" types on a chain of command. We need…'

'Bottom feeders, I get the picture. We need stand-up street level blokes I can personally vouch for, who I can get to and work with "off-grid" as you'd say, yes?'

'Well yes, and…'

'Don't stop me now Ames, I'm getting the flavour. Let's see…so it's you, little Andrew Glass the wonder beard and your auntie Zaida and Joey fucking Jupiter – plus me and a gaggle of old paratroopers and whoever else I might be able to round up versus the Russian Army, probably, in the middle of a state of emergency. Have I got that right?'

'That's about the size of it, H. What do you think?'

'What I think, Ames, is that you and your aunt probably do need help…from doctors, as well as the likes of me…'

He paused for a few seconds, lost in thought, and pulled out his phone. '…and that I'm going to need a proper right-hand man. What time is it in Krakow?'

***

Amisha left H to make his call. She walked around for a bit to clear her head and then went back to the car. She popped the boot open, took out a small cardboard box and got back inside the car. H was sitting quietly, lost in thought.

'All good H?' she said, 'is your man on board?'

'Yep, on his way. What's in the box?'

Amisha cracked it open and pulled out a vaguely familiar gadget.

'These,' she said, 'are going to be crucial to our endeavours. Zaida managed to get hold of them, and she's souped them up herself.'

'Well come on then, what are they?'

'Military grade field phones. Double-encrypted at both ends, six of them locked into their own network. They can call one another from anywhere – if you're in the middle of a desert or the Arctic they'll take a signal from a satellite – and nobody can hack in and listen to what's being said.'

'Nobody?'

'Well, almost nobody. You'd need a Zaida-level genius to crack these. I couldn't do it.'

'Good enough for me.'

'Zaida and I have one, there are four in the box.'

Handsome. Me, Kuba, one other guy I know can help ...and one for Olivia, to be on the safe side.

H took the box, and felt the old tingle, the old urge to action rising within him. He wanted to jump out of the car and get cracking, straight away. But something was holding him back, and he could see Amisha was feeling the same.

'H,' she said after a few moments' awkward silence, 'it's good to see you. I didn't know if it would be...but it is.'

'Same here Ames, same here. Look, I...'

'No need for speeches H, or a review of all the horrors. Not now. But I'm glad to see you're still you.'

'Who else would I be? Listen, why don't you come around and say hello to Liv and Little Harry?'

'Not now H, no. Let's not get ahead of ourselves. Say hello to them for me though, won't you?'

33

Vladimir Agapov was enjoying his reprieve. It was well over a year since he'd been beaten to within an inch of his life by H, and left in a heap in an old lock-up at the Elephant and Castle. But he had a depth of resourcefulness that enabled him to survive the ordeal, and get away from what, for most, would have been their tomb.

After breaking free, patching himself up and stopping the bleeding from his various wounds he limped sorely out into the world and proceeded to keep his head down for several months. He slept on the street in quiet corners by day and travelled around the country by night, stealing cars, hiding out on night trains, doing a few muggings and robberies to keep the cash flowing. His focus was not on simply avoiding the law, but evading the even longer arm of the worldwide organisation controlled by his former employer, the oligarch Kyril Kuznetsov. It was Kuznetsov who had provided the IT and security for the high-level paedophile ring that had been responsible for the murder of Ronnie Ruddock's wife, although he'd soon given them up when things got a bit tasty. Evading Kuznetsov had proved to be far harder than evading the law – and the consequences of capture would have been far more severe

He'd slept on the streets in Brighton and Glasgow, and everywhere in between where rough sleepers don't make too much of an impression on the locals who ignore and swarm around them as if they were street furniture.

Some months after his escape he started to get himself together in earnest. He returned to London and took a room in a house off the Walworth Road, livening up his rehabilitation by chasing his Romanian landlady up and down the stairs, much to her delight. He worked out, got himself back into shape and focused more and more on the fantasies of retribution he'd been cooking up since his beating. He tracked H down and watched him and his wife and child from afar. He learned where they lived, and gave much thought to the most diabolical methods with which to serve up a cold dish of merciless vengeance. He hung about in dodgy south London pubs and procured the necessary weaponry required to take on his adversary. Six months after his ordeal at H's hands he was ready, and plans were in place to take care of all three of them. He would show none of them any mercy.

And then his luck changed; and so, by extension, did the luck of the Hawkins family. One bright morning, when he was lying on his bed in relaxed post-breakfast mode, running through a wide range of lingering-death-of-Hawkins scenarios in his mind, he was confronted by a team of Kuznetsov's grimmest underlings, swarming in through the double-locked door of his room like it wasn't there. The hammer, at last, was falling, as he knew one day it must, and he readied himself for his back-seat car ride into oblivion. But no sooner had he balled his fists and readied himself for his last, futile battle for survival than the group of men moving towards him stopped and stood easy, their hands at their sides. At the centre of the semi-circle they'd formed he saw the diminutive and dapper figure of Kuznetsov's right-hand man. This was the man with no name, as far as the likes of Agapov were concerned, but a man who spoke directly for Kuznetsov. He was all business, dismissing his hulking crew from the room, pulling up a chair next to Agapov's bed and gently motioning him to sit back down.

Vladimir Agapov – veteran of the Chechen wars, former leader of one of Kuznetsov's most feared drug and people-running gangs, ruthless dispenser of murderous violence and untold misery – did as he was told, and, sensing that this was not in fact to be the last of his days on earth, cried like a baby.

'OK, my brother, it's OK,' said the man with no name. 'It is time for the black sheep to return to the fold. Mr Kuznetsov has shown you mercy. He needs you – the Motherland needs you.'

34

Something big was afoot, that much was clear. But Agapov was told only the details of the small part of the big picture that he needed to know. His orders were issued verbally, slowly and meticulously, and he listened hard – he knew there would be no documentation coming down the pipeline later to remind him of anything.

He was to begin, Kuznetsov's man told him, by leading a carefully scheduled series of raids on a number of prisons. Agapov soon realised that this, whatever it was, went all the way to the top. A few inmates were to be killed and the rest driven out into the streets. Spectacular explosions were to be used upon initial entry into the prisons – mostly for effect, as all internal security and surveillance systems had been hacked and would be under control. Key moments in the drama were to be livestreamed on social media.

Agapov was liking what he heard, and he ran through in his mind a short list of individuals he would take care of personally. Very personally.

What came next sounded much riskier: after the prisons were dealt with he was to make his way to an isolated compound in the Kent countryside and secure and defend it at all costs; he would be leading a group of thirty hand-picked former Spetznatz men.

'I emphasise at all costs,' Kuznetsov's man told him, 'and if the cost be the life of you and all your men, nobody, not even the British Army, is to gain access to the compound. Do you understand? We are making history…sacrifices will have to be made.'

***

'Faster, faster, what do you think this is, netball practice?' he screamed at his men as he put them through their paces in the fully equipped gym that had been put in place to help keep them occupied and in trim. Protecting a compound was boring work, most of the time. This one had been selected with great care, and bought and paid for several years earlier through the correct channels – Mr Kuznetsov always went through the correct channels in his business dealings in the UK.

It was a large place, deep in the heart of Kent. Nonington College had extensive grounds and had once been a specialist training centre for sports teachers, but had been sold off by the government in the 1980s to a new age religious sect from Germany who wanted, by and large, to be left alone. In an attempt to fit in and curry favour with the locals they developed a side-line making toys, and sold them at village fetes and suchlike; within a couple of years they had more or less become part of the landscape. They didn't bother anyone and nobody bothered them.

After fifteen years of living in peace and harmony their talismanic leader died after one mammoth session too many on the marching powder and the sect fell apart, riven by infighting for the succession. The fragmented remnants of the sect managed to cooperate sufficiently to sell the place to a London businessman and headed back to Bavaria.

John Stables, so the locals thought, was a working-class wide boy from London who'd got into property and done alright for himself. He turned up at the local village pub once in a while, full of plenty of chat and easy-going charm, to let the locals know their beautiful listed building was in good hands; this ensured there were no objections when he applied for planning permission to carry out a few modifications.

On the outside the modifications looked like they were in line with the permissions granted by the local council. On the inside, they were anything but. At the heart of the compound, twenty feet below ground, a bunker was built containing what not even John Stables was to know. The building was also beefed up with reinforced concrete walls lined with lead and a security system that would not have disgraced GCHQ headquarters in Cheltenham.

Agapov himself had no idea what the bunker contained and he and his men were under strict instructions never to visit it. They were to protect it with their lives but enter it under pain of death. Even if the Russian President himself turned up, with the Secretary General of the United Nations in tow, the instructions were clear – no one, but no one except the six operatives who lived and worked down there – and who only came out to eat and stretch their legs from time to time outside – were allowed in.

As he put his men through their paces Agapov reflected on his new role and the work he'd done so far, and was pleased. He'd helped take down a few prisons and dish out some primitive justice, which was all very satisfying work. He didn't care about what the big picture was; what was being planned was many pay grades over his head. He'd done his bit, and he took pride in his role in the bigger, violently destructive drama that was unfolding.

His men had been required to surrender their gadgets, and all communications went through him; beyond the compound he knew that fear, loathing and mistrust were now the order of the day. His Russian brothers – as he could see from the clips he watched when he was alone – were wreaking havoc across the land, and the British hadn't even figured it out yet; how could they? And it had all been so easy – the internet and social media revolution that people had thought was going to be such fun and make them all so free had turned sour: it had already created the environment of ignorance and separation that made things all so simple. It had fashioned a world of mistrust in which liberals and conservatives screamed at each other in echo chambers about how evil and stupid the other side was, in which minor differences had been massively amplified and in which nobody trusted anybody or anything they heard. His masters knew the potential for mischief in all this – had known it all along – and now they were in the driving seat, years ahead of the curve when it came to the info wars and media manipulation.

Yes, it had all been so easy, thought Agapov, as he shouted another command to keep the men on their toes. And when his work here was done he still had another appointment, an appointment he was looking forward to with joyous anticipation. He smiled and relaxed, a man at ease with his new situation, proud of the job he'd already completed with shocking success, the job of butchering the best friend of the man he hated most in the world.

I hope you survive the coming storm, Inspector Hawkins, so I can make you suffer like your friend.

35

'OK H, I'll book a week off for next week and come straight over,' Kuba had said, responding without hesitation to his friend's call for help.

'You're going to need more than a week son, the way things are shaping up.'

'OK H, let's cross that bridge when we come to it. I'll start with a week.'

'Alright son, text me the flight details and I'll meet you at the airport. You can stay at ours.'

***

H had known Kuba Bukowski for twelve years now, he recalled, as he sat in the arrivals lounge at Stanstead Airport waiting for the flight from Krakow to come in. Around 2005, just after Poland had joined the European Union, London had seen an influx of Poles: the bold and the brave, the good, the bad and the ugly – everything Poland had to offer, it seemed, rocked up in the metropolis in search, for the most part, of an honest living.

At the sharp end of things, where H was, this meant an influx of villains and moochers coming to London to chance their arm, and before long he was finding people with new kinds of unpronounceable names on the list of people he needed to talk to as part of murder investigations. One case, involving a thug from Nowa Huta who kicked someone to death in a bar packed full of people who saw nothing, took H deep into a new slice of London life: a community of hardworking people being preyed upon by the kind of parasites H was very familiar with, but could not talk to.

He needed more than a translator – he needed someone who knew how things worked, who knew people the way he did, and he got more than he bargained for. Kuba, a no-nonsense, larger than life giant with a colourful past who was almost as much a handful as himself, was seconded to the Met by the Krakow Police Department.

They hit it off immediately, on the basis of a shared love of Frank Sinatra, WWII history and hard drinking. H listened in amazement as Kuba related stories of crime and punishment in Poland, not so much at the stories themselves as the way they were being told.

'Fuck me mate, your English is better than mine. Where'd you learn to talk like that?'

'My mum was a big Anglophile, she had me reading English books from when I was young. We spoke English in the house, there were always British and American films, a lot of music. Then I studied engineering – before I joined the army – and a lot of that was in English.'

'Blinding,' said H.

'Not really, a lot of people in Poland can speak good English, you only think it's amazing because you Brits don't know languages – half of you can barely even speak your own properly. What is all this jabber I'm hearing around me...not exactly the Queen's English, is it?'

'You having a pop at me, son?'

Kuba stared at him, letting the silence build for a few seconds, checking him out. He liked what he saw; a proud man who would not back down, even in little things; a man like himself.

'No H, just making an observation about the strange people of your country. Have a drink,' Kuba said, refilling their glasses liberally with vodka.

'Cheers,' said H, 'God bless you.'

H took the vodka hit, and relaxed.

'Speak any other languages do you, Brainiac?'

'Well, my German's pretty good, and my Russian's ok.'

'Russian, eh? That must come in handy in our line of work.'

'You have no idea, H. You have no idea.'

***

The Krakow flight landed. It took Kuba ages to get through customs. H hadn't seen him for over six years, and noticed him as soon as he saw a tall, lean figure head and shoulders above the rest of the crowd, striding purposefully through the gate. Not much had changed, with the exception of a modish sprouting of facial hair.

'Fuck me mate, they allow comedy beards in the Krakow police now do they?' said H through the bearhug they gave one another.

'Yep,' said Kuba, 'in fact they encourage it – much the same way the Met likes to employ massive fat drunken bastards.'

'I'm not with the Met anymore.'

'Can't say I'm surprised to hear that,' said Kuba, smiling and holding H at arm's length to look at him. 'It's good to see you my friend.'

36

Olivia laid a chicken curry on the kitchen table, something H had become rather partial to over the last few years. Kuba, who'd been bouncing the baby boy on his knee and making a fuss of him while he chatted to Little Ronnie, took a deep breath and said 'Ah, I love English food.'

'You're good with the boy,' said Ronnie. 'The old man tells me you've got three kids?'

'Four, now. Kuba junior, the youngest, is four. I have Zosia, Kasia – your dad's goddaughter – and Andzrej.' He looked at the boy on his knee and smiled: 'So, Little Kuba and now Little Harry,' he said, ruffling the boy's hair. 'I hope this one grows up to be like his dad…well, up to a point anyway.'

Olivia smiled to herself; Kuba clearly knew her man.

'So, you worked together here, in London, before?' Ronnie asked.

'Yes, for about six months. Eleven or twelve years ago. Some thugs from my part of the world were terrorising people, it all went too far, a couple of people were killed. It was very heavy, your dad saved my bacon on more than one occasion. Literally saved it…we became good friends, and he even visited me in Krakow, came to Kasia's christening. We stayed in touch for a long time and then…you know.'

'It must be good to see each other again,' said Olivia, 'even in these terrible circumstances.'

'Well, yes. But I can't believe how bad things are here. You see it on the news but being here, seeing what's going on.'

'So, what's H up to Kuba?' said Olivia, changing the subject abruptly. 'What is he planning? I know there's

126

something going on, but he won't tell me. It's not like him. He usually tells me everything.'

'I don't know Olivia, I only have a rough idea of what's going on. But H said he needs help, he asked me to come. H asked, I came. Simple as that. He would do the same for me.'

***

After dinner Olivia took the boy upstairs for his bath and H and Kuba went to the living room, the condition of which required H to go through the story of Ronnie Ruddock's murder and his reaction to it once again.

They settled into their chairs, Kuba noticing that there were still tiny fragments of glittering glass embedded in the carpet.

'OK H, why exactly am I here?'

Kuba listened quietly as H took him through everything he thought he needed to know, and about the situation in general and the particulars of his discussion and agreement with Amisha, whose name he didn't reveal.

When H was finished Kuba let out a long, long breath and nodded, letting his friend know that he understood the scale of the problem.

'It comes down to this, mate. We've got to try and do something. My technical firm are drilling down into the dark web. They're certain everything we've seen so far is just an opener, a starter for ten. We need information, but until we start getting it we have to act on the assumption that nobody in any official position, in any institution, can be trusted. We don't know who might've been got at.'

'OK,' said Kuba, 'so you are what…trying to put some kind of team – or "firm", as you say – together? And you thought of me?'

'Mate, the situation here is absolutely dire. Our technical team are the dog's bollocks, but sooner or later we're going to need some proper men on the ground, dealing with these fuckers. I made a list of everyone I know, professionals who can handle themselves and who can be relied on; and then I made a list of people I trust completely, I compared the lists and finished up with two names – it would've been three up until a few days ago, until they killed my mate Ronnie – but now it's two. One of them I haven't seen for three years, and one of them is you.'

'And what about this other guy?' said Kuba.

'We find him, and take it from there. He's good as gold, and will know other people – he's probably already active on this, knowing him.'

'So how do we contact him?' asked Kuba.

'Well that, my old son,' said H, 'is a good fucking question.'

37

Amisha, Andrew and Zaida approached the roadblock on the south side of Waterloo Bridge in Andrew's car. Amisha flashed her warrant card and they got through on the fast track, heading towards the West End. Many of the central parts of the London boroughs were now under curfew after nine o'clock in the evening, but the West End and City were still open for business and pleasure round the clock under the watchful eyes of the Army.

It was 5.00pm as they crossed the bridge. The scene that greeted them along the sky and river-line of the great metropolis was extraordinary, like something out of a dystopian sci-fi movie: helicopters made their concentric circles overhead, swooping and wheeling around the now tiny-looking St. Paul's and the giant new signature global towers alike, scanning, searching, homing in on trouble. The bridge itself was dotted with gun emplacements charged with taking down the multitude of unidentified small drones that now buzzed overhead daily. Most of them were harmless and had been deployed by someone as a form of stress-building psychological warfare, others had been flown into key areas to create panicking crowds, and a small number carried insignificant explosive payloads which made them something like glorified and unpredictable fireworks. Rumours were rife that some were also spraying the streets with toxic biological or chemical agents, though this had not been officially confirmed. The Army's policy was to shoot them all down on sight, and Amisha, Andrew and Zaida watched with interest as a black, circular one was hit in the air not far from the Shell Building, spun and fragmented as it fell and came gently to rest, lightweight thing that it was, on the surface of the Thames.

Andrew swung a left into the Strand and headed towards the West End. Halfway down towards Trafalgar Square they passed a small fleet of parked-up ambulances and a stretch of pavement littered with the prone forms of people mown down in yet another attack on pedestrians by a hacked driverless car – another new feature of daily life in the city to which the population had become quickly accustomed.

'This is insane. Absolutely insane,' said Andrew, 'why don't we just put the whole city in lockdown? How can we have this every day?'

Zaida met his eyes, from the backseat, in the rear-view mirror. 'Two main reasons, Andrew,' she said. 'Firstly, it's completely impractical – London is too big, and too complex, to be shut down. Impossible. Secondly, London is London. Bad actors – worse actors than these – have tried before and failed to bring it down and destroy it. This city does not capitulate to terrorists, or militaries, or anything else. It does not surrender. We have to show the world that Britain is still Britain.'

Amisha was put in mind – not for the first time when listening to her aunt speak – of H. They were much more alike than their very different backgrounds, lives and surface features might suggest: Zaida, like the big man himself, was a patriot. She loved her adopted country and the opportunities it had provided her, and was showing Amisha and Andrew once again the calm, steely determination with which she would fight its enemies.

This was food for thought, and Amisha was impressed. Andrew, not so much:

'I don't know, I wish it were just that, Zaida,' he said through a heavy expulsion of breath. 'Terrorism, I mean, I wish that was all it is. If this is just the starter, I dread to think what sort of main course we might be in for.'

38

Amisha directed Andrew to park in a side street close to the BBC's broadcasting house, and led the party to a nearby coffee shop. She knew that the BBC had a well-organized and resilient internet system and thought they may need to feed off or hack into its wi-fi if the web got wobbly or dropped out – as it was tending to do, here and there, now and then, as unseen hackers jerked the coverage around.

They occupied a quiet booth, and got set up for work; Detective Sergeant Andrew Glass was about to receive a masterclass in internet surveillance, espionage and the dark web. True, he was becoming a top-notch, research-intensive detective in his own right, and he knew his way around online. But he'd never gone as deep as Zaida or Amisha – nowhere near as deep, and his general sense of this nether region, this sphere of anonymous hitmen, drug and weapons dealers, paedophiles and terrorists, was about to be seriously updated.

The hunt for clues that might connect oligarch money to what was happening on the streets was on. Zaida started Andrew off with a couple of breadcrumbs to try and make a trail out of: some offhand references to a location she'd noticed when tracking down the purchase with oligarch money of some expensive scientific equipment that, as far as she could tell, had been exported to the United Arab Emirates, before the trail went cold. It wasn't much, but it had turned up twice, along with some words that her programme had identified as slightly out of sequence. The words were: innocent, glen, log and on.

'And who or what might glen be?' he asked.

'Don't know,' said Zaida, 'it's just that a programme I ran identified the words as not being used in a normal way, throughout some emails that had been intercepted before all the current troubles started. Not long after I reported these findings I was assigned to a different role with less access than I had before.'

Andrew started to follow the breadcrumbs, which was a perfect job for Andrew, being that he was a follow-the-breadcrumbs type of guy.

'And me?' said Amisha.

'I want you to try and find out where all this equipment was delivered,' said Zaida. She showed her niece details of the equipment she wanted found. 'It was ordered two years ago. I discovered it while running some pattern searching software on GCHQ bulk data. It was ordered from and manufactured in Singapore to very specific requirements. I found the location where it was built, and then exported to the United Arab Emirates, but after that the trail goes cold. But it's a lot of real-world equipment with a capacity to cook up some very serious mischief. Someone, somewhere, moved it around, by plane or ship or lorry. We need to find out where it went.'

Amisha studied the list of equipment and researched what it all was. Being a bright young thing, she cottoned onto the possibilities quickly.

'Oh my God…Zaida, you don't think someone's making a..'

'It's within the realms of possibility, but I just don't know what happened to the equipment. What I do know is that it was all paid for with well-hidden Russian money – and it's had the most money poured into it of any of the things I've found so far.'

The gears moved swiftly in Amisha's head, and she felt her stomach churn. Zaida's concern was about a much bigger picture, a much bigger scale of threat than anything they'd seen so far. A whole new level of grief and chaos might be awaiting them – awaiting them all – if they didn't get on top of things. She got to work.

Zaida herself explored a third avenue of investigation. Some of the information she'd come across, before she'd been moved, had included a code name for what she believed to be a 'boots on the ground' operative who had been planted somewhere in the United Kingdom. She resolved to track down this 'secret agent' and discern his identity.

She'd taken a huge risk in downloading some bulk data onto her personal area of the cloud when her suspicions of infiltration were first aroused. She accessed it now and started to run a full indexed search of all references she previously thought suspicious. This gave her more than she bargained for, with thousands of possible avenues to explore. Without access to GCHQ interrogation software, which helped refine and prioritise possibilities, she was finding she had no choice but to explore them one by one.

She went down one cul-de-sac after another, spending time breaking into several not very secure databases, joining obscure websites and leaving messages pretending to be people she was not – 'spratting to catch a mackerel', as H would have said – to see if anyone would bite. She also scattered pictures and messages with hidden spyware in them everywhere she went and set up an automated message system so that if anyone opened her stuff she'd be alerted immediately.

The three of them worked on into the evening, sitting in their booth, guzzling coffee, undisturbed by the outside world. They worked quietly, methodically, for several hours, before Amisha called the meeting to order.

'Andrew, what have you got?'

'Nothing, really. Nothing worth reporting.'

'Zaida?'

'About the same. No real progress on the identity of our mystery operative – if there even is such a person. And not a bite on any messages I've been leaving.'

'And you,' said Zaida, 'any progress?'

Amisha displayed her computer screen to Zaida and pointed to a PDF file of a delivery note she'd discovered.

'The equipment,' she said, 'I traced it through several changes of delivery point and it eventually went into the world shipping database. I managed to access the database – I've been here before, so I managed to do it quickly – and here's the end point, as far as I can tell.'

The other two looked at the delivery note in horror.

'Southampton docks! Fuck!' exclaimed Andrew.

'Yes,' said Amisha, 'the equipment is in Britain.'

39

Olivia gave Little Harry a bath and read him a story. H usually read him *Where the Wild Things Are* but she was beginning to be alarmed by her husband's somewhat obsessive attachment to it. She knew he'd read it for years to Little Ronnie when he was a young boy, and he seemed reluctant to move away from it now and branch out.

She tucked the boy in and collapsed, exhausted, onto her own bed. Her anxiety level was peaking, and the voice of Kuba Bukowski, booming up loud, clear and Polish from downstairs, was doing little to calm her down. She liked him well enough, admired him even, and could see why H had so much time for him. But his arrival portended something frightening; she didn't know what H was planning, but she was sure he was going to be around less now, and out there much more, on the front line, in mortal danger.

She sighed heavily, took her tablet from the bedside table and brought up Joey Jupiter's page, automatically, without enthusiasm. She knew reading it was not likely to raise her spirits, but she also knew there were not many other places she could go to that would offer her perspective.

Her heart was moving down, through her stomach and towards the floor, before she got to the end of the first sentence.

GREAT BRITAIN, LAND OF LIBERTY LOST

So it has come to pass; the disaster most of us assumed could never happen has happened. To this land of the freeborn Englishman, of the mother of parliaments, the home of Magna Carta, this Sceptered Isle, etc., etc., etc. has been

135

introduced Martial Law. Full Martial Law. Read your papers, people, flick through your websites, gawp at your screens for details. Read it and weep: freedom is dead – in Great Britain, of all places.

We will not rehearse the details of the straitjacket to be placed upon us all here, but make only one point: the terrorists, the agents of chaos, have won. They have torn wide the fabric of our civilized society in not much more than a week.

And consider this: the mission – the duty – I have set out here in recent days just got much, much harder to fulfill. To find and band together with others who can be trusted; to search for the truth; to track down and confront the agents of chaos – all this must be done in a nation now pinned down by curfews, roadblocks, armed patrols, restrictions on movement, association and media access of all kinds.

The agents of chaos hit us hard and made us unsteady on our feet, and the state has now cut us off at the knees.

But still, somehow, we must rise.

40

The tech musketeers had shifted location a couple of times throughout the night, and then throughout the next day, just to be on the safe side; they didn't want to make use of their home wi-fis so they stayed out, moving from coffee shop to hotel to early morning breakfast bar.

It was now evening again and they'd already used up a full 24 hours, and were back in the place they'd started. The night was clearer, but the stars remained hidden from view, subsumed into the lights of central London. They were tired and irritable – long hours staring at their screens had taken its toll on their eyes – when Amisha got in another three coffees and once again called the team to order.

'All we seem to have so far, then, is that some high-specification scientific equipment, equipment that can be used to breed highly toxic viruses, is probably in the country.'

'Yes,' said Zaida, 'and I'm tired, and losing concentration. I need to sleep.'

'Let's get to another hotel, I know one not far from here. They'll have wi-fi and we can sleep and work in shifts,' said Andrew. 'It's a bit low-grade but they'll take cash and won't ask any questions...it's a spicy sort of place.'

'And how would you know that?' asked Amisha.

Andrew shrugged his shoulders and pulled a face, but said nothing.

***

The lobby of the dive in Camden was seedy and dimly lit, and a strong smell of bleach made it feel like they were in a toilet. A couple of semi pornographic oil paintings adorned the walls. The receptionist, an old and overweight man who looked like he could do with more than a lick of soap, looked on in admiration as the young, nerdy looking man with the comedy beard, accompanied by two absolute beauties, handed over the cash for one double room. He looked Andrew up and down and handed over the keys with an envious smirk.

Fuck me, this little bastard is either absolutely loaded or he's got one hell of a trouser snake.

The room had the same overpowering smell of bleach as the rest of the place but was surprisingly clean, Andrew thought, as he threw the keys onto a side table.

'Welcome to paradise,' he said.

Zaida made straight for the bed, laid down and was asleep within minutes. Amisha and Andrew took out their computers and accessed the hotel wi-fi, silently praying that it was working.

'It's going to be another long night,' said Amisha. They got down to work, Amisha on the bed next to her snoring but restless aunt, Andrew on one of the two old upright chairs by a small table near the window.

Several hours went by. Zaida woke up and got back on track. Andrew had a few hours kip. Amisha worked all night. It was early morning before the three spoke again.

'Nothing,' said Andrew. 'Not a sausage. I can't find anything of significance. These breadcrumbs are leading nowhere. Whoever is behind all this knows what they're doing.'

The other two concurred; it was time for a change of scene.

'Let's get out of here,' said Amisha, 'and go and get some breakfast. It's going to be another long day – there's no way we're giving up.'

As they descended the stairs the same receptionist was still on duty and he gave Andrew a smile and a wink as the threesome left the hotel. Given the place's usual usage and clientele, he couldn't be blamed for misjudging the situation.

Lucky little bastard.

41

Amisha, Zaida and Andrew were beginning to lose hope. Could the three of them really break highly secure computer systems with three laptops and hotel wi-fi? Were just the three of them enough? Did they have enough time? Did they have enough brainpower?

Amisha, who hadn't slept for almost three days, switched track while the others were sleeping and was using software developed by one of her friends at Cambridge University, designed to break codes in high-end security certificates. She'd found some servers she suspected were sending and receiving messages relating to the chaos gripping the country – that was the easy part – but accessing them was more or less impossible, and she was only trying out of sheer desperation.

She always kept up to date with what was going on, tech wise, with her old chums at Cambridge and made sure she had the latest versions of the code cracking software. But she knew before she started that it was as pointless as trying to catch wind in a net given the level of security involved. She explained to the others what she had been up to.

'I can find the servers and messaging channels that are being used, I think, to co-ordinate some of these activities, but getting into them is close to impossible. They're using a 2048 bit RSA modulus, which means we are dealing with a 61-digit number which, as far as I know, is the world's record for factoring the largest general integer.'

Zaida nodded her head vigorously, and frowned. Andrew wondered why Amisha had stopped speaking human language, and tried desperately to retrieve some morsel of meaning from what she was saying.

Amisha continued: 'Even if my software could find the average probability of time to factor the RSA Modulus associated with the key in the certificate to efficiently try all possibilities, given the processing power we have at our disposal it's going to take a very long time to crack the code. A very long time indeed.'

'How long?' said Andrew, at last hearing a phrase he could work with.

Amisha did some rough sums on a piece of paper. She often turned to the old technologies when the sums got super-tricky.

'Well, that's 4,294,967,296 x 1.5 million, which would be 4.3 billion years more than doing it for a 1024-bit certificate, which means that ...'

'A ballpark figure will do ma'am,' said Andrew, 'just something rough for me to get my teeth into.'

'About 6.4 quadrillion years,' said Amisha.

Zaida closed her eyes, sat back and began to breathe deeply. Andrew laughed out loud and felt a sudden craving for beer. Big beer.

'So,' said Amisha, 'I conclude that we are dealing with people who know what they're doing.'

'Yes,' said Zaida, opening her eyes, 'we won't crack their codes and, Amisha my love, I'm surprised you're even trying. All we can do is follow breadcrumbs and leave messages and spyware, and hope that someone somewhere clicks on something we can follow-up on. Human error always kicks in at some point – even the most sophisticated system can be compromised by a moment of thoughtlessness, or tiredness. This is our best hope of finding something we can use to send H and his boys out on the offensive.'

'Or…' said Amisha, holding the thought about going on the offensive.

'Or what?' exclaimed Andrew.

'Or maybe we're going about this the wrong way. Maybe we need to go on the offensive.'

'And do what?'

'Launch a cyberattack of our own.'

'How?' said Zaida. 'We'd need a heck of a lot of computing power.'

'I know what we need, and I have an idea of how we could get it.' Amisha launched a piece of software that identified the servers she was sure were controlling the messaging, and showed her screen to her aunt.

'This DNS server, it's outside the firewall of whoever's doing this. It has to be, in order to control general internet traffic.'

'Go on.'

'What if we launched a full-scale attack on it, overloaded it, and brought it down.'

'What,' said Andrew, 'in the same way the Chinese took out the government websites and the BBC for a time last year?'

'Exactly,' said Amisha, warming to her subject, 'if we could take it down, simply by inundating it with simple requests it would need to check and reject, when they bring it back online there would be a moment of vulnerability, before it was fully rebooted and all the post-operating software was loaded. We'd have a few seconds when we could access it.'

'Brilliant... I think,' said Andrew. He looked at Zaida.

'Well, as I just said, we'd need some huge servers or around seventy-five thousand separate personal computers to have that sort of capacity.'

Amisha played her trump card. 'But we also have H... don't forget we have H.'

Zaida and Andrew looked back at her in utter, blank incomprehension for a few moments.

142

'Well,' said Zaida, 'H has certain qualities Amisha, I am the first to admit that, but you're pushing it a little if you believe he can lead a sophisticated cyberattack involving seventy-five thousand devices. He doesn't even know how to operate smart phones, does he? I seem to recall you telling me stories about him launching them out of windows, or into oncoming traffic and suchlike when he gets frustrated with them. Doesn't his wife usually operate his for him?'

'That's all true,' said Amisha, 'but I'm thinking sideways, H has other skills. He can be very persuasive when he wants to be, and there's someone I know who could help us, with the right kind of persuading.'

'Who might that be?'

'Someone,' said Amisha, 'who has the ear of significantly more than seventy-five thousand people.'

42

Joey Jupiter wasn't used to clandestine late-night meetings at his loft in Shoreditch; he liked his privacy and few people ever got past the threshold of his door. But he'd received an early-morning, anonymous phone call – made by Andrew – telling him to expect visitors in the evening. He'd been having off-the-record meetings with Amisha, and the caller had used the code word they'd agreed, but he wasn't sure who else was coming. This made him nervous; these were dangerous times. Years of running his mouth from the side-lines was one thing – but suddenly, unexpectedly, he was now on the inside track, having cloak-and-dagger meetings with someone who was trying to do something concrete about the situation.

Doing something positive, he was learning, was far more difficult than commenting on what was wrong.

The hour of the meeting approached. His guts somersaulted, his throat and mouth dried up. He sipped on his cup of peppermint tea for comfort and munched on a piece of wholemeal toast. It was the first thing he'd eaten all day.

What if it wasn't Bhanushali? What if someone else was coming for him, from the other side? Who was on whose side anyway? Questions without answers swirled through his mind as he peeked, for the umpteenth time, through the blinds.

And there they were, crossing the road and making a beeline for his building. Amisha, accompanied by a big man in a dark Crombie overcoat, collar up, barrelling confidently across the road, like he owned it. Joey recognised him immediately.

Oh fuck, fucking hell.

He opened the door. Amisha gave a smile and said 'Hi'; H just stood there, looming over him, like a silent, brooding giant.

'Inspector, er, Mr. Hawkins – this way.'

H said nothing, brushed past Jupiter like he barely existed and made his way to the loft. Joey and Amisha followed. The three of them stood awkwardly, in a circle.

Amisha spoke first: 'Joey, we don't have much time. In the last meeting we had you said you were willing to help us. Well, we're here to call in your offer.'

'What do you want me to do?'

Amisha explained the situation, and the plan. As H had expected, Joey did not react decisively. The big man kept his own counsel, but began to bristle.

'But if I do as you ask I'll be in the direct line of fire of whoever is behind all this. I'll make myself a target. Even if I do it, the reach of these people appears absolute, my post will be taken down within less than an hour.'

H spoke for the first time.

'I fucking told you Ames, that this spineless prick wouldn't be up to it.'

H turned his attention to the subject of his ire.

'Jupiter, you fucking clueless mongrel, I've spent years thinking about how I'd like to turn you inside out – don't tempt me now. I've had a bad day and I've got the raving hump. Just listen to the lady, before I lose my fucking rag.'

'H, calm down,' said Amisha, 'You promised me you'd stay calm.'

It was like old times; the classic good cop/bad cop operation was in full swing. Amisha and H were well versed in the technique – few people could resist it.

'Joey, listen. You of all people know how serious this is. You've been explaining fake news to your readers and you've seen through so much of what's going on, and you've changed lately. The maturity and seriousness of your writing…you're ready for this now.'

'Do me a favour Ames, this useless little ponce ain't going to help us. He's hasn't got the…'

'H, please!'

Jupiter was looking wobbly on his feet. Amisha took him by the hand and sat down with him on the sofa. She locked her eyes onto his and appealed to him in earnest:

'Joey, it's half-past nine and you usually post at ten. That's why we've come now. There are millions of people out there waiting for your post. They're lost and frightened, and many of them are looking to you for information and guidance. You've already got them on alert – now it's time to send them a call to action. We need a minimum of 75,000 of your people to come on board.'

'I know. I get it. And if I do they'll come for me. Nobody will be able to protect me.'

'Well Joey,' said H, taking a more conciliatory tone, sensing that Jupiter was almost ready, 'you're right. They might come for you, and if they do we can't protect you. The question is this: do you have the balls to stand up now and do the right thing, and prove you're not a snivelling little hypocrite. Do it, or don't do it…your call, son.'

The words had a finality about them, and they hit a nerve. The time for more talking had passed. This was Joey's do-or-die moment. He took the piece of paper containing the technical instructions for the cyberattack from Amisha, went to his computer and started typing.

YOUR COUNTRY NEEDS YOU

Friends, this is likely to be my last post for some time. It may be my last post ever – so pay attention. I cannot go into detail but, as you know, our country, the very fabric of our democracy, is under attack. I am asking you to trust me. I am going to ask you all to do something. At the foot of this post are some instructions – those of you with technical understanding will be aware that they are instructions for a full scale cyberattack on a network we need to disable. Send this post to everyone you know, share it again and again on every social media network you use. Repeat the actions in the instructions again and again and again – and when you are exhausted, go repeat them again. Start the attack at midnight.

THIS IS VERY PROBABLY THE MOST IMPORTANT THING YOU WILL DO IN YOUR LIFE. THE SURVIVAL OF OUR COUNTRY DEPENDS ON IT.

By the time Joey finished typing, it was ten o'clock. His finger wavered over the send button and he gulped hard.

'Fucking send it!' shouted H. Joey Jupiter summoned all his reserves of courage, tapped the send button and put his head in his hands.

Amisha put her hand on his shoulder. 'Well done Joey, that took guts.'

Even H, who understood that Jupiter just stuck his neck way out there, felt a surge of admiration. He too put his hand on Jupiter's shoulder. 'Good man. Well done.'

'Yes, well, but…what now, do I just sit here and wait for them to come? They'll know where I am.'

'No. Get your coat on son, you're coming with us. We might have a use for you,' said H.

'But the curfew…it's already in place.'

'Better keep your fucking head down then,' said H. Without waiting or looking back he left the loft, ran down the stairs and surged out into the cold London night, Amisha and Joey tagging along behind him.

'Not big on pleasantries, is he?' Joey said to Amisha as they stumbled after H, struggling to keep up with the pace like small children following their father on a trip to the shops.

'No,' said Amisha, 'pleasantries are not his strong point, not when there's a job to be done.'

H stopped at a junction and waited for the stragglers to catch up with him. He was already thinking through next steps – his plans to put his crew together were already in motion.

'Right Ames, you make your way back to the hotel with our new recruit. Bring this server down and find out whatever you can. I've got a few things on the go to deal with.'

'Ok, guv,' said Ames.

'Ames, for the last time, I'm not your fucking guvnor.'

'Well, we have a mission, someone's got to take control of our newly formed group and you're giving the orders.'

H smiled. Amisha still knew how to make H smile.

'What is it you're going to be doing, just so I can inform the others?'

'Well, said H, 'you said you don't know what we're up against so we have to assume the worst. At some point, this is going to move out of cyberspace and into the real world. When it does we need to be ready. Best I can do is to put together a small firm ready to conduct guerrilla warfare, and I'll get in touch in a day or two, when I'm ready. I'm also going to need some funding. There are still some patriots out there who'll do whatever it takes for no reward, but others,

I'm talking about some old-school scoundrels now, will need to be incentivised.'

'Zaida has full working knowledge of big Russian money trails and accounts; she said she can divert some funds. Money's no object on this one H.'

'Sweet,' said H, 'give Zaida my regards.'

'Villain vigilantes, just like Kelly's Heroes,' said Jupiter.

H stared at Jupiter and gave him the look, with an extra portion of disdain, and Jupiter looked down, like a beaten dog. H was loyal to the core, the flip side of which was he could hold onto hatred for a lifetime, and he wasn't yet ready to forget the indignities the man with the poison pen had heaped upon him. But now wasn't the time for a reckoning, and by the time Jupiter raised his head to return the stare H had merged like a shadow into the dark London night.

43

Amisha and Joey Jupiter entered the lobby of the hotel that had now become the unofficial headquarters of the technical wing of the New Resistance. Amisha smiled at the receptionist, who appeared to be there all hours of the day and night, and gave him a wave. It was 12.40am, well past curfew, but that was not his concern. He returned the wave and hid the upsurge in his jealousy as a second bearded wonder went upstairs with her.

Maybe her and her mate have a fetish about weird looking little gimps with stupid beards.

They entered room 33 and Amisha introduced the new recruit to Zaida. Andrew was asleep on the bed.

Zaida didn't look up – she was captive to her laptop, staring intently into an inner world, a world in which a war was taking place. The citizens' cyberattack had started as planned, at midnight. The target DNS server was coping well with the initial charge, and rebuffed the attacks as if they were no more significant than a group of school children charging Fort Knox with toy spears.

But the attack was building, the word was spreading. Joey, who had brought his laptop with him, logged onto the hotel wi-fi and checked the analytics on his post.

'Over 300,000 clicks, and they've nearly all shared it. The attack level is going to increase, I'm sure of it.' He refreshed his screen but now got no more than a *page cannot be found* message. He tried again. He double-checked his connection by accessing some other sites.

'I think my service provider has been taken out. But the blog is all over Twitter and Facebook and Instagram. I don't think whoever is behind this can bring them all down. Can they? Those guys spend a fortune on protecting themselves.'

Amisha checked Twitter: #citizenscyberattack was trending. The attack was building, fast.

Zaida, still mesmerized, continued to check and recheck the status of the DNS server they were besieging. It was holding firm, although the level of the attack had been upgraded from boys and girls with toy spears to adults with axes and baseball bats. But you couldn't break into Fort Knox with baseball bats.

As well as the citizen cyber army on full frontal assault, Amisha had written a programme that kept sending a simple message, on an infinite loop, to the DNS server. It was running in the background of all the devices they had at their disposal. It was helping, at the margins, but they needed more power, more attacks.

'What actually is the plan?' asked Jupiter, who knew a bit about computers but was way out of his depth in this company.

'Well Joey,' said Zaida, 'it's not that sophisticated, as cyberattacks go. Often at GCHQ, where I work, or worked, they plan these things for months, attacking certain aspects of foreign networks with sophisticated code that tries to trick servers into thinking it's part of the usual systems the computer uses. Then, if we can get some software onto a target network, we can use it to spy on it and send us messages. But we just don't have that level of sophistication available.'

'So?'

'So,' said Amisha, 'we go for the numbers. Sometimes the numbers are what you need. Like in a battle, the side with the most bodies wins, all other things being equal. If we can overload the server we've located we can cause its operating software to seize up.'

'But what does that give us?'

151

'An opportunity. When they bring the server back online there will be a moment, perhaps two or three seconds, between the operating system being loaded and the security software being reloaded. Usually they build the server and then put it on the network after all that's been done and checked and, under normal circumstances, they would take it off the network before rebuilding it. But that takes time and if, as we believe, it's the server through which instructions are now being fed to whoever's co-ordinating the general chaos, they might just reboot it. If we're alert we can install a Trojan that will start reading files and sending us information about what's on them.'

'Got it,' said Jupiter, who understood the theory, if not the technical aspects.

Zaida and Amisha were monitoring their laptops even as they explained what they were doing, and Amisha gave an update: 'We've well above 75,000 hits now, your readership is certainly doing their bit Joey, but the server's holding. It's more powerful than we thought.'

The room went quiet. Andrew made some tea. There were only two cups so he passed them round, and everyone had a couple of swigs.

Then Zaida screamed something, in Hindi; something along the lines of 'Krishna be praised' – the boys didn't understand this but the tone of voice was universal and they knew it was good news.

'The server's down,' said Zaida, with quiet intensity, 'stay focused everyone.'

It was time for phase two. Amisha had another small program that just sent out a test message to say hello to the server three times a second. As expected the standard *server not found* message kept coming back. And then it didn't.

'It's back Zaida, it's back up,' she exclaimed, like an overexcited schoolgirl.

Zaida was ready and hit the install button; her software loaded onto the enemy DNS server.

'Now what?' asked Andrew.

'Now we wait,' said Amisha. 'The server's anti-virus software might find my program immediately and destroy it in milliseconds, or it may survive seconds or minutes, or even longer, and if it does it will start to send us the contents of some files – which might be useful or completely useless.'

'So, what you're telling us, DI Bhanushali' said Joey, 'is the whole success of this plan depends on some software you and your aunt knocked up in a hotel bedroom; a bedroom, from the look of it, that's usually reserved for a different kind of knocking up?'

'Yep,' said Amisha, as she swigged the last of the brew, 'any danger of another cup of tea, Andrew?'

44

Bradley, Brad to those who knew him well, walked into the pleasant and comfortable guesthouse in the Cairngorms National Park in northeast Scotland that had been his home for over a month. It was the largest national park in the British Isles. It included the spectacular landscape of the Cairngorm Mountains, and was designated as an area in which no activity likely to have an impact on the natural environment was permitted. The park encompassed the skiing resort of Aviemore, a highland wildlife park and the Dalwhinnie distillery that produced a celebrated single malt Scotch whisky which, by lucky coincidence, was Brad's favourite tipple.

He headed directly to the bar and ordered a double – he'd had a long walk, was tired, and felt like he needed a wee dram to warm himself up. Walking the Scottish Highlands in winter was a tough ask, and he felt his efforts deserved a reward.

The National Park was a hive of tourist activity in the summer, but mostly quiet in the cold winters. Brad, though, was a hardy man and his research into his book on the landscapes of Scotland could only be written if he experienced said landscapes in their primeval splendour. Yanks with Scottish heritage were commonplace in Scotland so nobody thought it too unusual, especially given his job, to have a freezing, lone American stay at an isolated Scottish guest house through the winter.

The dour Scottish barman proffered up the liquid refreshment and Brad downed it in one.

'Gees, that hit the spot. Another please.'

He tried to engage the barman in some small talk but the barman didn't do small talk, so Brad drank his next double, a little more slowly this time so he could savour the flavour and sensation on the roof of his mouth.

The manager of the guesthouse entered the bar, gave the barman a few orders and said hello to his guest.

'Ah, Brad, how was your day?'

'A little cold, but rewarding nonetheless,' said Brad, who had now finished his second whiskey and ordered a third.

'And how's the book coming on? Be sure to send us a copy when it's published.'

'Just fine – absolutely, of course.'

The manager ordered up another dram, on the house, which Brad drank with relish before retiring to his bedroom. He opened a map of the Cairngorms National Park, laid it down on his bed and started to plan his next day.

He fancied visiting an olde-worlde castle so he did some googling before he found one that was of interest to him, just six or so miles east of Braemar. An interesting spot, he thought to himself. With all the trouble in the British cities he felt peaceful and contented to be out in the wilderness, the perfect spot to escape the mayhem.

He smiled to himself as he considered the route he'd be taking. The castle and grounds were only open to the public from April to October, and much of the surrounding land was private, reserved for the fun and games of people who loved to blow birds to bits with shotguns. This didn't bother Brad – what bothered him was what route he could take. How he could get into the grounds and mooch about without being noticed? Brad did like to mooch about in places he didn't belong.

45

The day was cold but by the time he left the guest house the mercury had crept above freezing point. The air was crisp and the sky was clear as he threw his rucksack into the rear of his hire car, a 4 x 4 black Range Rover Vogue with all mod cons – diesel turbo, satnav, tinted windows, Bluetooth. He hit the ignition and heard the sweet sound of the engine fire immediately. A freezing Scottish morning was no match for this baby.

He made a few adjustments to make himself comfy, tapped the coordinates he'd got from his map into the satnav and he was off and running. The grounds he'd identified covered 50,000 acres of varied landscape and Brad was going to have a proper look at the whole spread. The varied landscape of the estate included seven Munros – Scottish Hills above 3,000ft – several lochs, and trees; lots and lots of grizzled trees that rolled on from one crest to another. About 8,000 acres of them. Brad liked trees and forests; you could climb the former and hide in the latter. He liked to hide himself away when he was working.

Red deer grazed among the trees and he spied several in the morning light, still and implacable as if captured in a Landseer painting. He drove around a little and got out a little, familiarising himself with the landscape, for now keeping within the allowable tourist areas. He came across one of the estate rangers and engaged him in conversation about his book and about the beauty of the area. As he strolled about, the distant high grey mountain of Lochnagar provided a backdrop to a truly harmonious panorama. He felt at peace here, that he would be happy for it to be his final resting place.

He made his way to Crathie Kirk, a small Church of Scotland parish church in the village of Crathie. The church was built in the Gothic revival style using materials from the surrounding area – the walls from local granite and the roof from Scots pine. Brad thought the church complimented the surroundings beautifully, as if it had risen from the ground organically, to provide spiritual sustenance to the locals. The church was an important focal point for people across the surrounding area, including those who liked to blow birds away or bring down a stag or two with a shotgun. Fair enough, thought Brad, someone's got to keep the red deer numbers down or the pesky things would eat the whole damn forest.

He went for another short drive around and about the town and then got out of the car. He took his rucksack and decided to go for a walk in the forest areas surrounding the small town. He came to what he thought was a nice spot and stopped for a refreshing glug of the local brew he'd brought along for the journey. He then started to climb a tree – he was good at climbing trees. He even had some tools for the purpose – sharp metal gaffs that he dug into the side of the trunk as he went up. He used them like a set of impromptu stairs as he slowly made his way to the top. When he arrived there, he took out a pair of binoculars to survey the panorama, and was stunned by a terrific view over Crathie and the little church. Distance-wise he calculated it to be 3000 meters away, about the distance a crack shot could hit a red deer, as long as he had a steady hand and a top-notch rifle with a decent sight. Brad had proven plenty of times he had the former, and he had the latter in his rucksack.

Everything looked so peaceful, and he considered the vantage point just about perfect. He descended, climbed another nearby tree and attached a small piece of cloth to one of its branches – when you were going for a long shot from this distance you had to understand which way the wind was blowing.

46

It had been a long drive up the M1 – enlivened by Sinatra, Sammy Davis, Dean Martin, and good conversation – and H and Kuba were tired as they approached the Army roadblock on the M62, just outside Leeds.

Kuba had dragged H, the previous evening, through a bottle of ice-cold premium vodka – Finnish, to H's surprise – and the pair of them had been gently nursing their mini-hangovers on the drive. But now it was time to focus. There had been a bomb in the city centre a few days before and rioting in the Chapeltown and Harehills areas of the city; it had taken the army forty-eight hours to bring it under control. These areas were now under curfew after dark, and the soldiers who slowed down H's car looked edgy and tired.

'Where you headed for, gents?' one of them said in a thick Scouse accent, leaning down and looking into the passenger-side window of the car.

'Just to see an old mate – I was in the Paras with him. Solid old school Yorkshireman. Lives in Armley. Hasn't been well, we've come to cheer him up.'

The soldier stared at H, pursed his lips and looked distinctly unimpressed.

'Can I get something out of my pocket?' said H.

'OK, slowly,' said the soldier, stepping back and raising his rifle.

H fished about in the inside pocket of his jacket, pulled out his old warrant card and handed it to the serviceman, who he could now see looked even younger than his boy Ronnie. 'Former Detective Inspector Harry Hawkins. Nearly thirty years in the Met, seven in the Army before that,' he said, 'there's no one you need to worry about in this motor, mate.'

159

'What about your pal here?'

'Kuba Bukowski, Krakow Police Department, former Polish Special Forces,' said Kuba.

'Any ID?' said the soldier.

Kuba pulled out and flashed his badge.

'Good as gold, this one,' said H to the soldier, 'me, him and the old boy we're going to visit did a bit of work together, back in the old days. You can rely on us to be sensible and keep the peace. All day long. That is absolutely nailed-on.'

The soldier smiled, and leaned in further: 'Got you – but be careful in Armley; it's not in lockdown yet and there's all sorts going off up here, everywhere. Stay away from Harehills and Chapeltown if you don't want some nutter to cut your fucking heads off. I'm not joking…we've had a couple of severed heads knocking about here. Literally. One of them got thrown through the window of a pub in Armley.'

'First I've heard of it.'

'There's a lot of things you've not heard about mate, there's a lot of things none of us have fucking heard about.'

H pulled the car away nodding sagely, then turned and faced Kuba. 'Welcome to the North,' he said with a wink and a smile, 'this is where the warm and genuine English people are.'

47

H pulled up outside a house he hadn't been to in a good few years, in a street that looked even less salubrious than it had the last time he'd seen it. Groups of young men loitered here and there along the terraced pavements, drinking from cans, cackling and guffawing at what H assumed were idiotic comedy clips on their phones. Kids hared up and down the middle of the road on their bikes, singing songs about Leeds United, their football team.

Sirens wailed in the distance and a helicopter circled in a tight loop in the sky overhead; the air crackled with tension, and H and Kuba were watched closely as they got out of the car and walked towards the house.

No one at home. H hadn't expected there to be. They hung around for ten minutes, asking questions, making themselves as visible as possible, and moved slowly and ostentatiously into the Pig and Whistle, the pub at the end of the street.

The interior was just as H remembered it, grim. A threadbare red carpet coated with the kind of stinky powder pubs always use when they try and cover up worse smells; tattered 'plush' seating around wrecked wooden tables; a taped-up broken window; half a dozen bored looking boozers around the place, their half-closed eyes following the horse racing on a gigantic screen. H was pleased to see the horse racing on. If people couldn't have a little flutter, civilisation really would be collapsing.

'Right my son,' H said to Kuba, 'it's your lucky day – time for a pint of good old Yorkshire ale.'

Kuba wasn't sure about this, but H was in the chair and he waited patiently for the beers to be pulled.

'There you are son,' said H triumphantly, passing his friend a pint of foaming liquid the colour of puddle water in a Silesian coalmine, 'get this down your fucking neck.'

Kuba took it, sipped at it, and grimaced.

'This tastes like washing up liquid H, no fucking way am I drinking this.'

'Shut up you old tart, get it down you, it'll put hairs on your chest.'

'I've got hairs on my chest already H.'

'Well, what do you want then? Vodka, I suppose?'

'No, scotch, I'll have a scotch.'

H turned back towards the bar. As he did so he felt a tap on his shoulder and heard a boy's voice say 'Mr Hawkins? There's someone waiting for you. In the garden,' in a Leeds accent so thick Kuba had to wait for a translation.

'In the garden,' said H, gesturing with a nod of the head towards a door at the back of the pub, 'our man is waiting for us in the garden out the back.'

They took their drinks out and into the small patch of concrete that H had called a 'garden', and before Kuba made it through the door he heard H roar 'Teddy…you old bastard! How the fuck are you?'

'Never better, you fat old Cockney fucker, how's yourself?' said a sharp, wiry looking man in his early sixties sitting on an old white plastic table, the remnants of a collapsed pub umbrella flapping against his shoulders in the breeze.

The two men bear hugged, and ranted and raved and insulted one another for a spell, and then H pulled back to do the introductions

'Kuba, meet Ted. Yorkie Ted. We were in the Falklands together.'

Kuba nodded, and stood his ground.

162

'Ted, this is my good friend Kuba – Kuba Bukowski. Visiting from Poland, he's working with me.'

'Why, have all the potato-picking jobs in Norfolk gone?' said Ted, winking and smiling at Kuba, who'd learned enough from H about the English sense of humour to smile back.

'Only joking mate,' said Ted, offering his hand to Kuba, 'any friend of H's is a friend of mine. Good to meet you.'

'Alright, alright, that'll do for the niceties Ted, we haven't got all day,' said H. 'You got somewhere we can talk? We've got work to do.'

48

Ted closed and locked the metal doors of the lock up he'd led them to, not far from the Pig and Whistle, and turned on the light. H and Kuba found themselves in a cramped and densely cluttered space, with boxes and bric-a-brac stacked all the way up to the ceiling, and a space in the middle of it all containing half a dozen office chairs.

'I do markets and boot sales to top up my pension,' Ted told his visitors. 'I use this place for storage, and meetings. It's coming in handy now, with all the fun and games going off and prying eyes everywhere.'

'Alright Ted,' said H, easing himself into one of the chairs, 'let's get to it. What the fuck is going on? What's been happening up here? What's your take on it all?'

'Well, right off I thought it was the Muslims – you know, the bomb we had here, and the others. A lot of us thought that, and a few of the chaps I know went into Harehills to look about. But what they saw there didn't make sense, you know…a lot of outsiders kicking off with everything that moved. Nobody we knew. Some of them were wearing Leeds shirts, acting like locals. They just sort of turned up and then melted away again.'

'So not anyone you know, or the BPF, or anything like that?' said H.

'No, these were Poles, or Russians, something like that.'

Kuba looked at Ted sideways, and was about to say something; H didn't give him the chance.

'What's happening in Chapeltown?' asked H.

'Similar sort of thing, except they're targeting the West Indians, but they're giving as good as they get. As you'd expect. It all seems to be a divide and rule kind of thing.'

164

'OK,' said H. 'Any thoughts on what the big picture might be? Across the country, I mean.'

'Not really mate, it all seems like an absolute fucking dog's dinner. Me and my boys are standing ready, and we're doing what we can, but the truth is we haven't been able to join up many dots.'

'Alright Ted,' said H, 'sit down. I'll tell you what we know so far.'

***

Ted listened intently, his head down, nodding occasionally, his hands stuffed into the pockets of his leather jacket. It was getting colder.

H summed everything up one last time and addressed Ted directly:

'The thing is, Ted, the thing is we need men. Trustworthy men with bollocks, if we're going to get anywhere. That's why I brought Kuba in, and it's why we've come to you. We don't know exactly what needs doing yet, but we might soon.'

'Well, I...'

'Well what? You want to sit up here scratching your arse, powerless to do anything useful, with no real fucking clue as to what's even going on? Or do you want to get on board with us – there's not a lot of us, I'll give you that, but the people we're working with are clever, and committed, and soon they'll start feeding us information about who's who and what's what, and then we'll have something solid to go on, someone to go and have a pop at. We'll have a chance to do something about what's happening to the country.'

'Well,' said Ted, grinning broadly, 'if you put it like that H.'

'Good man,' said H. 'Now, you said you've got a few chaps here. What are we talking about?'

'I've got half a dozen good men. All as good as gold – out of the Paras most of them, after our time, but I'll personally vouch for all of them. One or two others, ex-forces. I haven't got any lightweights around me mate.'

'What have you been up to?'

'Just getting ready, really. Keeping in training. I could tell something was going to happen, that a time was coming.'

'OK Ted, got it. What about gear? What are you lot holding?'

'We've been stockpiling bits and pieces, proper gear, for a while now. Rifles and small arms, a good number of rounds, a few other bits and pieces.'

'What are we talking about Ted, enough for one proper turnout against a well-armed force? Or more than that?'

'Well, more like one, to be honest H, against someone with plenty of gear, who knows what they're doing...one.'

'OK, we'll get you more. You'll have to come south and plot up with us, OK?'

'Who's us?'

'I've got one or two more people to see yet, there'll be a few of us.'

'OK.'

'Say Saturday? That'll give you a few days to sort everything out, get your people ready.'

H wrote an address and a time on a piece of paper and handed it to Ted.

'Right, memorise this and then burn it, or eat it, or whatever it is they do in the spy films. You can't phone me, or email me, or any of that. You'll just have to be there, end of. Come in ones and twos, have your stories straight for the boys on the roadblocks, have your gear well tucked away – you know the drill.'

166

'You can count on me H, if I say I'll be there, I'll be there.'

'Good enough for me mate,' said H, rising from his chair and extending his hand, 'see you Saturday.'

49

'I've been thinking,' said Kuba.

'Good man,' said H, 'it's a start. Keep practicing, you might get good at it.'

Kuba looked out the window for a moment, watched the cars and lights flash by in the darkness as they sped south towards London on the M1.

'No, seriously, I've been thinking about our aims, and what they might be, and what we might be up against. I was impressed with Ted, I see he's a capable man, and he can bring some good men with him. And your idea of bringing in your old London guys is good…'

'But?' said H.

'But is it enough? We're probably going up against some very formidable firms, well trained, organized and ruthless, and who knows how many of them we may have to deal with, in what situations?'

'Spit it out Kuba, for fuck's sake. What exactly are you saying?'

'That we need more. We need more men, who know what they're doing, who understand Russians, and who are motivated to fight them, to the death if necessary.'

'OK, makes sense. Speak to me son: who are you talking about – who do we need?'

'Poles,' said Kuba. 'we need Poles.'

'OK. Tell me more.'

'Well, there are two things to consider. One, if it's really the Russians we are up against, it can't be good for Poland. It never is.'

'And number two?'

'They've fucked us over for hundreds of years, so those of us who know our history, which is most of us, will fight against them.'

'I thought you all hated the Germans,' said H.

'No, the Germans have changed, the Russians haven't. I'm not saying we're all Germany lovers now, but try finding a Polish family that didn't have its grandmothers and great-grandmothers raped by the Red Army. And then fifty years of fucking communism. Basically H, if you want someone who will take it to the Russians, find a Pole.'

'Alright,' said H, nodding vigorously, 'what have you got? Who are we talking about?'

'I know some people here, in England. And, of course, back home. Men I can vouch for...patriots, ex-Special Forces guys. One of them you know.'

'Who?'

'Andzrej. Andzrej Boczar – you met him when you came over for Kasia's christening. His wife is her Godmother. You and Andzrej got on like a house on fire, remember?'

'Sure, yes, I liked him. Impressive guy. I had no idea he was ex-Special Forces.'

'Well we don't talk about it, do we? Do your ex-SAS guys sit around all day telling everyone what they were involved in?'

'No,' said H, 'they write books and make TV documentaries about it.'

Kuba laughed. 'OK, fair enough. But my point is, I've got some top-notch men I can talk to.'

'How many?'

'Maybe a dozen.'

'Will they keep their mouths shut?'

'What do you think H? What the fuck do you think?' said Kuba, exasperated.

'Bring them in son, bring them in.'

169

50

Sunday morning was usually the best time to find people at home in H's experience, and he was on the road and heading for Welling on the London/Kent borders – this time without Kuba – while it was still dark. He parked up and was barrelling up the walkway of a mid-sized terraced house by six o'clock. There were no signs of life as H hit the knocker – this was not the first time this knocker had been used to wake Barry Marshall up at six in the morning.

H was on his third cycle of hammerings at the door when he saw, through its frosted-glass pane, a light come on at the top of a flight of stairs, and heard heavy footsteps making their way unevenly down into the hallway. The door opened to reveal a tall heavyset lump of a man in his early sixties, with thinning hair and a ravaged, florid face set back behind two wobbling chins.

The man squinted, identified his visitor, and said 'Mr Hawkins, what the fuck are you doing here, if you'll excuse my French? What time is it?'

'Time you got dressed son – I need to talk to you.'

'What for? I ain't done nothing in years.'

'I know, Baz, I know. I'm not here to nick you or anything like that, just need to talk to you. It's urgent…have a quick sluice and sort yourself out, we can talk on the way.'

'On the way where?'

'To see an old mate of yours.'

***

'I don't really need all this, Mr Hawkins,' said Marshall, shifting uncomfortably in the passenger seat. 'I had a skinful last night, I haven't had a lot of kip, I'm feeling a bit choice. Can you tell me what this is all about?'

'Basildon.'

'What? Basildon? Basildon in Essex? Basil-fucking-don? I don't know no cunt in Basildon.'

'Yes you do. He lived in Bethnal Green when you were having all your little fun and games with him, back in the old days.'

'Who? I...'

'Terry Pendleton.'

'Terry Pendleton? West Ham Terry Pendleton? You're taking me to see Terry West Ham fucking Pendleton? Have you lost the plot Mr Hawkins? Why? I haven't even seen the wanker in ten years.'

'Slow down, son. Listen: you two need to talk. You need to bury the hatchet. I need your help. The country needs your help, believe it or not.'

***

H set the meet up in the café of a DIY superstore on the road to Southend. He'd filled them in on the essentials in the car, and now parked the two men at a table in the corner, out of the way of the other early morning customers, while he went to the counter for coffee.

He knew that putting together a street level contingent of foot soldiers on the basis of a Millwall-West Ham coalition would not be a walk in the park – this old, bitter football rivalry had lasted for decades and deaths had occurred on either side over the years; but the old-school Millwall and West Ham boys were second to none and likely to come in handy when it came to the crunch, and he hoped he might be able to have a sit down with these two seasoned old growlers without all hell breaking loose.

He was wrong; he heard their voices rise, and their chairs fall to the floor as they stood to confront one another. He turned back quickly with the coffees, made them restore their chairs to their rightful places and sit in them, and gave them the look. There was no arguing with the look, not unless you were ready to disregard it and go all the way against Harry Hawkins.

Barry Marshall and Terry Pendleton were not, formidable as they were in their way, ready for such a thing, not on this Sunday morning. They sat waiting, like schoolboys, with their heads down. The bollocking began:

'Will you two listen to yourselves? You're grown men, old men, squabbling over a bit of argy-bargy you had at football matches thirty years ago. For fuck's sake! Someone is trying to take over our city, make it ungovernable, turn everything to shit, and I'm giving you a chance to get involved, to do something about it, and all you want to do is quarrel like kids, and sit at home, drinking beer and watching stupid films on your giant fucking televisions. I'll be honest, boys – I was hoping for more from you.'

H understood these people, what they were about, how to appeal to them, motivate them. 'Are you patriots, or not? Do you care what's happening to our city, to our country, or what?'

51

'Yes, they were very heavy, in their day. Very heavy indeed, proper nutters. They'd blow your head off soon as look at you. They were about as tasty as it got, among the British firms…mind you, we only had British firms to worry about in those days. They gave the South London boys, the Butcher firm, a good run for their money, put it that way,' said H.

Suburban Essex sped by. H had picked up Kuba for his second visit. Kuba, his long frame crammed once again in to the passenger seat, had been listening intently to H's history of gangland London and the armed blaggers of the seventies and eighties.

'What makes you think they'll be any use now though H?' said Kuba, 'haven't they been retired for years, how do you say it, "put out to pasture"?'

This would be a different type of meeting from the Basildon one – once again H knew what was needed to get them on board.

'Money. Money's what always motivated them. These people are all the same: lazy, greedy, and prepared to do anything to get it. Plus the love of violence, for some of them. Albie Bradford and his firm always loved violence, enjoyed hurting people.'

'And patriotism? They'll get involved for love of their country, to help us try and save it?'

'Nah Kuba, these sorts of people only care about themselves, they don't go for all that stuff. A lot of my grandad's mates, my old "uncles", were villains during the war. They couldn't be got by all the King and Country stuff, refused to be drafted. A lot of them cracked-on they were conchies.'

'Conchies?'

'Conscientious objectors. Pretended to be pacifists and suchlike. Spent the war in military prisons, a good few of them, so no, it's no good us trying to appeal to their finer instincts – they don't have any.'

Kuba shook his head, not understanding. 'How can a man not want to save his country when it's under attack? In Poland...'

'We're not in Poland mate, these blokes don't know what patriotism means. What we're dealing with here are horrible bastards with no morals, no interest in anything but themselves. They'll do practically anything for money, and never lose a wink of sleep over it. That's why they'll come in handy now, if we can get them on board.'

***

The long driveway of the large Mock Tudor house, set well back off the road, was filled with an assortment of people carriers and sports cars, and H had trouble parking. He'd put the word out that he'd be coming, and was glad to see someone was home. Albie Bradford came to the door himself, three or four stones heavier than the last time H had seen him, looking about as happy to see the two visitors on his doorstep as a man who'd just been told his mother had died.

H and Kuba were ushered into a large, ostentatiously decorated lounge filled with acres of expensive leather seating. Three men were already in place, one of them was Kenny Keeler, Bradford's long-time right-hand man. They were all nursing tumblers of scotch. H declined the offer of one for himself, Kuba accepted. They took their seats.

52

'Alright, Hawkins,' Albie Bradford said wearily, sipping his scotch and eyeing H and Kuba with undisguised loathing, 'what exactly is it you want?'

'I want you and your chaps to help us, to do a bit of work for us.'

'Who's "us"?'

'Me and a few people who are trying to do something about what's happening. We're finding out about what's really going on and looking into ways of slowing it down and dealing with it.'

'Don't give me all the *Land of Hope and Glory* bollocks Hawkins, I don't give a fuck. I'm alright, I can look after myself. What possible reason could I have for wanting to help you?'

'Money. Proper money.'

'Meaning?'

'I give you a few little jobs to do, you do them, I get my people to transfer absolutely fucking ridiculous sums of money into your offshore accounts, or wherever it is you hide your dough.'

Bradford leaned back into the leather, stretched his legs out, drank deep and said: 'Are you sure I can't get you a drink, Mr Hawkins?'

Kuba had never heard sarcasm like it, you could cut it with a knife; but he felt sure now that things would be developing favourably.

'No thank you Mr Bradford, I'm driving, and I'm not the man I was. But if you'd like to take a turn around the garden with me, just the two of us.'

***

175

The garden turned out to be the size of a football pitch, and immaculately tended. It was a cold afternoon; both men pulled their overcoats tight around themselves as they walked.

'What I'm going to need,' said H, 'is a few people taking care of.'

'Tell me more,' said Bradford.

'You might not care, but we're at war. With someone who's trying to fuck the country up. We know a number of very important, high-up establishment types are involved, and once we know for sure who they are we'll need to have them taken care of – quickly, professionally, no-questions-asked, as they come up.'

Bradford paused for a moment, then pulled out his phone.

'What are you doing?' asked H.

'I'm phoning the police, to tell them I've got a man at my house impersonating Detective Inspector Harry Hawkins, hero of the Yard, London's top copper – or ex-copper – scourge of the murdering classes.'

H laughed out loud. 'Funny,' he said, 'I'll give you that one. But these are desperate times, and I'm being serious. I've got good people about me on this, and we're not going to sit around with our thumbs up our arses while these fucking traitors try and destroy our country. At the very least, we're going down fighting. I...'

'Alright, alright, no need for speeches. You know I don't care. What, exactly, are we talking about?'

'Hundred large per head, if dealt with within forty-eight hours of you receiving the order. Fifty grand down up front, the remainder upon completion.'

'How many head are we talking about?'

'Not clear at this stage. Something in the region of a dozen or so, from what I'm told, to start with.'

176

'A dozen, Mr Hawkins? A dozen? According to even my basic math that would come to something in the region of one point two million sovs, wouldn't it? Have I got that right?' Bradford said, laughing. 'On second thoughts, I'll phone the local nuthouse, tell them I've got a stark raving lunatic in my garden.'

'OK, it seems a bit strong, I can see that. But I'm working with some big brains, people who can make things happen online that you would not believe. Like hacking into deep places and moving money around. We're going to use these bastards' own money against them.'

'All I'm hearing is words, Mr Hawkins. Where are the readies?'

If you shake hands with me now I'll have a hundred grand in an account of your choice tomorrow, by way of a down-payment on two jobs and marker of good faith. How does that sound?'

'Handsome. Absolutely fucking handsome. Send me the money, and feed me their names. As many as you like. My boys and me will take care of them like you will not fucking believe.'

53

It was three o'clock in the afternoon in H's old family lockup, in one of the arches under the railway bridge at the Elephant and Castle. Men had been trickling in, quietly and in ones and twos, and now all the elements that H and Kuba had put together were in place.

The Kuba Bukowski and Yorkie Ted contingents – sixteen men of military background in all – sat together, chatting amiably, with Kuba doing whatever interpreting was necessary, though most of his guys had at least some English. Albie Bradford's firm had refused to show – they would have to be managed remotely. Terry Pendleton and three others from the West Ham leadership, Essex men all, sat with the main group. Barry Marshall and three other Millwall men sat apart, by themselves. Both Pendleton and Marshall had pledged to H that they would bring in two hundred and fifty men each from their core firms – a total of five hundred streetfighters.

Thus, then, was H's army: an intelligence section and a dozen gangster-mercenaries absent but fully signed up; sixteen veterans – seventeen with H himself included in the count – of armed combat in warzones; and five hundred or so foot soldiers, many of them now advanced in years, all of them experienced in toe-to-toe fighting. And Little Ronnie Hawkins, not so little now, and not the loose cannon he once was, but a young man with a CV full of the kind of extreme violence many of the others envied – and feared.

H stood up at the front and called the meeting to order.

'Alright boys – let's get started. We're ready to roll now. I'll be meeting with our boffins later today, and I expect them to have something concrete for us. We'll meet again here tomorrow morning for operational planning. Kuba's

178

and Ted's boys will be staying here, in this lockup and one a bit further down. We'll need Barry and Terry to stay here as well…we can't risk using phones or other gadgets for communications, so we'll be using a lot more direct word-of-mouth than you might be used to, with everything filtering out from here.'

Some sections of the room were becoming restless, and a hubbub was rising.

'Right,' shouted H. 'No speeches, just one message:

'Someone is taking liberties in our city, in our country, trying to collapse everything and turn it to shit. Maybe with a view to swanning in after it's all done and taking control. This has got to stop.'

The odds are against us: we're up against a massive conspiracy – big power, and big money, and they've covered their tracks and made it very hard for us to figure out what the fuck is actually going on. But our intelligence people are as good as gold, and they're finding things now that are going to put us in the game and give us a chance. We are fighting men, and the time for righteous violence is now at hand. The fightback starts here. Be bold, be decisive, be ruthless. Take no prisoners. That is all.'

54

The software lovingly crafted by Amisha and Zaida had survived for all of two minutes before it was discovered and annihilated with ruthless efficiency by the server's anti-virus programme. It didn't give up many of the server's secrets, but it was there long enough to send out an extract of a file which had an IP address located in the United Kingdom. Amisha performed some jiggery-pokery and traced it back to a machine somewhere in Kent, within a fifteen-mile radius of Dover, on the Kent coast. A big area to search with only four people on board.

'We need a drone,' said Zaida. 'There's no other way to cover that much land area – assuming it's on land.'

Jupiter was confused: 'But why do we need a drone? What are we actually looking for – a computer somewhere near Dover?'

'No,' said Zaida, 'not exactly. Based on what we know, or think we know, we're looking for some sort of complex, or building, in which some very specialized equipment has been installed. If what we're thinking is correct this place will be defended, fortified and built to hide a state-of-the-art laboratory. It will be big, probably isolated, and have substantial, defensible grounds. You don't set up a lab like this above a McDonald's. So we need to look, from the air, for places that fit that description – that's where the computer Amisha has identified will be. I think.'

'OK, so where do we get one – a drone, I mean?' said Jupiter.

'We can't buy one. All drones are grounded and the government have made ongoing sales illegal,' said Andrew. 'We'll just have to steal one, it doesn't have to be that sophisticated, and we can add an infra-red camera and fly it at night.'

'Where would we steal it from?' said Amisha.

'A drone shop,' said Andrew, with a shrug of his shoulders.

'And where might one of those be? Where do you buy a drone, I've never seen one for sale in a shop, only ever online.'

'Maybe that's because you haven't looked,' said Andrew as he got back online. He'd been side-lined while the ladies were working their technical magic so was pleased to be useful again.

'There,' he shouted, 'Hobbies R US', it's in South London, on a retail park in Charlton.'

'What kind of drone do we need?' said Amisha.

'Er...' Andrew returned to his screen, and learned that there were several types of retail drone. Ready to Fly, Bind to Fly, Almost Ready to Fly – and that they came in various degrees of flying difficulty.

'One that's easy to fly,' he said.

'And one that can hold an infra-red camera,' said Amisha.

'And can cover a range of at least fifteen square miles,' said Zaida.

Andrew pored over the specifications, and learned quickly about retail drones, their capabilities, specifications, distances, ease of control.

He concluded his research quickly and addressed the team:

'This is the one, the *Night Scout XXX7* – it's got a three-mile flight range, holds a camera and you can programme a route in through your mobile, so we don't have to waste any time trying to learn how to fly the thing. Looks like the highest specification you'll get in a retail outlet, and it's on the Hobbies R US website – guess they haven't had time to take drones off their web marketing yet. They won't be selling them but I'm betting they still have them in stockrooms. We'll have to steal one.'

The London dawn was breaking and the curfew hours were ending. Perfect timing for an early morning drive through London – down from Camden to Charlton and thence, by the look of it, to the coast.

They all piled into Andrew's car and headed south.

'There's nothing for it,' said Amisha to no one in particular as they sped towards Waterloo Bridge, 'I'm going to have to call Hilary…I can't avoid her any longer.'

She drew a deep, deep breath and hit the Chief Inspector's number.

'Ma'am, it's Amisha.'

'Amisha, where are you? Where have you been? I've been trying to contact you for two days…actually, it's nearer three. What the hell is going on?'

'I'm with Andrew. We're in the East End, following up leads on the Imam murder case,' she lied, 'we've had to go deep…but we're starting to get somewhere. I can't speak now, we'll be back as soon as we can.'

'Get back Amisha, the place is in chaos. Your team needs some direction. You can't just go off-grid like this whenever you feel like it, who do you think you are, Harry Hawkins?'

'Hardly…alright ma'am, we'll be as quick as we can, and I'll fill you in.' Amisha abruptly ended the call.

Andrew was feeling uncomfortable. He'd never gone rogue before. Amisha was used to it, having learned from the master himself.

'We should tell her the truth. She might be able to help. Surely we can trust her?'

'Sure, we probably can trust her. Probably. But can we trust the people she reports to, or the ones they report to? Somewhere along the line integrity has broken down. The situation is far too serious for us to be telling the truth to superiors, Andrew.'

They pressed on through South London. Empty roads meant good progress, and they pulled up outside 'Hobbies R US' in Charlton well before opening time.

'Great,' said Andrew returning to the car after a quick look around, 'it won't be open for another hour and a half – plenty of time for us to get in and out.'

Amisha laughed. 'Have you actually stolen anything before Andrew?'

'No, but I've seen all of Guy Ritchie's films,' said Andrew excitedly, to general laughter.

'What about charging?' said Jupiter when it had calmed down. 'These things don't come pre-charged, it'll take a few hours to juice one up. Sometimes chargers come separately.'

The two computer geniuses and the police officer known for his meticulous attention to detail were taken aback. Amisha was the first to recover.

'OK, good point. We better get moving then.'

The building was part of a retail park of large buildings and had all the standard stores found on plots all over the country, selling furniture, carpets, computers, food, discounted clothes. The 'Hobbies R US' building had a large windowed frontage to display its many wares, which was fortunate because all the other doors had multiple reinforced locking systems.

'Here's the plan,' said Amisha, 'Zaida and I will be in the car. I'll reverse directly through the windows and then pull up. Old-school smash and grab. The alarm will go apeshit and it might freak you out, but don't worry. With things as they are it will be several minutes, at the very least, before anyone shows. Andrew, you go in with Joey and find the boys' toys we need. Get two drones if you can. We then go and find a quiet spot somewhere to charge them up.'

Zaida's face was a blank; Andrew's face was as animated as a schoolboy thrill-seeker's; Jupiter's face was beginning to wear its trademark smirk.

'Right,' said Amisha, 'unless somebody has a better idea I suggest we get cracking.' She revved the car up like Steve McQueen in *Bullet* and got set for the ram.

'Ready?' she shouted out to the boys.

'Ready.'

'And Andrew...'

'Yes guv?'

'Don't forget the fucking chargers.'

☐

55

Andrew and Jupiter charged the drones up at a service station just outside Maidstone, keeping them out of sight as best they could, while Amisha and Zaida drank coffee inside, occupying the counter staff with warrant cards, security passes, spy stories and fluttering eyelashes. When the drones were ready they moved on, driving into the Kent downs and finding a good high vantage point in the Lydden and Temple Newell Nature Reserve, a few miles from the centre of Dover but with a view of the channel and the white cliffs – those great old symbols of patriotism and defiance of invaders. It was mid-afternoon, so they parked up and had a picnic in the car – with one of the drones in the boot and one on Andrew's lap in the backseat – while they waited for dark to descend.

Amisha gave the nod to Andrew when she considered the conditions gloomy enough to get started; he jumped out of the car, bellowed out what he could remember of *White Cliffs of Dover*, which wasn't much, fiddled with the practice manoeuvre he'd programmed into his phone and sparked his baby up. They all felt the thrill as it buzzed up into the air and seemed to take on a life of its own: it went up, it went sideways, it fizzed about for a bit like a maddened giant hornet, and it span out of control and back to earth with a plastic tinkle.

'For God's sake Andrew, let me do it,' said Amisha.

Amisha's initial efforts were not much better. Jupiter was beginning to start up with the wisecracks; Amisha, stressed and exhausted, wished H was around to shut him up with a little slap or suchlike. She passed the phone to Zaida – and the other would-be drone pilots looked on with admiration as the thing went up, sideways, performed a short circular route and landed gently back where it had started.

'Right,' said Amisha, 'Zaida, you are the pilot. We need to cover the area in a series of grids, let's draw up a search pattern that …'

'Amisha, sweetheart, I'm a spy. I have this covered. It's what I do.'

Amisha smiled. 'Andrew, you're driving the car, we need to make sure we stay within two miles of the drone, or the signal will break. I'll monitor the image from the camera on my tablet as we go.'

The search began. They were looking for a 'compound', which could mean anything. A farm, of which there were many, or a country estate perhaps, of which there were also a good few, where they might see something suspicious – whatever suspicious might look like.

The drones each had only a two-hour battery life, which made everyone tense, and it was slow, painstaking work. The kind of work spies and police officers are used to, but that writers of blogs are not, and Joey Jupiter was getting bored, especially as he had no real role to play. He started wondering how he'd managed to get caught up in all this.

'Can I help anyone?' he asked.

'No.' said Amisha, 'Just keep quiet please Joey, if you don't mind.'

The evening wore on, and after two hours Zaida brought the first Night Scout back to earth.

Jupiter was first out when it landed; he detached the camera from the first drone, set it up on the second, and jumped back into the car. Zaida programmed the flight path into her phone and launched drone two into the air with a silent prayer, and the foursome set off once more. The quiet, slow motion of the car was inducing a kind of fatigued boredom, on the boys especially. Every now and then the

186

atmosphere was enlivened by Amisha zoning in on a possible find and then dismissing it; each time this happened the tension went up a notch and stayed there for a while until the fatigue reasserted itself. Then, nearly three and a half hours in, they found something. They'd completed a sweep of the west side of Dover and its hinterland, and had moved to the southern side when the drone passed by a large building set in extensive grounds, surrounded by a substantial-looking perimeter fence. Amisha zoomed in and noticed, she was almost sure, a person standing outside the building; he was holding something and smoking a cigarette. The building was a mile or so from their present location.

'Zaida, change the flight path,' said Amisha, flashing her tablet and pointing. 'Hover over that building.'

Zaida did as requested.

'Go lower, I need to take a closer look.'

Zaida lowered the altitude of the drone.

And then there was gunfire, and then the images stopped coming, and that was the last they ever saw of their second Night Scout.

'Fuck,' said Andrew, 'what is that place?'

Amisha brought what they needed to know on her tablet.

'It's the old Nonington College, a specialist PE college, which Wiki tells us was closed down in the 1980s. It was bought by a community of the Bruderhof who, it says here, are a bit like new-age Quakers – they preach non-violence and peace-making, and so on.'

'Except when they see a drone,' said Jupiter.

'Yes,' said Zaida, 'except when they see a drone.'

Zaida continued the research – the Bruderhof had sold out some years earlier. It was now in private hands.

'This would appear to be a high-security compound of some sort. It may or may not be what we're looking for, but at last we've got something to get our teeth into. It's time to

187

get boots on the ground. Amisha, send H and his people in to take a closer look.'

56

She had to keep busy. That was all she knew: she had to keep busy.

Little Harry took up most of her time, of course, but Olivia still felt that she needed more to occupy her mind, and disperse her energy. She was living – like many others – in a sort of limbo, enduring the present in the hope that things would get better. She knew H was working on that, and she felt her usual glowing pride in him. But he wasn't around, and she was lonely and restless.

She decided to decorate the house, starting with the living room. H had given it a fair hammering, and though the windows had been fixed there were still bloodstains on the walls and the room felt like it needed cleansing.

'Little Man, come to mummy when that cartoon's finished, OK? We've got to go shopping – we're going to do some painting,' she called out from the kitchen. The boy burst immediately out of the living room and came barrelling along the passage, much like his dad, in high excitement – Peppa Pig would have to wait. Olivia held out her arms and he launched himself into them like a rocket-propelled grenade. For a moment Olivia was happy.

And then the letterbox banged open, and shut again, and a letter fell onto the mat.

Olivia threw the boy over her shoulder in a fireman's lift, H-style, and carried him back along the passage, singing 'Postman Pat, Postman Pat, Postman Pat and his black and white cat…let's see what Pat's brought us, shall we Little Man? Maybe it's some good news.'

She picked up the buff envelope – no stamps or postmark, she noticed – and sat down in the living room with the boy on her lap. It was addressed to her and him.

189

Just the two of them. She began to feel uneasy; she held her breath and ripped it open, and she began to read, with mounting horror:

> *My Dear Olivia and Little Harry. I hope you are well. I have prepared fun and games for us. You will not believe the fun we going to have. You can pack bag with a few things if you like – but you will not need much. This is one-way trip. I be back to pick you up later.*
> *Yours Sincerely*
> *V A*

Olivia stood bolt-upright, choked down a wave of hysterical fear, threw the boy back over her shoulder, charged upstairs to the bedroom and dug out the encrypted phone H had left her, along with strict instructions as to its use. She was to call him on it once a week, unless there was an emergency. She figured a one-way trip to God-knew-what with Vladimir Agapov qualified.

H listened calmly as she blurted it all out – the fear triggered by the letter, and all the other things that had been building up inside her since they last spoke.

'Shhh…shhh babes, it's alright,' said H when Olivia had calmed down. 'Think it through, doll – he's delivered the letter himself, so he could have taken you if he wanted. He's just trying to get into my nut. Stay calm, listen carefully – here's what I want you to do…'

190

57

'Fucking hell,' said Kuba as he took another look at the compound through the infrared binoculars before passing them back to H, 'this is not going to be a walk in the park.'

They were in the grounds of Nonington College, in a small thicket of trees at the edge of a vegetable garden. It was now four o'clock in the morning and they'd been hunkered down in their current position for over an hour. The job of scaling the outer perimeter and getting within viewing distance of the main compound had gone OK, considering H's age, his injuries after his Ronnie Ruddock murder meltdown and his aching limbs. The grounds didn't seem well guarded, and H thought he could get his men up close; but the residence itself was a completely different matter. The residence itself was going to take some taking.

***

Two days had passed since the drone had been blown out of the sky and Amisha and co. had made their way back to London. H and Kuba had reviewed the camera footage before travelling to Nonington to scout the area and see what was what.

They'd booked two rooms in the local pub – The Boar's Head – and H insisted on a couple of late-night sharpeners, before their real night out in the grounds of Nonington Manor began.

'Hi, just showing my friend here around the Garden of England,' he said to an aging drinker who looked like he'd spent many years in the corner of his local, having quiet drinks and soaking up the gossip, 'what's the story with the big manor house, who owns it? Don't suppose they'll let us have a little mooch about if we ask them nicely?'

The aging local was 79 years old, bent over and as wrinkled as the skin of a baked apple. He was glad when people spoke to him, which wasn't all that often given his appearance, so he readily opened-up to H's questioning.

'I doubt it. It's owned by a bloke called John Stables. He comes in here from time to time, has a quick pint and a little chat. But mostly he keeps to himself.'

'Why do you think he bought the place?'

'Your guess is as good as mine son.' This wasn't an H type 'son' as in 'my old son', but was used as a reference to a younger man, which was something H wasn't used to being seen as these days, and he rather liked it.

'I heard he was something of a big shot in construction; his wife was killed in a car accident so he sold up, bought the old place and now lives there on his own, with one or two staff who you never see.'

The story tallied with what Amisha and Zaida had found out since they'd returned to London. There was no evidence to indicate that Mr Stables had been involved in any kind of monkey business, no evidence at all. Since moving to Nonington a few years earlier he'd just kept his head down and lived the quiet life. Devastated by the loss of his wife, he had become a recluse, the Howard Hughes of south east Kent, and seldom if ever returned to his old stomping grounds.

'Look after the place, does he?' H continued.

'Oh, yeah. When he first came here he had the place completely renovated. Gutted it. Took over a year. Trucks were coming up our little High Street day and night for what seemed like forever. After he finished he invited the local paper in to see it and take pictures. Looked nicely done, classy.'

192

H and Kuba had already seen the photos, which showed nothing of any possible access points.

'OK fella, nice talking to you. Be lucky,' said H with a wink.

They retired to their rooms to plan the evening's activities, and got cracking. Neither of them presented a pretty sight as they clambered down the drainpipe that took them into the pub car park; dishevelled and puffing heavily they then made their way on foot to the perimeter of the manor, which was about a mile from the pub. Late at night in the middle of a small Kent village there are few lights, so moving around unnoticed was easy.

After an hour watching the front of the building they had seen only the one guard, who was stationed at the one front door. The ground floor windows looked new; observation of this fact drew from Kuba his comment that things were not going to be particularly straightforward.

'That's metallic glass, very strong,' he said, 'we won't be able to smash through it with any hand-held implements, no matter how heavy they are.'

'Hmm…' said H, as he continued to survey the manor. If there were more people in there then lights should be shining through the window, but apart from a single guard H could see nothing but dark, hear nothing through the blanket of silence.

'Let's creep round the back,' he said.

They got down and slithered along the ground, just as they'd both been trained to do in their respective armies, one slow and painful yard at a time. Kuba heard H ranting and raving beneath his breath, something about being too fucking old for all this bollocks and where were the brave young men prepared to step up when you fucking needed them. Kuba kept quiet until they had reached a vantage point at the rear of the manor.

They spent a few minutes surveying the rear with their infrared binoculars before talking tactics.

'You are fucking right my friend,' said H.

'What about?'

'As you said, "this is not going to be any sort of fucking walk in the park".'

There was no entry at the rear – only the same metallic windows.

'Key question: why is there only one way into a building this size?' said Kuba.

'Modifications,' said H. 'This place has been modified to keep people out.'

'Yes, even people like you and me, my old friend.'

58

The night wore on, and the two men resolved to stay until early morning. They were close to freezing and H cursed the cold in his inimitable manner. Kuba laughed for a while and then got bored with the 'old bastard', as he sometimes referred to H, so he moved the subject on. They talked about the old days, some of the old cases, and became a little philosophical about the lives they'd lived, the deaths they'd seen, the lives they'd taken. After all they had been through, all they'd seen in their violent lives, here they still were, giving everything they had to keep the devil down in his hole.

'There's no way round it son, people like us, it's why we're here,' said H, 'it's who we are, it's what we do. It's what we have to do.' The reflective night passed on and H gave a few more philosophical gems from the school of hard knocks until, away in the east, a blood red dawn broke over the horizon, throwing out enough light to allow for an improved view of the manor house.

'Up there,' said H, pointing to a curtain twitching in one of the upper windows. Then the curtain was pulled back, and H saw something he hadn't expected, and didn't much like the look of. A large man, maybe 6ft 4in, stood in the window frame and stared out at the new dawn. He only had the curtain open for a few seconds but it was enough. Behind him a group of men were filing past the window on their way, thought H, for an early morning shower.

'Shit,' said H, 'it's like a fucking barracks. They've got a small fucking army in there.'

The two watchers watched on.

'Look at that,' said Kuba, pointing to another area, 'that seems odd.'

'What?' said H, unsure as to what he should be looking at.

'The grass, over there, it doesn't grow in the same way as the rest of the garden.'

'So?'

'In Poland, back in the old days, I helped to make many underground bunkers, on farms and in the countryside. Some for the government, some for private citizens who wanted them for their own reasons.'

'And?'

'And always the grass around the area looked a little different. The frost, it is slightly less.' H could see a large square area where the frost was not as strong as the rest of the garden.

'So you think there's a bunker or a room below, and heat is coming from it, and it's reducing the frost?' said H.

'Yes, I would say so.'

Having seen enough of the rear H decided to crawl back to the front of the house, to look at that side in the daylight. Same hard going, same moaning.

They'd already seen two surprises that morning. A small army. An underground bunker of some sort. As they got to the front it was followed by a third, which was the biggest surprise of all. A man came out of the door and approached the lone guard. He was gesticulating and giving orders, clearly in command. H raised the binoculars to take a closer look. Then his body started to convulse in uncontrollable spasms as he attempted to suppress pure, animal rage. His instinct was to rear up and charge at the object of his hatred like a rampaging rhino, and tear him limb from limb. He controlled the urge to do this and instead took out his pistol and started to aim.

Kuba grabbed his arm. 'What are you fucking doing? If you fire now we're finished. Compose yourself. What are you doing?'

196

H turned himself over onto his back and stared hard at Kuba, and passed the binoculars.

'That man, take a look. It's the man who killed Ronnie – of that I am certain – and now he's putting the frighteners on my Olivia. Vladimir Agapov. He needs to die.'

'They have a bunker, used for we know not what, and lots of men to protect it. Do not reveal our position. Take control of your emotions now.'

H grunted an animal grunt. Kuba was right, now was not the time to extract revenge. That time would come soon, H thought, as the two men crawled slowly to the perimeter, slinked cautiously back to the pub and snuck back into their rooms.

A few hours later they met in the bar area for breakfast.

'So,' said Kuba 'what's the plan?'

'The plan, mate,' said H as he munched appreciatively on a slice of salty bacon, 'is to get our firm up here and take that fucking manor house, pronto. It's a tricky set-up, but we've got good men, and the element of surprise – we can handle the situation. But show your boys Agapov's picture and make sure they know he's mine. Mine alone. I am going to gut that dirty no-good cunt, slow and sure, from stem to stern, and make him rue the day his mother shat him out. Agapov is mine.'

PART THREE

59

Brad woke up early. He had a busy day ahead of him. He packed his rucksack and made his way to reception to check out. He exchanged pleasantries with the guest house manager and paid his bill in cash. Brad always used cash – he had brought plenty with him from the States. As he was leaving the manager slapped him on the back and wished him the best of luck on his travels and with the new book.

Brad returned the smile and the handshake and departed the guest house for the last time. His real name wasn't Brad, but the hotel manager didn't know that. Nor did anybody else in Britain. His real name didn't matter anymore, at least not to Brad.

Brad got to his hire car, threw his rucksack in and set off. He found the A93 and then the short drive to the small village of Braemar. Braemar was thought of as a quaint little place. One or two small coffee shops, a couple of hotels and a golf course ensured a regular supply of tourists in the spring and summer months, and an annual highland games gathering in September always brought in a good crowd.

But there were no crowds on this freezing cold January morning when Brad dropped his car off at the Braemar Tourist Centre. He took the paperwork into the office and the administration was soon done. The car was looked over, papers signed. No drama, nice and easy, just the way Brad liked it. He then made his way to the post office and sent the letter he'd written the previous evening. He didn't want to send it by email, it was too personal. The letter was to his wife, telling her he loved her and how sorry he was he would never see her again.

He then set off on his walk. It was about nine miles to Crathie and he intended to take it at a leisurely pace. He'd planned for around three hours, along a gentle and picturesque walking path that followed the River Dee. It was cold but it was dry, and Brad was thankful for that as he adjusted his backpack and threw his second piece of luggage, a long black bag, over his right shoulder.

Brad was a seasoned walker and the nine miles were eaten up in no time. He arrived in Crathie in fine mood, in exactly the time he'd planned, and made his way to the tree he'd climbed a few days previously. He laid his luggage on the ground and checked the contents. The backpack contained supplies for the period he would be staying at his new home. Freeze dried vegetarian ratatouille with pasta; crackers; almond poppy seed pound cake; peanut butter; tropical punch powder; salt; seasoning blend; sugar; chewing gum; wet wipes; matches; toilet paper; plastic spoon; can of petrol; and one other fluid-filled container. Everything you would expect in a US Army ration pack. He had enough to last a couple of weeks; he'd get his water from the little stream a few hundred yards away.

He opened his long black bag and took out his waterproof winter clothes. He put them on, including the fur-lined balaclava. Brad knew the importance of the balaclava for keeping warm and had always remembered the words of his commanding officer on those long cold nights lying low in Iraq – *When your feet are cold, cover you head.*

He ate some rations and took out the small spade from the long black bag and started to dig his foxhole. He would be here, probably, for several days so he ensured it was large enough to keep him comfortable.

He then took out his Remmington M40A6 sniper rifle, which had been professionally adjusted to ensure it could be folded into small spaces, yet still have a full-length rail to accommodate a 12x50mm night scope. He assembled the weapon as if engaged in some purging religious ritual and checked, as best he could without firing, that it was fully operational, before disassembling and placing it tenderly back into the long black bag. Then the pain hit again, deep in his bowels, so he took a swig of the liquid morphine he had brought with him. Brad was covered for all eventualities.

It would be a difficult shot, no doubt about that. Over 1.5 miles. No knowing the weather conditions until the day came and no base to rest on up in the trees – he'd have to have a steady hand. But it was a shot he'd made before, and he had no reason to doubt his ability to do it again.

It was now 4pm and already the sun was making its westerly descent. As the night drew in around him Brad felt relaxed and confident as he settled into his foxhole.

60

'We're going to need a lot more weight than what we've got now,' said H. 'Automatics are a must, given the size of the firm at Nonington and the firepower they'll likely have. A lot more rounds, and something to go bang – grenades – and some shoulder-held rocket launchers to smash through those metal windows.'

Kuba and Yorkie Ted both nodded emphatically, hunkered down around the tea chest that was serving as their desk, and cradled their coffees; H's old lockup was not getting any warmer as the night wore on. The Elephant and Castle train station was directly above where they sat, and the night time rumblings and thundering from the trains in and out of Blackfriars or Victoria were wearing at their nerves. But H was laying out essentials now, and they were focused.

'My policy is always to assume the worst, and be ready for anything. I'd say these blokes are likely to be tasty: well trained, possibly Spetsnaz or ex-Spetsnaz, and very well armed. We'll have the element of surprise, but we've got to throw the kitchen sink at them from the word go, all at once. Total shock and awe – you boys getting me? We're going to have to make openings in those windows, grenades in straight away and then men following up immediately, before they know what fucking day of the week it is.'

'Loud and clear H, loud and clear,' said Ted. 'My lads are chomping at the bit, no problems there, but...where are we going to get the gear we need? If we were in Leeds we could...'

'I know some people, or at least one of my guys does,' said Kuba. 'Jarek. He's lived in London for about eight years now. Does personal protection for people that need it.'

'You mean he's a bodyguard?' said Ted.

'I mean he protects high profile people with real enemies, enemies who would have them killed in a heartbeat. He ran the Presidential security team in Poland for a couple of years, and he's been in Afghanistan and Iraq. Special Forces. Is that good enough for you Ted?' said Kuba, the anger rising in his throat.

H put an arm on Kuba's shoulder to calm him, and waited until he settled. A freight train rumbled past at walking pace overhead.

'So,' H said at length, 'humble pie for you in the morning, Ted. A nice big breakfast. Will you be able to get it all down?'

'Yep, that I will H,' said Ted, crisply. 'And I shall probably ask for a second helping when I've finished. What's the plan Kuba?'

'Haven't really got one. What I'm saying is that from time to time Jarek has to find hardware, and he deals with a reliable guy who usually gets him whatever he wants, within reason.'

'How do we contact him?' said H.

'We don't. He always works through third parties. The last time Jarek used him he went through a drug dealer.'

'Where?' asked H.

'A place, I think, called...something "Hill". In south London.'

'There are a lot of hills in south London,' said H. 'Herne Hill? Streatham Hill? Gipsy Hill? Brixton Hill? Tulse Hill?'

'That's it, Tulse Hill. Is it far from here? What sort of place is it?'

'Well, it's a step or two down from Windsor, put it that way,' said H. 'But I'm sure you'll get the flavour once you see it. You better get down there now.'

'Now?' said Kuba, 'it's half past two in the morning.'

'Yes, now,' said H, 'what do you think this is, a fucking holiday camp?'

61

Tulse Hill at three in the morning turned out to be something of a disappointment, being neither a couple of steps down from Windsor nor a complete hellhole, as Kuba thought H might be implying. He was still getting to grips with some of the nuances of English irony. The four men, Kuba, Jarek Dydowicz, Little Ronnie and Marek Kucharski, stepped out of their cars – two of these, as H had instructed, for the benefit of any roadblocks – and into a grubby, moonlit side street. It was quiet for the most part, the silence broken only when a police chopper making a wide circuit over Brixton was overhead.

Jarek tapped lightly on the bay window of a squat terraced house and the door was answered almost immediately by a wiry, dishevelled and grey looking middle aged man with an otherworldly air about him. Another disappointment, of sorts, for Kuba. He'd expected to be dealing with some larger than life, drugged-up headcase, something out of *True Romance* or *Harry Brown*, which he'd watched with Little Ronnie on his tablet. Yet here was a weedy, mild mannered guy who looked like he sold second hand plumbing requisites on a Sunday morning market stall.

They were invited into a record and magazine strewn living room smelling of weed. The stereo was playing King Crimson. Still no vicious Pitbull terriers or crazed, gold-toothed nutters gurning at them. Kuba, Marek and Little Ronnie made themselves comfortable, as best they could, on a tattered grey velveteen sofa. Jarek stood and addressed their host.

'How are things, Martin?' he said.

'Not too bad mate, what can I do you for?'

'I need you to speak to Mr Bosanquet. I want to make an order.'

'Same as usual, more or less?'

'No, more this time, and heavier.'

'OK, give me the list.'

Jarek began to recite H's wish list in full detail. Kuba listened, incredulous, for fifteen seconds and stopped him.

'Jarek, what are you doing. Why don't you...'

'Oh, this is how it works, old son,' said Martin, turning to Kuba, 'Mr Bosanquet works on a verbal-orders only basis. No lists, nothing written down, no evidence trail. Jarek knows that, him and Mr Bosanquet are old mates.'

'But you've been sitting here all-night smoking weed,' Kuba said, 'this room smells like Amy Winehouse just spent the last two days in it. How the fuck will you remember all this?'

'It's no problem. It's what I do, it's how we do things. Mr Bosanquet's instructions. Business is business. We've never had any problems, have we Jarek?'

***

'What do you need all this lot for Jarek?' drawled Mr Bosanquet – a tall, lean, expensively dressed man with an Oxbridge accent – twenty-four hours later, in a field outside Guildford. 'This is a lot of weight, much more than usual.'

'Well I've got a big job on, Mr Bosanquet.'

'How big? What are you doing, invading Russia?'

'No, nothing like that,' Jarek said with a laugh, appraising the stock in the back of a white minivan. *Plumbing Materials*, it said on the side.

'Well, it's your funeral.'

'That it may well be, Mr Bosanquet, that it may well be...how much do I owe you?'

Mr Bosanquet mouthed the figure silently, then traced it with his finger in the air by way of confirmation.

Jarek walked back to the car Kuba was waiting in and gave him the figure. Kuba punched it into the laptop on his knees. They waited a few moments, until Mr Bosanquet withdrew his gaze from his phone, smiled and gave them the thumbs-up. He threw a bunch of keys towards Marek in a high arc, turned smartly on his heels and walked across the field, away from the van.

62

They met in Bermondsey Street. H could hardly believe how the place had changed. The wealth and tentacles of the Square Mile had reached out across the river, like the limbs of a giant octopus, and drawn the area into its orbit. Gone were the working men's cafes and the warehouses, replaced by art galleries selling the kind of modern art stuff H hated. Frothy coffee shops and swanky flats offered a slice of the new London, right next to the Thames. A canny buyer could pick up a one-bed rabbit hutch for little more than a million.

It was late afternoon; helicopters and drones buzzed above the churning grey river but in this part of town things were proceeding reasonably normally – the gallery owners were back in their galleries and the office workers were back in their offices. The coffee shop was quiet when Amisha walked in. She ordered a black coffee and a strong tea, two sugars. H spied her through the window as he arrived, right behind her. One of the things they had in common was never being late, all other things being equal.

'Hello Ames,' H said, parking himself on the stool next to her. He thanked her for his tea and took a large gulp. She slipped a note across the table. It contained a list of names that looked as if it was taken from *Who's Who*, the bible of the British establishment. Names that had received eye-watering payments from the oligarch accounts Zaida had accessed. Names that would have to be dealt with. H took a look.

'That is Zaida's preliminary list.'

There were ten names on it.

Jesus…this is unbelievable.

'Fuck me, are you sure Ames, really sure about this? This is a preliminary list? How many of these fuckers are there?'

'We don't know. But yes, we're sure. All of them are involved, have been paid off in one way or another. Zaida's been as rigorous as rigorous can be. She's not doing this for a laugh, H – we always used to call her Ms Meticulous. She's famous for it. Trust me H, this list is bulletproof. It's not complete, by any means – but what's here is bulletproof.'

H indicated with a nod of the head that he accepted the fact.

'Look at them,' Amisha continued, 'it's the Dream Team for wrecking Britain: Lords and politicians for passing laws and shaping public opinion, senior army people for throwing spanners in the works of efforts to control what's going on, media executives for shaping "news", hedge fund managers for destabilising the economy.'

'Jesus Ames, this is absolutely fucking mental. And there are more where these came from?'

'Yes, we believe so. A full array of top-level players for a hybrid war.'

'What's a "hybrid war" when it's at home?'

'One that's not declared, or defined. One where no one can be entirely sure who the enemy is, or what their motives are. One in which force and disinformation are blended, where the media stops being a source of reliable information, and nobody can tell who's who. Designed to destabilise and weaken an enemy, either as part of a bigger geopolitical strategy or a prelude to full-scale takeover. Zaida's money is on the former, and I think she may be right. Whatever, the Russians are the best at all this – that's why it all makes sense. Sort of.'

***

H fell silent. Amisha could almost hear the gears winding in his head, trying to match the theory up with the practice. She went back to the counter for refills.

'Alright then Ames,' he said when she got back, 'we're ready to roll. We're going forward on two fronts. One, I've got people all set to take care of this little lot on the list. These fucking traitors are going to get what they used to get in the old days: the full treatment, no beating about the bush. We'll do them all and let God sort them out. That ought to slow things down a bit. We've put a deposit down for the first couple already; make sure Zaida stays focused and disburses the payments as soon as I give her the details, which I will on a case-by-case basis. These blokes don't care about the country, only the money. Anyway, they'll start to wobble double-quick if they don't get paid on time.'

'Second, I've finished putting my team together now; we're well-equipped and ready to take down the compound at Nonington. Also scheduled for tomorrow.'

'Who's on board.'

'Well, I'm working closely with Kuba, the Polish bloke I told you about. But apart from that I'm keeping everything on a need-to-know basis, and you don't need to know any of the others at this stage – what you don't know can't hurt you.'

'So H's army is ready to roll?'

'You better believe it,' said H. 'These bastards wanted blood and chaos? Well, they're to get more than they ever bargained for. See you later Ames.'

He stood up, gulped down the last of his tea and swarmed out of the coffee shop, moving fast in the direction of the Elephant and Castle.

63

Something was telling H it had all been too easy. They'd navigated the roadblocks without too much trouble – he never expected many problems on that front. But from the moment they had parked up in the woods surrounding Nonington and made their way under cover of darkness to the compound they'd met no resistance. He had a gut feeling something was wrong. But what? And they had no choice, they had to go through with the attack.

'If this is such an important site why don't they have any scouts, nobody on the ground. If I was securing that compound I'd make sure I had an early warning system.'

'I was thinking the same thing,' said Kuba, 'what if they know we're here? What if they're just waiting to pick us off?'

'No,' said H, 'makes no sense to let us surround the place and get our positions set-up. If they knew we were here they would have attacked. Something's wrong, but I don't know what.'

'You thinking of calling it off?'

'No, we're too far in, and the risk of doing fuck all is greater than the risk we're looking at here, in the bigger scheme of things. Let's go through the plan one more time.'

H and Kuba gathered the inner firm – Yorkie Ted, Little Ronnie, Jarek – and gave them the news.

'Right,' said H. 'What we think is this. Inside this place there's an underground laboratory, and it's being used to cook up something very nasty indeed, something that could make what we've seen so far look like a vicar's tea party. It will likely be very secure and it's unlikely our attack will disturb it – which is just as well because from what I understand we really don't want to do that.'

Our objective is clear. Take control of the manor house quickly. Find and secure the laboratory. Once we have done that I'll stay until the Army show up. With the racket we're going to make they should be along sharpish, even under the current conditions. Everyone else clears off. Some of you will get caught, some of you will escape. If you get caught stick to the story – basically, the truth.'

As H had told Amisha, they were working on a need-to-basis; only H and Kuba knew the details about Albie Bradford's kill squad, and only Little Ronnie knew it was Amisha heading up technical division – all the other members of which were unknown. If anyone got caught they wouldn't have to lie about what they didn't know.

Having confirmed the objectives H moved onto specific tactics.

'Yorkie, you and your boys at the front with me. Kuba, your lot at the back. One RPG each. We'll give you five minutes to get your men within fifty feet. Stay down low. Then I'll give the command here for the first grenade, which is going to blast through this window at the front, here.'

H pointed to the drawing of the compound he and Kuba had made after their first survey.

'Kuba, on hearing the attack begin, hits this window here. Then both RPGs reload and take out windows here, and here. That gives as four windows open at different points in the house. The snipers take down any guards who show themselves while everyone else gets to their allocated window, one grenade per window popped in before every man storms the building with the utmost speed and urgency – we need to hit them hard, fast gentlemen, hard and fast. Speed is of the essence.'

H then opened the layout of the interior he'd got from Amisha. It was an old architectural drawing she'd found on a website about the history of Nonington. It had gelled with what they had studied from the archives of the local papers that showed pictures of the place after John Stables' modifications – so they were confident it hadn't changed in any major way.

It showed a flight of stairs at both ends of the building.

'I'll lead a team up this set of stairs, Kuba will lead the other team up the second set and into the upper bedrooms, which are being used as dormitories, as far as we can tell.'

'And then?' said Jarek.

H held the thought. And then…and then what? Agapov was inside and he hadn't told anybody since he'd nearly lost the plot on his first visit with Kuba. As desperate as he was to get hold of him, Kuba had forced him to reconsider his animal thirst for vengeance. Having men looking for individuals would slow them down, make them think twice before firing. In short it would jeopardise the mission – put his men in danger. Things couldn't be personal with so much at stake. Kuba stared at H but said nothing, although he knew what H was thinking.

'And then, my old son, you shoot the fuck out of anything that moves – with extreme prejudice,' said H.

64

They got into position quick, without any trouble. No one fired on them, no one seemed to notice they were there. H had a nagging feeling he just couldn't shake. With just a little bit of luck – and H knew that despite all the planning these attacks often failed or succeeded on a turn of fortune – the element of surprise might see them wrap this up quickly. Everyone was in position: the two RPG shooters, the snipers to take down any guards, the teams with grenades at the ready, and Little Ronnie, who stood side by side with H at his command post.

The two had argued the previous evening, H insisting that Little Ronnie stay at home. He couldn't bear to lose a son, not after losing his lifelong friend. But Ronnie had been adamant, relentless in his determination to be part of the assault. In the end H conceded, but he was going to make sure Little Ronnie was at his side. He turned to face him.

'OK, son,' said H, 'this is the serious stuff. This is war and you haven't been trained for it and you haven't been here before. We know you can dish it out when you have to, but what we're doing here requires discipline. We're not here to run amok chopping people's fucking heads off, so do what I fucking tell you and keep your wits about you. You ready ?'

'Ready,' said Little Ronnie. His heart was all but leaping out of his mouth, his pulse was accelerating faster than a fat man in a spin class and his breathing was erratic. But he felt ready, he felt like he was where he should be, standing shoulder to shoulder with his dad in a moment of extreme danger. 'I'm ready as I'll ever be, Pop.'

H stared into his son's eyes and knew he had what it took, saw and knew that the boy had whatever it was that he himself had. But this was no time for happy families, it was time for war. H raised his hand and gave the signal for the attack to commence.

It was well planned, with good men who knew what they were doing. The RPGs fired and hit their targets, the snipers took out a solitary guard and the two teams were straight in with the hand grenades. H had timed his run to perfection and surged through the window within a second of the grenade exploding.

'Fuck me,' said Yorkie Ted to no one in particular as he followed close behind, 'how the fuck is that old bastard moving that fast?'

H surveyed the scene. No one. He coursed forward towards the stairs. No one. He ran upstairs and swarmed into one of the bedrooms, letting off several rounds as he entered. No one.

Kuba had entered at the other end of the house with the same deadly hostility. His actions were almost a mirror copy of H's. Up the stairs and into a bedroom, blasting with everything he had as he smashed his way through one of the upper doors and into the room where he'd seen a group of men just a few days earlier. The room was sparsely furnished, just a row of beds either side of a long, wide room. They were all empty. No men, no clothes, nothing.

H and Kuba met in the middle of three upper rooms. Each was the same as the rest. They made eye contact as their men followed them in.

'The bunker, they're in the bunker,' shouted H. He barked orders, telling everyone to get back downstairs and find the door to the bunker. Getting through it would present problems – he'd had visions of some kind of computer-controlled, ten-inch thick titanium job, but when they got there it turned out to be a just an oak door, a heavy one for sure, but nothing insurmountable.

H was furious, as concerned with the thought that Agapov had eluded him as much as with the general fuck-up. He started to kick at the door. He kicked at it again and again with every ounce of energy and effort he could muster. Then he kicked it again. It was frustrating work. Kuba understood and let H wear himself out before he ordered everyone back and rolled a grenade up to the door's bottom. The bang was deafening in such close quarters. The door itself buckled but stayed where it was, hanging from its hinges.

Little Ronnie stepped up to the mark and gave it one almighty kick. It still held. He gave it another. And another. H, recovered from his prior exertions, sensed its final moment had come, palmed Little Ronnie out of the way and hit the door with everything he had. It flew open. H surged into the room and took stock of the surroundings.

Nothing. H was perplexed. The walls were just whitewashed stone. No scientific equipment, no germ-generating technology, no bomb factory, nothing. Not so much as a power supply. It was just a small room with a set of bunk beds on both sides, and another door.

Kuba tried it. It was not even locked. It led to a tunnel.

'Fucking hell,' said H, 'staring hard into the eyes of Kuba, who'd come to the same understanding as the big man, 'the bastards have sold us a pup – an absolute fucking pup.'

65

H looked about him as more of his rag tag army made their way into the bunker, itching for a tear-up, primed for action. The Poles vented their displeasure at the outcome explosively, while Kuba shrugged his shoulders. Yorkie Ted's boys also went large, hollering and hooting like there was no tomorrow. Full on adrenalin overload, thought H, ready to explode himself. There was nothing he could do about that now.

Overhead an army helicopter had arrived and was scouring the area. The pilots had located and seen the damage and called in the location. It wouldn't be long before the foot soldiers arrived.

'Right,' barked H, 'there's fuck-all point in standing here like tits in a trance. Let's get going.'

'As our enemies have made a point of preparing an escape route why don't we use it,' said Kuba. H thought for a few seconds about the possibility of booby traps; but they could have left these anywhere and hadn't. He decided to take the risk. The tunnel was well-built and surprisingly large, high enough to walk upright if you were under six foot. It was also surprisingly long.

'This must have taken some digging,' said H to Kuba as they inched their way along. Kuba was using his phone as a torch, his keen eye on the lookout for a tripwire or anything else that might impede their progress.

'What if it's a dead end, and there's someone hiding in the manor who creeps out and closes the door?' said Kuba.

'Then we'll all die a slow and unpleasant death,' said H.

It took over twenty minutes to reach the end, by which time they were well into their second mile. The exit was just a manhole covered with twigs and leaves. It flipped open easily and H slowly poked his head out into the cold night air. Nothing but the sights and sounds of a cold English woodland at night – birds twittering, the rustle of wind through the trees.

Kuba passed him the binoculars and he did a 360-degree swivel of the landscape.

'Fuck all out here,' said H, as he pulled the rest of his body out of the tunnel and got to his feet. With the help of Kuba's phone and a map of the area they'd pinpointed their position by the time the rest of the men had emerged from the tunnel.

'They knew we were coming,' said Ted, 'there must be a grass on the firm.'

'Not likely,' said H. 'we're too tight. This wasn't an inside job.'

'Well then,' said Ted, 'these so-called great leads from the so-called technical team, whoever they fucking are, are bollocks. You said the information was nailed on. They're not as smart as you said.'

'Turn it in, dozy bollocks – sort yourself out. It's not just that they knew we were coming, they knew we would come before we knew ourselves.'

'How would they know that?'

'Think about it, there's no other explanation. They knew we would come because they led us here – they've been yanking our chains all along.'

'But why?' said Kuba, 'why go to all that trouble?'

'I have no idea mate,' said H. 'But I know it's not good. We knew we were outnumbered, and now we know we're being outsmarted. We've got to up our game, fast.'

66

Christopher Mannering, a reliable creature of habit, groaned, turned onto his side and switched off his phone alarm. Five o'clock. He rolled himself out of bed without thinking and set his routine in motion: shower and shave, dressing room, breakfast while he reviewed overnight developments in the global markets, short drive to Reigate station for the 6.15am into Victoria, behind his desk at Bluesky Capital Assets on Threadneedle Street by 7.45am. The big daddy himself, the head honcho – CEO of one of the largest hedge funds in the City of London. If you were in the market for bespoke complex portfolio construction – for ways to tuck vast sums of money away where nobody, or almost nobody, could find them – he was your man.

Kenny Keeler was also a creature of habit. Like the rest of Albie Bradford's firm, he'd been issued with a Glock to do the business with, but he'd been a sawn-off man all his life and had no intention of changing at his age. Tucked away off-road behind a hedge a short way from Mannering's handsome fourteen-room pile – a mansion, really, set in huge and perfectly manicured grounds – he checked his old blagging gun one last time and slipped it back down the front of his leather jacket. He sat tight, relaxed and confident as he let the bike's engine idle, and laughed to himself.

Hiding behind a hedge, waiting for the hedge-man.

Keeler knew he didn't have a big window to get the job done in. The drive into the centre of Reigate was short, no more than ten minutes door-to-carpark. He liked to do things with a bit of panache, really go to town with the dramatics and put the frighteners on people. But there was no scope for that sort of thing today.

'No collateral damage Ken,' Bradford had warned him the previous evening, 'or Hawkins will do his nut. Just the target. Don't get carried away – it's just about the money.'

All things considered, then, this one would have to be clinical. Keeler had decided on the layby he was going to force Mannering's car into, about a quarter of a mile from the house. The road into Reigate was relatively quiet, given the isolated splendour in which the gilded elite of Surrey lived, and the layby also benefitted from being secluded from the road at one end by a line of trees.

Mannering came crunching over his driveway gravel in the Baby Bentley he liked to use for short runs. Keeler peered at the car – through his crash helmet, through the hedge – and nodded his head in appreciation.

Good man…bang on time.

67

Keeler pulled out from his hiding place and held back, fifty yards from the car. Traffic was light, as he'd hoped it would be. He visualized what he wanted to happen one last time, then he made it happen. There was no oncoming traffic as the Bentley approached the layby, five hundred yards out, and Keeler saw in his mirror that the closest thing behind him – another motorbike – was about a half a mile back.

He accelerated sharply and was alongside Mannering within seconds, steering the bike with one hand and indicating with the shotgun-waving other that the car should be slowed down and brought to a stop behind the trees. Mannering panicked and did as he was told; Keeler was close enough to spit through the partially open driver's side window.

Both vehicles came to a halt, just out of sight of the motorbike as it flashed by. Keeler stepped off his bike and motioned with the gun that Mannering should get out of the car on the passenger side.

The two men stood face-to-face, or face-to-helmet.

'Don't do anything stupid and you won't get hurt,' said Keeler.

'Sit down – here, next to the car. I want your wallet, phone and car keys. Now!'

Mannering fumbled in his pockets for his things. He'd half-expected to be robbed, sooner or later, driving a car like his. Coming out of a house like his. Now it was actually happening it felt unreal, like he was watching someone else go through it in a film.

'Alright, good man,' said Keeler, filling his pockets with Mannering's offerings.

'Now, lie down on the ground. Face down. I'm going to drive away now, OK? I want you to stay there, head down, for ten minutes. Understand?'

Mannering nodded, his face working itself into the grass, his mouth taking in dirt.

'Good man. What did I tell you? No need for anyone to get hurt. Sensible – very sensible. No wonder they love you in the City.'

Keeler stood back from his man, enjoying the early-morning silence, and waited until he heard a vehicle coming on. It sounded like a van, heading into Reigate. He waited until it was parallel with the layby, and gave Mannering both barrels, where his head met his neck. The head exploded like a watermelon falling off the back of a moving lorry, spraying chunks of meat and watery goo in all directions.

Keeler wiped down his leathers, put Mannering's effects onto the driver's seat, and pulled his bike out into the road, satisfied with his morning's work.

68

The meeting wasn't going well. At all.

'Let's just say it as it is Ames. It's a total fucking cock-up. Cyberattacks, malware spy software and all the other fancy strategies you and your little firm cooked up have been a waste of time. We're nowhere nearer than we were at the beginning. They've turned us over like a bunch of mugs.'

H was angry. He was angry because all their efforts had got them nowhere, angry because something big was coming and he had absolutely no idea what it was, and angry because he'd had Agapov in his sights and let him slip away. He was also smarting because he'd been tucked up like a kipper. H hated being done over, he always took it personally. He was also a little paranoid and, despite his belief that his army had not been compromised from within, had cut Andrew and Joey Jupiter out of the meeting.

'It's true they tricked us H, but then they've had a lot of time to prepare. They've probably set up multiple decoy scenarios,' said Zaida.

'Yes, but why exactly?'

'To keep the most capable people occupied – to get those most likely to figure out what they're really planning thrown off the scent. There may be others like us out there, clever people working independently of the security apparatus, which we know has been compromised. It's a way of decreasing the likelihood of anyone figuring out the big thing, by putting carefully planned, brilliantly conceived dummy operations in play. Probably even the people on the ground – like your friend Agapov – think they're doing something real.'

'Fuck. We're up against some exceptionally formidable people here ladies.'

225

'Yes,' said Zaida. 'They've had all the time in the world, limitless resources, and have extreme cunning. They've played us like fools, it's true. But we had to go in, and on the bright side, we've learned something crucial.'

'And that is?'

'That they are planning something massive, their game-changer – there's no other explanation for their going to all this trouble.'

'OK, good point. Fair enough. Got it,' said H. 'Now, back to basics: so they fed us a location and then disappeared. Do they know who we are?'

'I'd say not,' said Amisha. 'They'll know Joey Jupiter led the cyberattack but they don't know who ordered it. My guess would be they believe we're a bit more official than we are, and had no idea it was a vigilante force coming their way.'

'They might know it's not an official force, if it was they might have found out about it. Their tentacles are everywhere,' said Zaida.

'We just have to keep going,' said Amisha, 'we just have to keep investigating the web. Zaida's the best there is – if she can't find something, no one can.'

'OK,' said H. 'But my instincts tell me that we can still get something from an actual human source. Someone must know something. I need to get back in touch with the firm I put on the traitors and slow them down. I need to pay a visit to some of the people on that list before they're all dead. It'd also be very handy if we could locate Agapov – get Jupiter to do his thing, will you?'

'Good idea,' said Amisha, 'so we'll just crack on. Though I'll shortly have to send Andrew back to doing official police work, at least for a bit. I can't keep telling Hilary we're out investigating murder and mayhem and show her no progress whatsoever.'

'OK, so that's a plan,' said H. 'I'll see you both later, I've got an abduction to arrange.'

69

The afternoon, and the evening, wore on. Amisha, Zaida and Andrew beavered away at their gadgets as usual, but being stuck in a hotel room day after day was getting old. None of them said anything, but it was getting old, and they were getting tired. Andrew decided a mood shift was in order.

'I'm going to get a few beers. Anyone care to join me? I can get wine, something stronger if anyone likes, maybe we can watch the telly for a bit. There's a big debate on tonight, on the troubles.

'Seriously?' said Zaida. 'nobody on those panels has anything real to say.'

'What about the old sweet talker, Lord Lambert's on tonight – he's usually good value, no?'

***

Lambert had been a regular talking head on all the major TV and radio channels for years. He divided public opinion: some, especially the ladies, found him charismatic and debonair. Others found him repulsively unctuous and know-it-all. But there was no doubt he had a real way with words - manipulating them, turning his opponents inside out with his quick-witted verbiage. Even so, it was not always easy to figure out what his real convictions were. Sometimes he was very much the New Labour man, put into the House of Lords by Tony Blair back in the late nineties as one of the youngest peers ever to have taken a seat there. Like his boss he looked good, and sounded good - with the added bonus of having a wicked, scathing wit. And he could always be relied upon to say something controversial, which was good for ratings, so the media executives loved to have him on air.

Andrew arrived from the local kebab shop with six beers, two bottles of vino collapso and a bottle of vodka just as the host was introducing the panellists.

'Not one of them with half a brain,' said Zaida.

The panel consisted of one harried and gormless-looking government apparatchik in a Chanel jacket; one representative of the Green party, her eyes twinkling faintly behind a face hanging like a bag of wet sand; one grown up but dull and blustering big-honcho type from the Confederation of British Industry; one stand-up 'comedian' with a huge beard and a fake working class accent; and Lord Peter Lambert, leaning back in his chair like an amused owl about to go to town on a field full of clueless rabbits.

***

With the exception of Lambert the panellists, looking drawn and exhausted as they circled around their evasions and non-answers to direct questions, droned on and on, shedding light on nothing.

Zaida fell asleep. Amisha opened the second bottle of wine, which numbed the boredom a little. Only Andrew remained animated, fizzing with beer and growing increasingly angry at the panel's refusal to offer any insights or forthright statements.

Lambert began to address the question of who was to blame for it all.

'It's no good just blaming everything on the Russians,' he was saying, 'they've just become the default bad guys. What would they have to gain by causing all this chaos in Britain? Is it part of a huge conspiracy to weaken NATO? The EU? Is that what we are all expected to believe?'

A good proportion of the audience obviously thought not, laughing uproariously and egging His Lordship on.

'This is all too preposterous. It just won't do. It seems clear to me that a right-wing terror group has declared war on our system – on our liberal values. Look at who and what is being attacked – our ethnic minorities and their institutions, our police and prisons… and criminal elements up and down the country have jumped on the bandwagon. It's as plain as the nose on your face.'

70

The boy had had a restless night, and Olivia was up and about early, before anything was open, trying to walk him back to sleep in his buggy. She'd always loved the seaside, and Brighton in particular. It had changed a bit lately, become pricier than the faded and down-to-earth place she knew as a girl – but she still loved it. She'd resisted coming, at first, when H suggested that she take the boy and get out of London for a bit after she got the letter from Agapov, but after a couple of days of sea breezes and walking around and rest and relaxation in the nicest hotel she'd ever stayed in – H said the money was coming out of 'funds' – she came around.

She came off the front and headed up towards town. It was quiet and peaceful as she approached The Lanes, a shopping area of tightly knit pedestrian streets, and she was trying to decide whether to stay on the move for another hour until the shops opened or head back to the hotel. Then the decision was made for her.

A roar came up from somewhere close by, a deep, guttural roar made by groups of aggressive men with the scent of blood in their nostrils. She doubled back on herself to get out of the area, and passed by a small side street filled with a throng of dozens of men, smashing the windows and pouring out of a bar. It looked like they'd just had an all-night boozing session, and were going on like football hooligans intent on destroying the place.

Olivia stepped up the pace and soon had sight of the sea, which calmed her a little, until a police helicopter wheeled into view, filling the area with its noise and settling into a circling pattern overhead. She walked faster still, and realized that there were tears in her eyes. She looked down at Little

Harry, now sleeping peacefully, and felt the mother's anguished wondering about what sort of world she'd brought him into.

There's nowhere to escape from all this…Nowhere to run, nowhere to hide.

She got back to the room, parked the buggy inside the door, collapsed onto the bed, and cried. She wanted H, here, beside her. Now. She reached for her tablet, looking for something to divert her and take her mind off the troubles. She surfed some of the entertainment sites she liked; this calmed her down, and she regained some of her composure.

She propped herself up on her pillows, and began to swipe and scroll for more serious things, looking to see if there was any coverage of what she'd seen earlier. There was nothing. She entered Joey Jupiter's site name out of habit, but it was still offline.

She entered his name into an internet search engine and discovered Joey had started posting on another site. Her crawling flesh and tightening stomach told her before her mind really processed it that she'd got more than she bargained for.

It was a short entry, just a paragraph, below a large picture of a face she recognized. A large, shaven head, with Slavic features and cold blue eyes, scars and scratches on the forehead and face. It was the face of the man who'd approached her in a shopping mall the year before, with a present for the boy and good wishes for H, and had more recently sent her the least welcome letter of her life. This man had been making her flesh crawl for a while, and he was making her flesh crawl now. It was Agapov…Vladimir Agapov.

She read the paragraph beneath the picture:

FIND THIS MAN

Hello People. Thanks for keeping the faith.

I can't go into details now, but things are happening. There are people – good people – beginning to deal with our problems. They are starting to get somewhere, but they need your help. First up, we have to find this man. Please send any news of a sighting or any other relevant information to me through one of my channels. I'll say it once more: we MUST find this man.

Stay tuned for more news on what's been happening, and how you can help.

Olivia sat back and tried to process what she'd read. She wondered who the 'good people' Jupiter referred to were. There was obviously some sort of pushback underway, against Agapov and his ilk – but how deeply was H involved in it? Or, knowing him, leading it? Feeling more distressed than ever, she swiped listlessly away from Jupiter and onto the website of the local paper, The Argus, and read its banner headline:

Breaking News: Two killed, more injured, in vicious attack on Brighton gay bar.

71

H – he'd sent Little Ronnie to go and spend a bit of time with his mum, and wouldn't take no for an answer – arrived back at the lockup to find Yorkie Ted and his boys in grizzly mood. Morale was not high. They were clearly in post-battle, restless-agitation mode; what goes up must come down, and H knew as well as anyone that this was especially true of adrenalin and cortisone and the body's fight-or-flight mechanism. The guys were coming down, which is hard to cope with when you've hyped yourself up and put yourself in harm's way for nothing.

A pep talk was needed, so H gave one, but to the northern contingent it sounded more like a bollocking.

H waited for them to settle and pulled Ted to one side.

'Listen Ted, are you and your boys in or not? I don't need your firm getting cold feet now. Keep 'em on board – new information could come through at any moment. We need to stand ready.'

'Have a word with yourself H, for fuck sake – we're in, you know we are. It's just we are getting a bit stir crazy cooped up in here all the time, and after that pantomime we've just been through me and the boys need to let off a bit of steam, like the Poles do. Look around you, where are they all? Out having a little drink somewhere, I should think. Don't get me wrong H, they're good men and they get the job done, but it's like their 303 squadron in the Battle of Britain all over again: those boys absolutely blew the fucking Luftwaffe right out of the sky, but controlling them was like rounding up three-year olds, they just wouldn't do what they were told. You getting my drift H?'

H nodded to indicate that he was. He knew enough about Kuba and his men to understand that they were fearless when it came to the crunch, but also had an anarchic streak in them that could make them difficult to manage.

'Plus,' Ted continued, 'most of Kuba's guys know people in London and have places to go, but us Yorkies don't know the place. The lads have got to get out and about for a bit. Find a boozer, just a few pints before the curfew.'

'Alright Ted, fair enough,' said H. 'But keep an eye on 'em, nothing stupid. Just a few pints, nothing major. Back before curfew,' said H.

'You have my word H, on my honour.'

H laughed out loud, and was about to start with the wisecracks when Kuba came in through the gate, alone. Ted and his men moved quickly through the gate while it was still open and swarmed out into the street, like ten-year olds let out of school.

'H, we need to talk,' said Kuba.

'I'm all ears, son.'

'H, you have to put me in the picture more. I understand why everything's going through you, and all this "need-to-know "stuff, but if something happens to you we'll all be running around like headless chickens.'

Kuba knew about Albie Bradford's kill squad, but little about exactly what all the football guys were supposed to be doing and nothing at all about the whereabouts or personnel of the technical wing.

H was reluctant to do as Kuba was asking, though he knew he was right. Taking Kuba to meet Albie and his firm was one thing, he didn't care too much for them. But Amisha, Andrew, Zaida. He wanted to protect them from all possibility of discovery, if any of his boys were caught by the other side. He knew that some would talk, under torture. Some always do.

Kuba pressed him.

'You obviously have a direct line to this Joey Jupiter. Who else is involved?'

H thought for a few seconds and realised he was making a strategic error as the only conduit between the fighting men and the boffins; his heart, as so often, had been ruling his head.

'Alright mate, but this is for your ears only.'

'Agreed.'

'Emergencies only.'

'Agreed.'

'I mean real fucking emergencies.'

'Agreed.'

'There's a young woman leading the team. Her name is Amisha.'

'Amisha who?'

'Just Amisha, that's all you need to know, mate.'

H gave him Amisha's field phone number. 'Only ever through this, got it?'

'OK. What's next H?'

'Next we pay a visit to Albie Bradford. I arranged a meet with him tonight, a kind of progress review, near his house in Essex. We need to find out where he's got to, who he's managed to get locations for. He'll be monitoring the people on his list he hasn't killed. We made a mistake, going straight for the executions. We need to change strategy, from kill to steal.'

'Kidnap them, you mean.'

'Yeah. Amisha and co. might come up with something, but they might not – and we also know now that we can't trust what they do come up with. We'll take a couple of these traitors and put it on them. It won't take long to crack them, they've got no moral fibre.'

'Amen to that,' said Kuba.

'Good man. Right, I'm going home to have a shower. Go and check on your boys, make sure they're keeping their heads down and doing the right thing, and meet me at mine in two hours. Six o'clock. I've told Little Ronnie to be there at the same time.'

'OK, just one other thing, out of interest.'

'What's that?'

'When are you going to stop calling him "Little" Ronnie?'

'When he's big enough to hold his own.'

'You don't think he's there yet?'

'No mate, I don't, not by a long fucking chalk. See you in two hours.'

72

H got to Eltham in good time, having talked his way through a roadblock at New Cross, crunched into his driveway, killed the engine and with it the dulcet tones of Nat King Cole, and jumped out of the car. He was tired and weary, having now to deal with his own post-adrenalin comedown and a succession of sleepless nights. These had been punctuated by nightmares in which a terrifying hooded figure, reeking of evil, forced pliers into the mouth of a screaming Ronnie Ruddock, before moving on to do the same to Olivia. He walked heavily up the driveway, concentrating less than he normally would on his surroundings as plots and schemes and priorities swirled and rearranged themselves in his head. There's a lot to think about when the fabric of your country is decaying faster than a dead body in a grave.

What happened next took him by storm: he was hit by two small dart-like electrodes, shot from the window of his living room as he approached the front door.

He lost control of his muscles as the current over-stimulated his sensory and motor nerves. He'd never used a Taser, nor been shot with one before – it hurt. H fought hard to gain control of his leg and arm muscles; roaring like a bull and straining every sinew in his body, he somehow managed to rip the electrodes off. This gave him another jolt of pain, given the design of the electrodes was engineered to prevent such actions. They were pointed and barbed, and penetrated both his clothing and his skin, and he lost two lumps of flesh as a reward for his efforts.

H looked up to try and locate the source of his pain and another two electrodes bit into him, inducing the same spasms, the same involuntary muscle movements as before. He hit the ground.

A white van pulled up. Four masked men jumped out of it, ripped the electrodes from H's body, put a sack over his head and deposited their victim into the back of their vehicle. Two more masked men came out of the front door of the house. One got in the back with the others and one sat in the front seat with the driver.

'Back to base. Let's get this party started,' said Vladimir Agapov as he ripped the mask of from his face.

***

Mrs Joan Simmonds lived a quiet life. She didn't go out much, not since her husband died. She had a son, but he'd emigrated to Australia over ten years ago. She spent much of her time doing crosswords, at which she was highly proficient. When she wasn't doing crosswords, she liked to look out of her window, see what was happening in her quiet residential street. Nothing much, most of the time. Every now and then she'd see a little argument to brighten her day, usually a mother telling off an errant child. Once she'd seen a full-scale row between Mr and Mrs Jackson at number 62. That had been a real highlight.

But this was her first kidnapping.

There was so much going on in the country it was just as well she didn't go out much. The riots, the bombs, the daily news of crisis. The authorities had told everyone to keep their eyes peeled, to watch out for anything suspicious, to call the emergency phone number if anything looked out of the ordinary.

She was nervous when she called it in. Her frail heart fluttered with uncontrollable spasms. But she was also excited – she'd be useful again, after all the years of staying in and doing nothing. It took her ages to get through to somebody – the phone centre was inundated with calls – but after waiting on the phone for over thirty minutes a polite young man answered and asked her what she wanted to report.

'A kidnap,' she said, 'of that nice Mr Hawkins, who lives opposite.'

The call centre operative entered all the details. He didn't know if this was another crank call, they'd had so many lately, but he put it into the system.

'When are you going to come around?' Mrs Simmonds asked.

'I don't know. All the calls go into the system and get prioritised. There's so much going on it might take a couple of days.'

'A couple of days, for a kidnapping?' she said.

'Yes, sorry madam, but we're doing our best, under the circumstances.'

73

H didn't have a couple of days. Agapov would keep him alive for a bit, while he returned the beating, measure for measure, he'd received at his prisoner's hands when last they met. This thirst for vengeance had become the central purpose of his life. He'd thoroughly enjoyed butchering H's best friend, but now he had the real thing in his hands. Time for the main course. Happy days.

The journey had taken less than ten minutes, so H knew he was close to home. He guessed at what he would see as the sack was lifted from his head – and was not disappointed. Agapov was all smiles and bonhomie as he greeted his tightly chair-bound guest of honour.

'Ah, Hawkins, how nice to see you. It's been too long.'

'Yeah. How you been doing? You're looking well.' H was zoning in. Options and possibilities were flowing through his mind. Thing was, none of them were coming out in his favour.

'I've been doing fine, H.'

'So, what's the plan?' said H, smiling.

'No real plan. I beat shit out of you, you beg for your life, then I kill you.'

'Fucking terrific,' said H 'then stop talking and get on with it.'

'No need to rush Mr ex-Inspector. We have time.'

It took a mighty effort but H suppressed his inner rage. It wouldn't do any good, unless he could find a way to free himself. For now, he decided, it would be best to do a bit of coppering.

'Who's behind all this? What's it all about? You might just as well tell me before you start knocking seven shades of shit out of me. What've you got to lose?'

Agapov, secure and arrogant in his victory, was revelling in the power he now held over the hapless H, and telling him what he knew would only increase the enjoyment.

'You still so fucking stupid. Kuznetsov of course, and other great Russian men even higher than him. We will fuck up your country, then we will take it.'

H had prior dealings with the oligarch Kuznetsov and knew he was the kind of guy who had his fingers in every pie worth having fingers in. He'd understood, for some time, that people at Kuznetsov's level and higher were behind things, that the attack on the UK was possibly state-sponsored, through back channels. But he wanted some names, people he could get to, who would know about the operational details. He had to use Agapov's arrogance, his need to be Johnny Big Bollocks, against him. Although Agapov didn't have the brains or the subtlety to make it to the top, he might know something useful.

'Your small fry,' said H, 'a little man. People like you don't deal with the likes of Kuznetsov. You know fuck-all.'

'I deal with his top man in UK, you know nothing.'

'I've got news for you, old son, you're not an engineer, just an oily rag… and twice as fucking ugly.'

Agapov was easily irked, and H had irked him.

'Ha ha. Top man in UK is your Lord Peter Lambert, from House of Lords. You know him, I'm sure. He's running things for Mr Kuznetsov here.'

'What about this major thing you lot are planning. What's that all about?'

H was right in that Agapov was a mushroom, cultivated in the dark, as far as the big picture was concerned. Like all mushrooms he and his men often speculated about where the madness of the past weeks was really heading, and Agapov presented the speculation as if he was in the know.

'Remember your Guy Fawkes?' he said, 'No country can function without government. A snake with no head is easy enemy to defeat.'

H tried to engage Agapov in further conversation but the Russian was getting bored; it was time for the talking to end.

Agapov smashed H in the face with a surprise blow, the force of which was shocking; it broke H's nose, opened a gash in both his upper and lower lips and sent him and the chair tipping over. Agapov lifted the chair back to the sitting position and repeated the blow. H didn't topple over this time but the force of the punch sent trembles coursing through his entire body. Agapov, with the absolute confidence that he was the master of the situation, wanted to see H squirm. He pulled up another chair, sat opposite H, and stared at him hard.

'How it feel, Mr ex-Inspector, now, as you say, boot is on other foot?'

Agapov was putting on a show, and turned to take in the appreciation of the men sitting around the perimeter of the room, looking on like an audience at an execution. H watched them and returned their stares.

'Blinding. I feel absolutely blinding. Never better. Now just get the fuck on with it,' he said, spitting blood, tooth fragment and gristle from his mouth.

74

Kuba was already at H's house when Little Ronnie arrived. The meeting with his mother had gone well and he was in good spirits, but his mood didn't survive first contact with his Polish ally, who was waiting by the front door.

'I've been here a few minutes. There's no reply. Nobody is in. Do you have a key?'

'No'.

Kuba didn't say another word. The five-lever mortice deadlock on the front door hadn't been secured and the simple dead latch gave way as soon as Kuba hit it with his shoulder.

They got in and performed a lightning-fast search.

'Nothing, looks like he never made it back into the house,' said Little Ronnie.

'Then something must have happened between the car and the door. If your father says meet him somewhere he's always there. Something is wrong, Ronnie.'

The two men went outside to look around. The car was in its usual place, no damage. All seemed calm.

'Front room window, opposite, two doors to your right. Someone's watching us. Follow me,' said Kuba.

Kuba did his best to look disinterested as he strolled past the door in question and strained to look inside the window behind which he'd seen a peeper, without turning his head, but saw little. The house was terraced and the windows were flat so it was just a few yards before Kuba and Ronnie were out of view from inside. Kuba was a man straight after H's own heart: no time for fucking about. The fake nonchalance turned to aggression with whirlwind speed as he took his pistol from his belt and surged back towards the front of the house. He was about to kick the door in when it opened.

'Hello,' said Mrs Simmonds, 'my, you were quick. They told me it might take a couple of days.'

'Er.. yes, we came as quickly as we could,' said Little Ronnie, arresting Kuba's momentum by pulling hard at the back of his jacket.

'Do you want me to tell you exactly what I saw?' said Mrs Simmonds.

'Yes, yes please madam, that would be great,' said Kuba.

***

Mrs. Simmonds did her best to string out her story for as long as possible. It was so nice to have company. She offered tea and biscuits, which were politely declined. When they thought she'd offered up all she had they readied themselves to leave.

'The number plate. Do you want the number plate of the van before you leave?'

'You know it?' said Kuba.

'Yes, I have a very good memory. I do more than ten crosswords a day.'

'Brilliant!'

Mrs Simmonds was pleased she had been useful and wished the two men good luck as they left.

'Oh, and I know who took him,' said Mrs Simmonds, just as they stepped outside.

Little Ronnie and Kuba started at each other, realising that Mrs. Simmonds' memory was simultaneously detailed and erratic. They hadn't asked her if she knew any of the kidnappers.

'He took his mask off when he got in the van.'

'Go on,' said Kuba.

'That man, on the blog.'

'What blog?'

'Joey Jupiter's,' interjected Little Ronnie.

'Yes. I've been reading his blog – my son in Australia recommended him to me when all the trouble started. He's changed the site he blogs from, but I soon found the new one. Information on the Internet is easy to find, if you know what you're doing.'

'That's brilliant,' said Little Ronnie, 'you've been a tremendous help. Thank you.'

Mrs Simmonds was glowing; she pottered back to the kitchen to make tea, forgetting they had already declined. When she returned Kuba and Little Ronnie had left, and were talking feverishly on the pavement outside.

'When we were watching the compound, prior to the attack, your father saw this man, it was the same man who murdered Ronnie Ruddock.'

'I know. He told me,' said Little Ronnie, 'but how would he even know what my dad was up to, where he was? How would he know that dad was even involved in all this?'

'Not sure. He's probably just an operative; he's told where to go and when and when not to fight. If one of their leaders knew what your father was doing they would have had him killed by now.'

'But they must know something? Why take dad otherwise?'

'Maybe it's personal. This guy knew where your dad lived before all this started. Which means…'

'What?' said Ronnie

'It means we might have a little time, before Agapov kills him,' said Kuba.

Little Ronnie gulped hard on hearing the truth spoke so bluntly; like his dad, Kuba was not one to sugar the pill.

'The people working for dad, investigating the dark web, we need to contact them now.'

'On it,' said Kuba, 'this Amisha is our only hope. Let's hope she's as shit-hot as your dad says she is. His life depends on it.'

75

Amisha was awoken from a nap by the sound of her field phone; even she had to sleep sometimes, if just to prove to her colleagues that she wasn't a cyborg, with cyborg energy. It wasn't H, she noted with alarm, but one of the others.

What the hell?

She took the call. The voice was one she'd never heard before: a man's voice, very deep and thickly accented. Was it a Russian voice? Had they been rumbled? Had all their efforts been for nothing?

'Who am I talking to please?'

'My name is Kuba Bukowski. I'm an old friend of H's. I'm working with him on the same project as you.'

'How do I know that?'

'I'm using one of the project's super-encrypted field phones.'

'Not enough. You could have stolen it. I'll need more details.'

'Such as?'

'What does H call his wife?'

'Her name is Olivia but he calls her Liv.'

'What kind of wine does he prefer?'

'I've never seen him take a glass. He drinks Scotch and beer.'

'Who are his favourite singers?'

'Sinatra, Sammy Davis, Dean Martin…and he's killing me with Nat King Cole at the moment.'

'OK,' said Amisha, 'tell me how he got all the cuts on his face and hands he's sporting at the moment. How he got them, and why.'

'He saw, on a Facebook live stream, the murdered body of his best friend Ronnie Ruddock and went on a rampage.'

'And has he told you who he thinks is behind this killing?'

'Yes, Vladimir Agapov, an old adversary of his. That's the reason I'm calling.'

'Tell me more.'

'H has been taken, from outside his house. By six men in a white van. Little Ronnie and I have established that one of these men was Agapov. He has very little time.'

'Fuck,' said Amisha, 'details. Now.'

'Around 4.30pm. Six men, standard white van with the following vehicle registration number…'

76

Amisha flew into action like a streak of lightning. Noting on her way out the door that the hotel room was now empty – she'd sent Andrew over to Brick Lane to forage for scraps they could feed to Hilary and McPherson, and figured Zaida must have gone for a breath of air – she bolted down the stairs and through the reception area and was in her car and on the way to Eltham before she even realised what she was doing.

She punched in Zaida's number en route, knowing that her aunt had long since achieved full, system-wide access to the police, private enterprise and local government networks that had made London the CCTV surveillance capital of the world. Zaida took the call straight away and Amisha breathlessly gave her the location, time and vehicle registration number she would need to figure out where H was being held.

'Alright my love,' said Zaida, 'leave it with me, I'm on it. Drive fast, but safe. Check your phone in a minute or two – I'll send you the latest on flare-ups and places to avoid. Or I can just feed a route straight into your satnav…'

'No, focus on finding H. Zaida, don't worry about me. Just find H.'

Amisha was frantic with worry, desperate to get south of the river and get down to H's place to meet with this Kuba. She was held up, almost as soon as she started, by some looting on Mornington Crescent, but once she got through the Waterloo Bridge checkpoint and onto Waterloo Road the traffic and streets were orderly and she made the Bricklayer's Arms flyover in less than an hour. She was surging along the Old Kent Road when Zaida called back.

Please God, let her have found him.

'OK, speak to me auntie – what have you got?'

'Right, so I found footage of the van coming out of H's road at the time you gave me,' said Zaida, 'and took it from there. Almost all the cameras we needed were working, believe it or not, and it was only a short ten-minute journey, so I've got a location for you…'

Amisha made a mental note of everything her aunt told her and ended the call. She pulled into Eltham in a state of manic agitation.

She turned into H's street, recognized Little Ronnie loitering on the pavement and assumed that the rangy, bearded and imposing man standing with him was Kuba Bukowski. 'In,' she said, as she screeched the car to a halt, 'we know where he is, it's not far from here, I'll fill you in on the way.'

77

'Amisha, this is Kuba,' said Little Ronnie, 'Kuba, this is Amisha.'

They nodded at one another in unison; Amisha resumed talking:

'The van went to a location in Kidbrooke, ten minutes away. They're in an old warehouse not far from the Railway Station. There's a railway track to the rear, an industrial estate on one side of it, and busy main roads on the other two sides. Whatever Agapov is doing in there, nobody's going to hear it,' she said, showing them an aerial photo on her tablet.

She passed it to Kuba, who was taking a little time to get his head in gear – he hadn't quite expected the leader of H's technical wing to be so forceful, efficient... and beautiful.

'How many?' he asked.

'There's the six that took H, and my colleague says she's seen at least four more on CCTV. Maybe more, we don't know. What weapons do you have?'

'Enough,' said Kuba.

'They will be well armed, and the location is open. Not much chance of getting in their quickly and surprising them.'

Kuba made no comment on Amisha's tactical advice and proceeded with his planning. He punched a number into his field phone. Yorkie Ted answered, and Kuba gave the coordinates of the warehouse.

'Ted,' Kuba said, bring your best men with you, and Jarek and Marek. Arm yourselves to the teeth my friend, and don't forget the RPGs.'

'OK, got it. Thirty minutes,' said Ted, 'if we stick to the speed limit.'

'Stick to it,' said Kuba, 'and pray that thirty minutes is not too long.'

Kuba punched the end-call button, enlarged the target building on the screen and thought things through. He motioned to Little Ronnie to get in closer and walk through the plan with him onscreen.

'We'll attack from south and east simultaneously. The RPGs take out the doors here, and here, with the main force going in here.'

'I don't know, it's a high-risk strategy,' said Amisha, with her dead boyfriend Graham on her mind, 'H might get caught in the cross fire.'

'H, if he is alive, they will try to finish the moment we reveal ourselves – these men will not negotiate. This plan is our best option and we need to put it into operation quickly; we will enact it.'

Amisha had already seen enough to understand that Kuba was H mark II, and that arguing with him would be pointless.

'OK,' she said, 'we follow your plan.'

'Yes. And one more thing.'

'What?'

'Eye witness reports of us and our capabilities must not get back to their handlers. None of them gets out alive,' said Kuba, 'none of them.'

78

The warehouse was just a long, rectangular, decrepit open space. Agapov's men lounged around relishing the sight – and sound, and smell – of their leader delivering his version of natural justice to the figure tied to a chair. At first, they'd assumed he was carrying out an order from on high but as the gruesome events unfolded the sharper among them realized that Agapov was making way too much of a meal of things for this not to be personal.

For Agapov himself the moment was delicious; he savoured the chemical taste in his mouth and smell of blood in the air as another right-hand rainmaker lashed across H's face. The big man's eyes and face were now so bloody and swollen his own wife might not have recognized him. Agapov lashed out again, and again, his fist driven forward by nearly two years' worth of stored-up hatred.

Most men would have been unconscious by now, but H was not most men – he blinked through the pain and gore in his eyes and stared hard, through what were now just tiny slits, at the merciless torturer before him. Agapov saw it was a stare from a man who knew his last moments on earth were at hand, a stare from a man whose resistance had gone, whose life force was evaporating.

'How do you like it now, Hawkins? How do you like it now?'

H slumped forward in the chair, his head down. Agapov gestured to a henchman to hit his victim with the smelling salts.

H looked up again and showed faint signs of life, but could do nothing to ward off the onslaught as further punches crashed into his body. Then the boots came for him. The kicks were expert, well timed, well placed and each one came with a surge of agony that cut through to the core of him.

'You are cunt and I am going to beat you to death, Hawkins, with my own hands. You should have killed me when you had chance. No one gets second chance with Vladimir Agapov.'

H thought this to be true, as he sat motionless and helpless in what he was now certain was his death chair.

The beating was having an intoxicating effect upon Agapov, giving him a natural high. He took a breather to revel in his moment and glugged down a swig of vodka before pouring the rest over H's head. He grabbed H by the hair and pulled his swollen face back, and prepared himself for a series of pulverizing punches, punches that would continue until H was dead. The first one hit H like a thunderbolt and sent yet another shock-wave rippling through his body. H was losing awareness of where he was, how he got here, even of who he was. His life was hanging by a thread.

And then the second chance came.

The world around H was already a blur before the grenades exploded, knocked through the outside doors and threw Agapov from his feet. What happened next would never be recalled by H except as in a hazy, half-remembered dream. Another explosion, gunshots, shouting, more gunshots. Was that Ronnie, his Little Ronnie, surging through the door and taking out a series of Spetsnaz operatives before they had time to comprehend what was happening? Was that Kuba he could hear, barking orders like a turbo-charged Genghis Khan? Was Yorkie Ted really smiling like a devil welcoming a new sinner to hell as he got around behind Agapov, pulled his head back by the hair and slit his throat from ear to ear? And was that Amisha, cutting the ropes that bound him, like an angel of redemption come to give him another chance, yet another lease on life?

Kuba threw off the ropes Amisha had cut, swept H up onto his shoulders and howled out more orders. H's army dispersed as fast as it had attacked, back to the meeting points, and their cars, and out onto the streets of Kidbrooke.

The attack had taken less than two minutes. No prisoners were taken.

79

'Lay him down over here,' said Amisha as she readied the makeshift bed at the lockup. Kuba did as requested and Yorkie Ted got to work. He'd seen plenty of mashed-up faces before, but none as swollen as this. The patient was semi-conscious, semi-delirious, mumbling things no one could understand.

Ted held H by the back of his head and tipped half a bottle of scotch into H's mouth, which was well received after it found its way past a swollen tongue. Next, he reset the nose, an action which was not so well received, but another glug of H's favourite snifter helped ease the pain.

Yorkie Ted had always been known for his magic medical box, having acted as a second to boxers for years, after he'd had to abandon the sweet science himself. He knew what he was doing as he started to put some stitches in the deeper wounds scattered over H's face, all the while trying to quieten the patient, who was trying to make himself heard.

Amisha pulled Kuba to one side.

'What next?' said Amisha.

'Don't know… Any news, anything, from your team?'

'No, no real leads. Except…'

'Except what?'

'It may be nothing. There's been some chatter we've intercepted about something happening in Scotland, but it could be nothing, or another decoy?'

'What kind of chatter?'

'That there's going to be some kind of attack. Nothing specific, just a few messages that we've interpreted that mention it's a possible location for something big.'

'Scotland's a big place,' said Kuba.

'I know.'

The two turned at the sound of H coughing up some unholy brew of scotch, blood, and bile.

'Are you sure you should be giving him that?' said Amisha.

'Yes love, that I am,' said Ted, as he sewed up another gash in H's face.

'Done. He's taken a good bit of punishment, but I haven't found anything broken, apart from the nose. He'll live,' said Ted, standing back and admiring his handy work.

One of Yorkie Ted's men passed Amisha a cup of coffee, which she accepted and supped with relish. H lay on the bed, drifting in and out of consciousness, mumbling incoherently.

'He's not with it. No telling yet if there's any kind of brain damage. Doesn't sound like he knows what day of the week it is. Maybe he's hallucinating,' said Ted.

Amisha sipped on her coffee, hoping and praying that the damage wasn't lasting. She crouched down at H's bedside, such as it was, and ran her hand gently across the top of his head. She got down low and tried to look into his eyes, feeling a mixture of emotions that almost overwhelmed her – fear, loss, heartache…but also tenderness, and love. She felt, once again, a kind of love for him. She thought back to a time when their roles were reversed, in a warehouse in Grays following her capture and ordeal at the hands of a loathsome pervert, when she, and he, and her Graham had all been together. Then it had been his strength, his compassion that had pulled her through.

'H,' she whispered, 'it's Amisha. I'm here.' His face was beaten black and blue, and other colours she couldn't quite put a name to, and was so swollen she could barely see the eyes beneath it all. But she knew H was inside them. He was mumbling again as he fixed a gimlet squint on her.

'H, what is it? What are you trying to say?'

258

He forced himself up onto his elbows with great effort, and got his head up. Amisha knew he wouldn't be able to hold this stance for long. She turned her head and pressed her ear up against the big man's mouth.

'Lambert,' he whispered, 'get me Lord Lambert.'

80

Olivia was awoken in the dead of night by two loud cracks of gunfire that sounded like they were not far enough away. Little Harry was not far behind her. She cuddled up closer to him in the big hotel bed and he was soon fast asleep again. But Olivia was not; anxiety was eating her alive. She hadn't been out of the hotel for a while. She'd stopped watching the news as it was either too depressing or too fake.

She gazed out of the window and saw two drones circling above the seafront.

Even at this bloody time of night.

She hoped the shots she'd heard were the police trying to bring them down.

She powered up her tablet, praying silently as it came to life that the wi-fi would be working. She was in desperate need of distraction, something to make her feel better, remind her of the human world. It was working, so she went to YouTube and searched 'black and white films', hoping to find the kind of reassuring thing she was in the habit of watching with H. Something with Spencer Tracey and Katharine Hepburn, maybe…but there was nothing she could settle on. She gave up and, with a heavy sigh, brought up Joey Jupiter's site in the hope that he'd posted something again. He had, and for the first time in what seems like an age she felt a surge of hope as she read.

THIS IS THE END OF THE BEGINNING – IT MAY EVEN BE THE BEGINNING OF THE END.

Be of good cheer, people. Take heart. I am paraphrasing Churchill today because I have good news, for a change, to report.

The fightback is underway. We've seen three breakthroughs in recent days:

1) The people I am working with have identified a number of powerful traitors who have been providing succour and support to our country's enemies. These people are being dealt with in no uncertain terms; a new broom is sweeping the corridors of power clean. This project is ongoing and we expect to meet with more successes in the immediate future.

2) Last week an armed vigilante force from our side attacked an enemy compound believed to be a site used to produce unspecified weapons. The compound was taken with no casualties on our side.

3) Our people are also bringing the streets back under control. I can report that, on at least five occasions in the capital last week, substantial and effective fighting forces at street level have got the better of the violent mobs with whom we have become all too familiar. On one occasion a force of five hundred or so fighting men drawn from two football clubs – old rivals from the south-east and east of London who need not be named – engaged our enemies on the streets of Limehouse, literally driving many of them back into the river. On another the same actors joined with a group of armed Sikhs to come out on top once more against a mob of thugs who had launched an attack on a Gudwara in Plumstead. You may not see this reported on the mainstream media, but it is happening: the tide on the streets of London has turned.

I'll be back with more news soon. Keep your chins up, and get on the front foot.

81

Brad awoke with the dawn. He loved these Scottish mornings – the mist on the mountainside, the crisp fresh air he could suck deep into his lungs. The sense of hope that comes with the birth of a new day. Odd, he thought as the sun started its daily struggle with the mist, that he still felt this hope, given that he only had a handful of mornings still to see.

He was in good spirits as he filled his water container from the clear stream that flowed through the forest below his foxhole, and took a refreshing nip. He walked back to his lair and prepared his breakfast of dried fruit and biscuits. He didn't need much.

A rush of pain gripped his body. He waited for it to subside before taking a mouthful of his liquid morphine. The pain passed and he set about cleaning up his little home. He packed away his sleeping bag in the watertight container and double-checked the explosives and bottles of petrol he would douse himself in after completing the mission. His funeral pyre would destroy all traces of him – except maybe his teeth, which in any case he'd taken the precaution of having replaced on the run up to the job. He'd made complete anonymity a condition of the job; his wife and children were to live on in obscurity after it was all done, with enough money to take care of all their needs for the duration.

His employers – whoever they were – had agreed to his terms, although they had other ideas. It had been easy enough to find him. A crack sniper, with years of experience across the Middle East picking off America's enemies, now forgotten and put out to pasture, full of resentment, with deep mental issues and dying of cancer. A perfect CV for the job in hand: leaked news of an American veteran being part of the offensive, when it came, would be useful propaganda, and would muddy the waters beautifully.

Brad finished his breakfast and went through the rest of his morning routine. A little stretching, pull ups on a branch to get the circulation going. Next, cleaning his weapon, climbing the tree that would be the scene of his final job, checking the line of sight.

Then back to the foxhole to turn on his mobile to check for instructions. Nothing, same as each day he had checked it since he'd made a hole in the ground his final home. He switched it off and prepared for the rest of the day. He was a patient man, well used to keeping himself company. Boredom never entered the equation for Brad as he sat quietly meditating, stilling his mind.

He was not sure of the day or the time that would seal his fate, but he felt it would be soon. He knew what he had to do and he would do it. One day soon the phone would have a message for him, details about time. When the time came he would be ready, and he would change the course of history.

82

'Let him sleep,' said Kuba, as H flopped back down. He motioned for Amisha, Ted and Little Ronnie to join him in a corner. 'We need to go and see Albie Bradford. He'll know where this Lambert is, and whether he's still alive.'

'Who the hell is Albie Bradford?' asked Amisha on behalf of herself and the other two.

'Top man of the kill squad that's been eliminating the people on the list you gave H,' said Kuba. 'We were supposed to go and meet him yesterday, but...'

'OK, got it...but will he talk to us without H?'

'I have no idea, but he's all we've got. He's certainly our best hope of getting to Lambert,' said Kuba. 'Plus, I've met him, he'll recognise me from the time I went to his place with H.'

'Alright then,' said Amisha, 'let's do it.'

***

It was midnight when the trio – Little Ronnie wanted to stay at the lockup and take care of his dad – arrived at their rearranged meeting on an industrial estate in Chigwell. It was a cold night and Bradford was every bit as charming and helpful as Kuba remembered him. The phalanx of goons behind him, led by frightening Kenny Keeler, did not look much more cheerful.

'Where's your fucking guvnor?' asked Bradford. 'And who the fuck are these two?'

'Team members, trusted by H,' said Kuba.

'Listen son, I do not give a flying fuck whether your guvnor trusts them or not. Nor whether they're his long-lost sisters.'

Ted bristled. Kuba placed his hand firmly on Ted's upper arm before he could take a step forward, and moved a small step closer to Bradford himself.

'It was Hawkins who gave me the work, and it is with Hawkins I will deal – not with you three fucking muppets.'

'Well, Mr Lambert,' said Ted from behind Kuba's shoulder, 'H sends his apologies, but circumstances beyond his control have prevented him from coming. We need to find an individual called Lord Peter Lambert. H seems to think you may know of his whereabouts...' Ted's decision to take the lead was risky, because these Essex growlers didn't like his northern accent and because he had no understanding of how to deal with the likes of Bradford.

'I said where's your fucking guvnor? Answer me or I'm out of here now.'

The hairs on the back of Ted's neck went up. He loathed these unpatriotic mercenaries almost as much he loathed the bastards trying to wreck his country.

'Fucking listen. Our country's future is at stake here, and we need some help. I asked you a question.'

'Do what, you fucking northern monkey,' said Bradford. He turned and signalled to his men that it was time to leave.

'Wait,' said Amisha, 'your kill list, the one H gave you. I prepared it.'

This intrigued Albie, who held up his hand in a signal to halt his men.

'And...?'

'And H is hurt. Hurt really bad, or he'd be here. He asked us to come. He said you'd help, and told us to tell you there's another big bonus in it if you do.'

'What kind of bonus?'

'Half a million.'

'For what?'

'You've taken care of eight of the ten people on the list so far, correct?'

Bradford nodded yes.

'Well, we don't want the last two killed.'

'Why?'

'Does it matter?'

'No.'

'OK then...'

'OK then...so you are saying to me five hundred thousand large to not do the last two?'

'Not exactly.'

'What then?'

'We need them taken. We are especially eager to get hold of Lord Peter Lambert.'

'Taken?'

'Yes.'

'Not fucking likely sweetheart. The reason we haven't got to these last two already is they've both got serious, top-notch security wrapped round them. Taking them would put my men at risk.'

'Then,' said Kuba, who understood Bradford wouldn't help with the kidnap no matter what the incentive, 'tell us what you know. About Lambert.'

'For the extra half million?'

'Yes,' said Amisha.

Now this, thought Bradford, is what you call a win-win; he didn't need asking twice.

'Alright, young lady. I can live with that. I'll give you full chapter and verse once I've received the usual down payment.'

'No, no time for that, Mr Bradford. We can let you have the full amount tomorrow.'

'You have heard that there is no honour among thieves, I take it?'

'But I'm not a thief, Mr Bradford. I am DI Amisha Bhanushali, of New Scotland Yard. Murder Squad. I won't be hard to find. If the money is not in your account tomorrow you have my full permission to come and kill me. I can give you a note to that effect if you like.'

Bradford nodded and, for the first time, smiled.

'Well well, a rozzer working outside the law because she doesn't trust anyone inside it – strange times indeed.'

Albie considered the proposition to be as tight as it was going to get.

'OK. We were going to take care of him tomorrow afternoon. He's doing an interview for ITV, at their London HQ.'

'South side of the Thames, right by the Southbank centre?' said Amisha.

'Correct.'

'What time?'

'Interview's at one o'clock. He's due to arrive between twelve and twelve thirty. Convoy of three vehicles. He'll be in the middle car. Black Merc.'

'How do you know all this?'

'We had to spend some of the money your guvnor sent us.'

'How were you going to deal with him?'

'A single shooter, roof opposite. Our man's already in place, keeping his head down.'

'Thanks,' said Amisha, 'stand your man down. You'll find the payment in the usual account.'

'Sweet,' said Bradford, 'nice doing business with you, doll. You can come again if you like – make sure you leave these two fuckwits at home though.'

83

Back at the lockup Yorkie Ted, frustrated at the lack of action at the Nonington compound, favoured a full-on bushwack on Brixton Hill, with all his guys in tow.

'Let's just throw the kitchen sink at them. Shock and awe. Wham-bam-thank-you-mam. Lambert's security won't be able to handle my guys, no matter what that thug Bradford says. Two minutes – that's all I need.'

Kuba was coming around to the idea, given there was no apparent alternative, and was about to say so when Amisha lifted her head from her screens and announced she'd found the name of the security firm Lambert was using

'It's all here gents, including the docket with the names of the drivers and minders booked in for the job. Nine bodies in all. That's what Lambert will be expecting.'

'Right you fucking are,' said Ted. 'if you'll excuse my French, Amisha. Lovely, me and eight others. I…'

'Hold up, Ted. Hold up.'

H was speaking.

He was still in a good deal of pain but had been following proceedings in silence from his bunk; now he rallied, with great effort, through his swollen mouth and messed-up head, and joined the conversation.

'I know him,' he said.

'What?' said Kuba, his ears pricking up like a dog hearing the whistle of its owner.

'The guvnor of that security firm, I know him. Eddie Jackson. He's knocking on a bit now, but I think he's still about.'

'And what did you nick him for, H?' said Amisha.

'Nothing. He's an old mate of my dad's. Him and the old man used to drive tippers together. Let me have a word with him.'

H heaved himself up onto his elbows; Amisha punched in a number, handed him the phone and put it on speaker; Yorkie Ted looked on, crestfallen; Kuba struggled to follow the conversation – H and Jackson spoke in a much thicker accent than he was used to.

'OK H, I'll take the job off the system,' said Jackson, after being put in the picture. 'It'll be like it was never booked. But no drama, please H. No trouble.'

'Trouble? Me?' said H. 'My people will handle this like the little old ladies who see schoolkids across pedestrian crossings. Just make sure your boys hand the vehicles over to them without any trouble.'

'You'd better keep the chauffer driver on board H. Lambert likes him. He's used to the other guys chopping and changing, but the driver's a constant. You won't have any trouble with him if he sees the driver.'

'Right you are, Ed. Your driver, eight from my firm.'

'OK. Get the cars back without any blood on the upholstery or bullet holes in the windscreen. Agreed?'

'Absolutely mate,' said H, 'we can valet them for you first if you like.'

84

It was natural, as the country descended into mayhem, that Lord Peter Lambert should become more ubiquitous in the media, pontificating on the causes and meaning of the disorder and devastation for all he was worth. Today he was making the rounds yet again. Phone interviews with BBC Radio Four in the early morning, followed up closely by LBC Radio. Then a spot on the ITV for the lunch time news followed up by a session on an early evening SKY TV debate about what the troubles meant for the future of the nation. All in a day's work for the great man.

He was picked up early from his townhouse off Brixton Hill. The security outfit he'd employed since things got wobbly sent the usual convoy of three black Mercs to deliver their man to the studios about town. They observed their usual routine, with his Lordship in the middle car with a driver and two minders upfront and two other cars, each also containing two minders in addition to a driver. The personnel changed from day to day but Lambert knew his own driver well enough by now, and relaxed in his company.

He sat in the back going over his interview talking points as they left Brixton and moved through Stockwell, before turning left at the Oval Tube station towards Vauxhall, past the Oval cricket ground. An unusual route, thought Lambert, though he was not unduly concerned. There were so many ways to get around the great metropolis, and different routes were the stock-in-trade of security firms.

The sight of the Oval cricket ground, now towering high above Harleyford Road, gave his spirits the usual lift. He was a debenture holder and went there often to watch Surrey play, as well as England in test matches. He was relaxed, and admiring the classic look of its *Pavilion End* entrance, when the car stopped at a set of traffic lights.

He'd once read somewhere that, in the event of a nuclear Armageddon or suchlike, English civilisation could be rebuilt if a copy of the rules of cricket were found under the rubble. Everything could be extrapolated from them – the reasonableness, the pragmatism, the peculiar playfulness, the quiet dignity – all the 'fair play' and 'level playing field' bullshit he'd been taught to believe in as a boy.

The car idled; he reflected on his long association with the Oval, and his boyhood. He'd been educated at a grammar school that overlooked the ground, and in the days before a new, higher wall was built the boys were occasionally allowed to watch matches from the roof. He recalled on one occasion watching the legendary Viv Richards heave, with a mighty blow, the ball clear out of the ground, across Harleyford Road, and onto the roof of the school. He and his companions were electrified, and fell immediately to fighting like demons for possession of the sacred object. Lambert had his heart set on it; he'd got to it first and clung to it, as at the bottom of a rugby scrum, as he felt the blows of older and bigger boys. But nothing could make him surrender it – neither the momentary violence nor threats of much worse in the future, and he emerged victorious, bloodied and unbowed. Viv Richards would have expected no less.

He set up a concession at the back of a classroom at which boys could come and touch the ball for ten pence, accruing cash in addition to glory. But later in the day his geography teacher – an old school disciplinarian – demanded he hand it in, only to keep it for himself.

Lambert recalled how bitterly disappointed he'd been. But he also learned a lesson that had served him well that day:

272

the people in positions of power always take the spoils. When he grew up he'd make sure he was one of the takers.

Happy days, he thought, as he returned to the present and the car began to move again. But his little convoy, rather than carrying on towards Vauxhall Bridge, turned right into the Oval car park. The gates were locked behind them.

The car park was quiet, as it always was in winter. Amisha had disabled the CCTV cameras and Yorkie Ted had a quiet word with a small gaggle of security staff, who were happy to make themselves scarce.

Kuba grabbed Lambert by the collar, dragged him out of the car and forced him into another one, where one of his men was waiting with a gun to ensure his Lordship complied with instructions. Kuba slipped into the driver's seat and exited the car park as Yorkie Ted's men melted away. No drama.

'Right,' he said to the now rather anxious lord of the realm, 'I have a friend who is very keen to talk to you. Important matters. Don't try and bullshit him – he's not in a good mood.'

PART FOUR

85

H had resisted at first but he needed to numb the pain and make himself operational, so he accepted a shot of morphine from Yorkie Ted's first aid box. He then asked everyone to leave the lockup, except Kuba and the Yorkshireman. The harsh fluorescent strips overhead cast their blueish-green light on the hapless Lord of the Realm H now had in custody, making him look like a ghoulish apparition from a nether world.

'Who are you?' said H, staring intensely from eyes he could still barely open.

Lord Lambert felt unlimited rage emanating from the man with the bloated, smashed-up face; he gulped, hard, and adopted his finest TV persona.

'I am Lord Peter Lambert, as I'm sure you know, and who, may I ask, are you?'

'But who are you. Why? Why did you do it? Was it just the money?' continued H, ignoring his captive's counter-question.

'I'm sure I have no idea what you're talking about.'

'I want to know two things before I kill you,' said H, unaware of the saliva that flowed from his swollen lips as he spoke. He didn't have the energy or time for too many words. He took out his Glock and pushed the barrel hard against Lambert's temple. Lambert was a bold man when it came to standing up in front of crowds and dishing out tongue lashings, but this was different.

Now we'll find out what you're really made of, you traitorous little piece of shit. I doubt it'll amount to much.

His Lordship was having a bad time – his body's involuntary fear-response mechanisms took over: his heart rate was going through the roof; he was breathing in irregular staccato bursts; the sweat was pouring out of him. Yet he had a bit more than H thought, and rallied himself.

'I don't know who you are, or why I'm here. What is it you think I can tell you?'

H signalled to Kuba to hit the prisoner in the face, which he did immediately and with considerable force. Lambert, a politician to the core who prided himself on his negotiating skills, responded to this, again, with more resilience than H had expected. He surfed the pain, spat out the blood and tooth fragments and turned his thoughts to how, or if, he could get out of this alive. He was a good judge of character and had no doubt the man with the beaten face would kill him if he played his cards badly, or maybe even if he played them well. He knew why he was here but had no clue as to how these people, whoever they were, had found out about him. But find out they had, and he knew what they wanted to know.

86

'I don't know who you are, or what you're up to. But I'll answer all your questions truthfully if you agree to let me live.'

'OK,' said H, thinking the path of least resistance would speed things along.

'How do I know you will keep your word?'

'You don't.'

'What do you want to know?'

'You've been receiving money. Russian oligarch money. Lots of it. What do you do for it?'

'Not much. Ask a few questions in the House of Commons, make some points in speeches.'

'Who is your contact?'

'It's all remote. I don't have contacts, as such. I'm just a pawn.'

'There's something about to happen, something even worse than what we've had until now. Something that's been planned for some time. What, when, where?'

'I don't know.'

'We had a deal. You answer truthfully and I let you go.'

'I know.'

'You're lying, so the deal is off,' said H.

There was a knock on the door. Amisha hurried in with the look of a wide-eyed messenger with a secret. She beckoned H over and thrust her phone into his hand.

'It's Zaida, she's found something.'

'Hello love.'

'H, we missed something'

'What?'

'Lambert, he didn't just receive money, he moved a lot of it on.'

'And?'

'He's moved a fortune to offshore accounts in the Bahamas. Money has been transferred and re-transferred in a complex web, but I'm sure he pays people to do things. I believe he's a player, he'll have knowledge about the big picture.'

'I was figuring that. Is there more?'

'Yes. I've being running checks on his background. In the 1980s, when he was in his late teens, he spent six months in Russia when his father was posted there in the Foreign Office. He's fluent in Russian and has kept in touch with his Russian contacts ever since.'

'So…?'

'Kyril Kuznetsov is one of them. He has had regular contact with him for years.'

Bingo! She's confirming what Agapov told me.

'Great work Zaida, now we're fucking getting somewhere.'

'There's something else, I'm not sure if it's related.'

'What?'

The chatter on the internet, its going crazy. Lots of stuff about a high-profile target, or targets. But I'm not sure what. Maybe a building.'

'The House of Commons,' said H. Agapov's beating had been so severe he'd forgotten some of the Russian's ramblings, but Zaida's information had jolted his memory. 'Agapov indicated that was the target.'

Zaida went quiet. H waited.

'There's another emergency debate tomorrow,' said Zaida after a minute or so. 'The whole of Parliament is sitting.'

'Blinding,' said H, 'absolutely fucking blinding. Great work. Looks like they want to give it the old Guy Fawkes treatment.'

H returned to his captive. He tried to smile a knowing smile, but it hurt too much.

'You lied to me.'

Lambert sat, stony faced. He didn't know what H's conversation was about but he had the feeling it was not good – for him.

'You broke our deal.'

'And?'

'And I'm going to kill you.'

Having shaken Lambert up H went in again fast and direct and keenly watched the prisoner's response.

'When's the attack on the House of Commons?'

H scanned Lambert's face intently, monitoring his response, but couldn't tell if he'd hit the spot. This fucker was good – he'd been conning people all his life.

'Alright then your Lordship, enough of the party games.'

H placed the barrel of his gun behind Lambert's right kneecap and pulled the trigger. When the screaming and heavy breathing and gnashing of teeth calmed down H put the gun behind Lambert's left knee and pulled the trigger again.

'Right, Mr Lord fucking almighty, you need to understand that I'm in charge here. We're not in your world, we're in mine. The next time I ask you a question you better answer me with the truth – or the next bullet is going straight into your fucking nut.'

87

Hilary Stone took her place around the huge oval table that dominated the New Scotland Yard priority incident room. Emergency meetings were the new normal. The Commissioner was not in attendance, having a prior engagement, so Deputy Commissioner Jane McPherson called the meeting to order. She needed to be well briefed – there was a meeting of COBRA that afternoon to review the ongoing need for martial law, and she was presenting the Met's view.

'Chief Inspector Stone, bring us up to speed on the Wembley and Brick Lane situations please. Arrests in these cases remain a priority.'

Hilary decided to get the bad news out in the open as quickly as possible.

'Polish police have picked up, in Krakow, a potential suspect for one of the Wembley murders. We've sent a man out to find out what's happening, but the Russian attaché there is accusing us of manipulating evidence and gaining evidence without proper process, and stalling progress. We still do not have anyone in the frame for the Brick Lane murder.'

'So what strategies, exactly, are you employing to remedy this situation?'

'Since the imposition of Martial Law the streets have calmed down a little, which means we've been able to get more officers on the ground on the murdered imam case. We are still going door to door, speaking again to every single person who lives in the area.'

'And you are still pursuing the right-wing conspiracy angle, I presume?' said McPherson.

'Well ma'am, we've been all over the groups we know but we haven't been able to tie them to anything much…certainly not this particular murder. Some of my officers are of the opinion that the far-right thing is a red herring – they're thinking in terms of some foreign actors.'

'Such as?'

'Well, some sort of Russian element is being looked into. Perhaps there's a connection between these two cases. I think that…'

'Russians? Murdering imams on the streets of Tower Hamlets? To what end?' said McPherson. 'Have you any evidence of connections between the cases?'

'No, but my people are saying that all these street thugs running around attacking everything that moves are probably not Brits.'

'Tell me more about Wembley.'

'Well, we've dragged in every known hooligan in the country but found only a few who actually attended the game, and not a single one who has any real idea of what happened. We are still in the process of talking to as many people as possible who attended the match. That's almost 90,000 people. We've poured over the details of all ticket purchases, and found that whoever planned the riots purchased them through intermediaries under false names. We have eye witnesses, of course, but none that have led to identifiable suspects, apart from the man picked up in Krakow, which we're still trying to find out more about.'

'God, what a mess,' said McPherson. 'No wonder the public has lost faith in us. They think we don't know our arse from our elbow, and on the basis of what you've just told me I'd say they have a fair point. Listen to me closely, Chief Inspector Stone. You have no connections between the cases. Put your conspiracy theories about Russia on the back burner – focus on the far-right angle. We've seen mosques and Islamic community centres smashed up and firebombed, gay clubs trashed…do you not see a clear pattern to all of this? Is this not exactly what the opening phases of a fascist revolution would look like?'

'Yes ma'am, but…'

'No buts, Chief Inspector Stone. We need results. Go with what seems most likely.'

'Yes ma'am.'

'Now, listen everyone,' said McPherson, scanning the room with a steely eye, 'I have an important announcement. The Commissioner is about to attend another COBRA meeting with the Prime Minister, Home Secretary and the head of the Intelligence Services. It has recently come to our attention, through GCHQ, that an attack on a very high value target is imminent. We have recommended removing some of the soldiers from the streets of our big cities and doubling numbers around possible targets. We also need now to think about how we deploy our own people. I'm talking about the Houses of Parliament, various sites in the City, some of the main tourist attractions. However unclear we may all be about what exactly is going on, this is starting to look like a war and if one of these targets is successfully hit it will look like we are losing it.'

88

Brad sat meditating in his foxhole. He didn't mind spending the last days of his life alone. He didn't even mind the nature of his impending death. It would be glorious, in a way, retreating into his lair with his possessions, after completing his final mission. His funeral pyre was all set. Everything would be destroyed long before the authorities ever reached him.

As a boy he'd always loved tales of Viking warriors, their fearlessness in the face of death. He'd liked watching films about their exploits and was awed by the scenes showing how they accepted their losses and came to terms with death via a ceremonial burning of bodies.

He would die like the warriors of old. It would be a good death, an honourable death. Far better than slowly dying without dignity, being bed-washed and drip-fed while the life slowly drained out of him as the stomach cancer spread.

Most importantly for Brad his wife and kids would have more money than they needed; and they would never know it was him that took down the British Head of State. He didn't even care about that – he had no time for all the king and queen stuff so getting rid of one was doing the world a favour as far as he was concerned. And what an impact he would have – he would be changing the course of history itself. A million conspiracy theories would abound and historians would be writing books about what happened a hundred, indeed a thousand years hence. What a way to go out.

His period of meditation came to an end and Brad started on his daily routine. Brad liked routines. Stretches, exercise, quenching his thirst in the nearby stream before morning rations. Each day Brad spent out in the wild made him feel more alive, more real than he'd felt lying around at home, purposelessly waiting for the grim reaper to come knocking. Another surge of pain spread through his body, and he rode it out. No more morphine; he wanted to feel himself dying as much as he needed to be focused. The closer he came to his death the more alive he felt.

He looked up at the sapphire blue sky and took a deep breath. The position of the sun told him it was midday. Check-in time. He took out and switched on his mobile as he'd done every day since he'd moved into his new home. For the first time there was a message, consisting of one word.

TOMORROW

The message never gave a time. The time didn't matter much, Brad had plenty of it. He turned off his mobile and took out his weapon and checked the sight. All in order, he thought, as he looked to the top of the tree, his tree, the tree from which a single shot would set in motion a series of unpredictable events that would change everything.

89

H turned his attention back to Lambert. His Lordship was still alive, although he'd lost a lot of blood. He only had a few minutes left. H decided to take it easy, see if he could entice him into a deep and meaningful conversation. He'd seen it before – the final justifications as the lights went out, the deathbed confession. People didn't like to die burdened with secrets.

'Listen, you're going to die,' said H, 'because I'm not going to lift a finger to help you. I'm sorry I've had to do what I've done. But you've been playing a high stakes game for years, you must have known it could end like this?'

Lambert looked at H and smiled. His time was up. He'd enjoyed it, mostly, but H was right. He'd long ago decided to play with the big boys, with all the risks that entailed.

'Who are you?'

'I'm Harry Hawkins, formerly of New Scotland Yard.'

'Oh, of course. I've read much about you. Seen you in the papers over the years. Didn't recognise you, what with the face and all.'

H touched his face and felt around its new lunar landscape – he realised he had no idea what he looked like.

'Who are you working with? How did you find out about me?' asked Lambert.

'That's no longer important. We know about your past and your connections with Russia and all that Marxist bollocks that turns people into traitors. But Russia gave that up long ago. Is it a question of old habits dying hard or did it just become about the power; the money?'

'The latter, in the end,' said Lambert, 'I got used to the money, the power. Power is a powerful drug, Inspector.

Being at the centre of the big things, with the kings of the world.'

'I know.'

'I started out by wanting to change the world, create utopia and all that. Over time the political dreams all dried up…but by then I was in so deep, well, I just kept going.'

'So, what's the big plan?'

'Archduke Ferdinand.'

'What?'

'You know, his assassination triggered the first world war.'

'Yes, yes. And?'

'And that's the plan. Hit a target so big, so symbolic of Western power and democracy it will unleash forces that will be uncontainable. There are lots of people out there who want to see the end of the west in its current guise. A new world order.'

'Fuck me,' said H, 'are you being serious? An attack on The Houses of Parliament, while it's in session? Finish what Guy Fawkes started? The Scotland thing is just another decoy?'

The life was draining from Lambert. H was right, he wouldn't take the secrets to his grave.

'No, the Scotland thing is for real.'

'What then? There's fuck-all in Scotland capable of starting World War Three.'

'Balmoral.'

A light exploded in H's head. They'd been thinking buildings, mass casualties. They'd got used to thinking that way. But Archduke Ferdinand, a single death, followed by unimaginable chaos. Balmoral, ancestral home of the Royal family. The Queen, these fuckers were going to assassinate the Queen. The Queen of fucking England.

'You cunts!' said H. He'd planned to let His Lordship bleed out peacefully - but this was too much. This was way too much. He pulled out his Glock and without ceremony put a bullet into the dying man's head. 'You absolute, no-good fucking cunts. Kill the Queen? I don't fucking think so.'

90

H left Kuba and Ted to hold the fort at the lockup and eased his aching frame into Amisha's car.

'We need to talk to Zaida as soon as,' he said as they approached the roadblock at the southern entry to Waterloo Bridge, 'this whole thing's just gone up another level. We've got to find out more about what these bastards are up to in or near Balmoral.'

'Won't be easy H, I doubt they've posted an itinerary online.'

H gave her the look – as far as she could tell through his mangled visage – but said nothing.

Note to self: the big man is in no mood for sarcasm.

'Well,' she continued, 'if Zaida can't put us on the scent, no one can.'

H closed his eyes and sat back in his chair, doing his breathing exercises as best he could through his sore ribs. He was just reaching a point of something like relaxation when the car swerved suddenly as Amisha was forced to avoid a large crowd of people spilling off the pavement and into the road outside a supermarket.

'Back on the pavement, now, the lot of you,' barked Amisha. She flashed her warrant card at her side window, and most of the crowd obeyed.

'What's going on here Ames? What is it, food shortages?'

'Yep. The bad guys have been disrupting food distribution. All of that goes through the Internet, like everything else now. But they're doing it in a stop-start sort of way, to show us they can, I think. They could have us all starving if they went all out and collapsed the big supermarket chains' logistics systems.'

'Fuck me, they can do all that?'

'Yep. It's not even all that difficult to hack these things. Remember the ransomware attack on all those hospitals the other month, before all this started?'

'Yes…very tasty. Some of them were shut down for days, weren't they?'

'Well, if you can stop people getting their operations, get wrong medicines prescribed, names all mixed up.'

'Jesus, Ames, how have we been so stupid?'

'Dunno H, we just have. I have a feeling that the attack on the hospitals may not have been a ransom thing, more a dummy run for the hackers to test their capacity and reach. Sort of dipping their toe in the water before they really got going.'

So you're telling me that these people could basically bring the whole shithouse down around our ears, just by fucking about with the Internet?'

'Yep.'

'Then why haven't they?'

'Maybe because they don't want to destroy everything, just get everyone feeling on edge prior to…'

'Shooting the Queen. They reckon that might knock the bollocks out of us.'

'Yes, and they may be right. Imagine the demoralisation if…'

'Yes, well, whatever. But no way are they going to knock the bollocks out of me, Ames. Are we there yet?'

***

Zaida was in the hotel room alone. Joey Jupiter, who wanted to keep out of sight, had moved to an unknown location, and Andrew was mooching about somewhere else now, pretending to be a normal policeman.

But Zaida had nothing to add. She was convinced about Scotland, and H was convinced about Balmoral. It made perfect sense, especially to the cunning bastards they were up against.

'Well kids, there's nothing for it. We'll have to take this to Hilary. She's the only person we know who can get anything done now, and she's sure as fuck the only person in the system we know we can trust.'

'You'd have to see her in person, H,' said Amisha. 'You cannot have this conversation over the phone.'

'Set up the meet then Ames. Tell her you've made a breakthrough on the Brick Lane investigation, that'll get her attention. In the park, not at the Yard. Tell her you want to meet her outside the cafeteria. Do it now.'

91

H spotted Hilary as he entered the park from The Mall, circled around behind her and whispered into her ear.

'Any chance of an ice cream Hilary? I've left my money at home.'

Hilary swivelled round in alarm, her body's fight-or-flight system kicking in instantaneously as she assessed the threat. Flight looked like a good option when she found her face inches away from the shattered visage of someone she seemed to know.

'H? Is that you? What in God's name happened to your face? Where's Amisha?'

'Amisha is indisposed. I've got to talk to you. It's urgent. Get the ice creams in and we can sit by the lake. I just need ten minutes of your time – please, for old time's sake.'

They sat. H talked, Hilary listened. She was a Chief Inspector at New Scotland Yard, an experienced woman who thought she'd heard everything in her time.

'Yes, I'm certain,' said H, 'the plot is to assassinate the Queen while she's spending time in Scotland. Don't you see – no matter what happens they know she'll try and stick to her routine. It's her job description, make things look like all is normal, even when they're not. Everyone knows that.'

'And you got this from the confession of a man you kidnapped.'

'Yes,' said H.

'And where is he now?'

'Gone to meet his maker.'

'Who was he?'

'Lord Peter Lambert.'

'H! Are you insane? You're even more of a liability than you were as a copper. You kidnapped Lord Peter Lambert and tortured a deathbed confession out of him? You've surpassed yourself this time H, and just made yourself a suspect in a murder that I'll have to report.'

'Hilary, listen: you're right – of course you are. But think about what's at stake. We're in a war here, and Lord Peter Lambert was on the wrong side of it. He was a traitor and he got exactly what he deserved.'

Hilary sighed – her old, hopeless, H-sigh. She'd been here before and, as before, knew that H's instincts were usually spot on.

'Where's the body?'

'Disposed of.'

'Any other evidence?'

'No.'

'OK, let's leave that issue there for now. But why shouldn't I assume that your Balmoral plot isn't just one of the million and one theories currently doing the rounds. Plots about the assassination of the Prime Minster, an attack on the House of Lords, or the London Eye, or biological attacks from all these drones, or nuclear Armageddon? The whole world has gone mad, and now you're presenting a theory about some Russian oligarchs or the Russian state or more likely both, taking the Queen out? Don't you see how crazy that sounds?'

'It's not a theory,' said H.

'Yes, it is, and besides, don't you think this has been considered. There are scores, maybe hundreds of operatives of one sort or another protecting Her Majesty, and everywhere she goes is locked down long before she arrives. We are talking about a security perimeter of one and a half square miles around her.'

'I know, but the planning for this has been years in the making. You wouldn't believe some of the long-term planning and organisation that's gone into some of the shadows they've had us chasing after. Trust me Hilary, they've found a way.'

'Was anybody else involved?' interrupted Hilary.

'With what?'

'Your kidnap.'

'No. Just me.'

'Where did the information come from, about Lord Lambert?'

'Sources.'

'You're not giving me much to work with here H.'

'You'll have to trust me.'

'God help us all.'

'Report it, just report it upwards. Get somebody to take notice.'

'H, as it's you and we go back so far I'll pass your concerns upstairs. At the same time, I'm afraid, I'm going to have to say where it came from, and how the information was obtained. They're going to require a source.'

'Fair enough,' said H, 'do what you've got to do. Put it on me. But get the word out. This is the biggest shit we've been in since the Blitz, we've got to do something. These fuckers are tying us up in knots, but someone's got to do something. Get on the right side of history Hilary – don't go down as just another mug.'

'And what are you going to do, Mr Hawkins?'

'What I always fucking do,' said H.

92

Amisha and H were forced to take the long and winding road back to the hotel room in Camden. Many of the streets around St James' Park, Parliament Square and Whitehall were closed – they assumed it had something to do with preparation for the big security lockdown they knew was coming – so they had to make their way through snarled, honking traffic back through Mayfair and Fitzrovia and get back eventually via St. Pancras. It took them over two hours, with H keeping his own counsel most of the way – screening out the chaos they moved through and brooding, Amisha thought, on his meeting with Hilary, thinking things through.

***

'Where have you two been?' said Zaida, 'I was worried Hilary Stone had arrested you, H. How did it go?'

'Well, Hilary sort of half-bought it, but I doubt she'll be able to do much for us,' said H. 'They won't go for it. They might increase security, if someone takes notice, but they'll still go through with the Queen's schedule. We're on our own. Let's think it through – what are we looking at up there anyway?'

'Well,' said Zaida, 'air space will be locked down over a much larger area than usual, so we can rule out an attack from the air. And inside the perimeter on the ground, forget it. I've studied the landscape; there's one area has potential – stands out as somewhere a sniper could dig in, and a place the Queen always visits when she's at Balmoral. The small church in Crathie, a few miles from Balmoral. She'd insist on going there, and the authorities would want to make a show of her visit, make sure it was on world-wide television to make it look like the whole country wasn't going to hell.'

'How would they know she'd go to Balmoral?'

'Partly it's the obvious choice. Create havoc in London. Balmoral is a safe place away from the madness, and she'd have to do public appearances, calm the panic. And for all we know they have someone feeding into her schedule.'

'Still seems so unreal, far-fetched,' said Amisha.

'No, it's obvious. They've been manipulating us all along, creating mayhem so a public appearance from the Queen ups the ante – millions upon millions watching, needing to see normality. I think they're planning a live assassination, when we're at our weakest.'

'Ok,' said H, 'Hilary says they've extended the usual security perimeter to one and a half square miles. Zaida, what's the record distance for a sniper kill shot? Didn't a Canadian Special Forces man break it recently?'

Zaida returned to her screen, and came back in seconds with 'Yep. 3,450 metres. 2.1 miles to you, H. In Iraq.'

'OK, so we're in business. We act on the assumption that it's going to be a sniper. It's a *Day of the Jackal* turnout. Let's have a look at the terrain around the church. Ordnance Survey if you please Zaida, none of that Google maps stuff. A sniper will want to be in an elevated position relative to the church for a shot like that – let's see what we can see. Print the map off and we'll take it with us, in case communications go down. Seems likely the shooter's people might want to take care of that, no?'

'Yes,' said Amisha. 'But what do you mean by "take it with us" – have you seen the state of yourself?'

'No. What I mean is we're going up there. Now. The Queen's in church when, exactly?'

'Day after tomorrow,' said Zaida. 'The service is at eleven o'clock.'

'How the hell are we going to drive up there, through all the roadblocks?' said Amisha.

H looked at her but said nothing. She had a point.

'We're not,' said Zaida.

'This is no time for riddles, Zaida. Please start making sense.'

'I mean we're not going through roadblocks, or observing curfews, or other such restrictions suffered by landlubbers. We can get up there on my boat. Remember my boat H? I invited you to come out on the seas with me, ages ago.'

Amisha saw that her aunt was surfing on H's energy, his way of doing things. She saw how in tune with him she was.

'What sort of boat is it?' asked H.

'It's an old power boat, a Fairey Huntsman 31. I got it cheap and I've been doing it up for years. Runs pretty well now. It's the love of my life. I renamed it the *Royal Mawalin*.'

'A power boat. Are you having a laugh?'

'No, really. It a classic from the 60s – quite small, but a cabin below deck, and seaworthy.'

'Where's it moored?' asked H.

'Whitstable, in Kent.'

'How long to get up there?'

'Well,' said Zaida, tapping at her keyboard and glancing at her screen. 'Stonehaven is our best bet – we can get into the Cairngorms through forested areas, other ways in would leave us exposed and the Cairngorms are actually up on a mountainous plateau. Not a lot of cover there, and very few roads. It's the sort of terrain that favours the watcher rather than the traveller. It's about 340 nautical miles. My boat has a 5.95 litre turbo engine and can hit 31knots. Journey time will be something in the region of twelve hours, give or take. Depends on conditions, of course. And it'll be dark.'

'Blinding. How many passengers, apart from me and you?'

'Three or four, at a push.'

'Alright kids, this is it. Amisha, put an info pack together – distance, terrain etc., etc., from Stonehaven to the church at Crathie, and anything else we might need to know. Do it now. Print off hard copies. You stay here and hold the fort. When we're ready me and Zaida will swing by the lockup to pick up some guys and then head out to Whitstable. It's all systems go people – we're rolling.'

93

Helicopters, airplanes, any form of motorised land vehicle – all these were meat and drink to H. He loved them all. But boats, and things that went on water, he'd never fancied. He'd been on the ferry across the English Channel once or twice, from Dover to Calais, back in the days of the beer runs with his pals, when you could get a good look at the White Cliffs of Dover, load the car up with duty-free French booze and get merry and bright for next to nothing into the bargain.

But this was different. It was going to be real seafaring in a smallish craft, very close to the water. As they boarded the sea seemed calm and placid under a sanguine moon, but Zaida learned there was a storm brewing and the advice from the coastguard was not to go out.

H would not entertain the notion of not going. He knew that Hilary, even if she tried to push the theory upstairs, would get nowhere, so they had to risk it. H, Kuba, Yorkie Ted, Little Ronnie, Marek Kucharski and Jarek Dydowicz might have been hardened fighters to a man, but they were like lost sheep as they were cajoled to get on board and told were to go and what to do by Zaida.

H's determination to keep the different elements of his private army separate was now dead in the water. He hated exposing Zaida to real danger but concluded there was no choice. Jarek was clearly agitated at taking orders from a woman he'd never met before. H noticed the agitation and moved to calm the tension.

'Kuba, tell your boy to calm down, pronto. She's the only one here who knows how to drive this fucking thing.'

***

Zaida and H took care of things up top; the boys played cards below. The boat left the safety of the port and H felt the power of the open sea as the vessel began to roll from side to side in concert with the rhythm of the waves. Zaida gave H the wheel.

'You steer H, I need to navigate. Just turn the wheel when I tell you.'

H grabbed it as instructed and watched as the skipper surveyed a range of instruments he didn't understand. But he was getting used to the rhythm of the waves and the open sea, which were still relatively calm.

'OK, I'll take over now,' said Zaida abruptly, 'things will be getting lively soon.' Her soft, bejewelled hands moved to grip the wheel, touching H's as they did so. H let his hand linger for a moment and the two stood side by side, feeling the energy that flowed between them. H's face was beaten, puffed and had more scars than a Viking's shield, but Zaida felt herself drawn, as usual, to this warrior from a bygone era. Beneath the impatience and the bluster and the non-stop cursing he was...heroic, in his way. He reminded her of the tales of Gods and heroes that had enthralled her as a young child in India. Tales such as that of Indra, the God of war who rode a four-tusked white elephant into battle with the dragon Vritra.

'Remember the night we met?' she said.

'Not really, no. Was it in Catford? At the dog track?'

Zaida laughed – because he was funny, and because she knew he was trying to slow her down and stop her getting too close.

'I can't say I wasn't disappointed when I heard you were completely committed to your lovely wife. If things had been different do you think we...'

'Maybe,' he said. H wasn't a poet, she knew, he was a pragmatic and honest man in love as in life; he was never going to whisper sweet nothings into the ear of a woman who was not Olivia Hawkins. But there was a romantic in him, a chivalrous heart, somewhere beneath the crust made hard by bitter experience. 'Yes, I've thought about you from time to time. You made a bit of an impression.'

H felt his heart beating and wondered what Zaida was thinking as she peered into the puffed-up mask currently doing business as his face. Under these conditions a kiss was out of the question – not that it was ever really a possibility, given all the circumstances.

The wind was picking up; the waves were increasing in strength and starting to chop into one another. The cuts and abrasions on H's face began to smart in the gathering salty wind, which livened him up no end.

'Get ready H, a storm is coming.'

'How bad?'

Zaida explained that the wind was coming in from the North Sea, which meant waves would likely hit at around forty-five degrees into the direction they were heading, and there was significant fetch – which was the distance the wind blew across open sea. 'The greater the fetch the bigger the waves, I'm afraid. We are also hugging the coast. That means extra swell.'

'Sounds grand. Do we need to wobble or can you handle it? Do we need to put to shore?'

'No. I can manage it. I've steered in a beam sea a few times before, and…'

'A beam sea?' said H.

'A sea in which the waves are hitting you from the side. It's a question of power management, working the throttle back and forward, in response to seas you encounter.'

H, exasperated by the fact he was about to become as useful as a concrete life vest, cursed and made a forlorn offer: 'Anything I can do?'

'Yes,' said Zaida, 'make sure you don't get rolled overboard.'

And then the worst happened. Without warning the night plunged into darkness and the clouds thickened, blotting out the moon and stars. The wind speed increased and the choppy waters morphed, it seemed to H, into mountains of angry waves intent on smashing their vessel to pieces. They were lifted on the surge of a forty-five-degree wave high above the waterline and then crashed back down, jarring the bones of all on board and tossing them from one side of the boat to another.

A bolt of lightning struck nearby, temporarily lighting up the sea, which now looked gigantic and limitlessly powerful. H was awestruck. For the first time in his life H experienced the sublime power of the watery world. And then the waves spun the vessel sideways. It seemed as if Zaida had lost control and H looked on as helpless as a babe in the woods as she spun the wheel and worked the throttle, all concentration and composure.

Now that is my kind of girl.

And then it passed, almost as quickly as it had begun, and they were easing their way through calm seas, moonlight, stars and stability. The storm had lasted just twenty minutes. But they were long ones.

'Fucking hell,' he said, 'that was incredible. Tremendous work.'

'Thank you, H' said Zaida, 'would you mind driving, I'm a little bushed.'

303

94

'Right gents, let's be having you,' said H. 'Morning has broken. It's nearly seven o'clock, Zaida says we'll be rocking up in about twenty minutes.'

He spread out his Ordnance Survey map of the Cairngorms on the table.

'We are disembarking here, in this cove outside Stonehaven. Distance to Crathie church is 53 miles as the crow flies. We're hitting the ground at this spot because we want to make our way into the Cairngorms under as much cover as possible, on the assumption that the area is being monitored by the bad guys as well as the good guys, at least outside the security perimeter. Phase one is here to Aboyne on the fringes of the Cairngorms by car, through lots of lovely Scots pines for cover. Any questions so far?'

'Yes Pop, if you don't mind,' said Little Ronnie, 'when will we be passing through Cock Bridge? And how many distilleries do we pass on the way?'

'All of them,' said H with a smile, 'and you need to sort yourself out and get focused.'

'So,' he continued, returning to the map, 'phase two is a bit tastier. We need to get up onto the plateau and make our way towards Crathie, where the church is, here. This will not be a walk in the park – a lot of it is open mountainous country, and the weather up here this time of year can get very naughty indeed. One minute everything's lovely, the next you're walking through dense fog or some sort of fucking blizzard.'

He looked around, inviting questions. None came.

'Kuba has already identified the most likely, really just about the only, vantage point for a shooter to be as here, up on this forested ridge. Scots pines again, and plenty of them

– it's about a mile and three quarters from the church, and that's where we need to get to, without being spotted by either the authorities or the bad guys, well before eleven tomorrow morning. I'd say by about this time tomorrow morning, seven-ish, at the latest, so we can have a good mooch about and see what's what.'

'OK,' said Kuba, 'I have a question I know must be on everybody's mind – what are the rules of engagement?'

'Well,' said H, 'Kill or be killed. If the enemy are about up here they won't be stopping us to ask questions. They may even guess we're coming – I told my old boss about all this. She's solid as a rock, but we know there are traitors further up the chain. As for the army and security services, our people, I'd say we play it by ear.'

'Ah, another one of your English idioms,' said Kuba. 'What does it actually mean?'

'What it means, mate,' said H, scanning the faces of his men one-by-one, 'is do what you've got to do. We're here to prevent the assassination of the Queen. Just do what you've got to do.'

95

'OK H,' said Zaida up on deck, 'we're nearly there. I'll bring us into this little cove, a little way outside the town?'

'How far out?'

'Two and a half, three miles.'

'No, take us further in. We don't want to be tramping about in the middle of nowhere for no good reason, we haven't got time to waste, and we've got cars to steal.'

'Bit risky, going into a populated area, isn't it?'

'No risk, no reward,' said H, 'and anyway, these blokes behind me, all of them, have been taking risks all their lives. Bring us in nearer to town please my love, soon as you start to see some nickable cars.'

***

Zaida spotted a cluster of a dozen or so cars parked a couple of hundred yards inland, close to the beginning of a tourist trail, and dropped anchor as close as she could get to the beach in a spot called Strathlethan Bay.

'Alright H,' said Zaida, 'you'll find an inflatable dinghy, and a gadget to blow it up with, in that compartment there. Better get cracking.'

'We're getting into a dinghy?'

'What would you like me to do, "drive" the boat straight up onto the beach?'

Kuba stepped in, quietly and efficiently, and dealt with the dinghy while H issued instructions to the men.

'There's not much to choose from, but if you can, get hold of something old,' said H, 'these new motors all have keyless push-button ignitions, they're harder to nick. Look for something from the nineties if possible. Me, Zaida and Ronnie in one car, everybody else in another one.'

H spotted a likely candidate, a worn and tattered Peugeot, as he clambered off the dinghy. He approached it directly, covered his hand with his coat and smashed the driver's side window. He opened the door, slipped inside with more elegance than his age, bulk and wounds should have allowed and popped off a plastic cover under the dashboard. He exposed three main bundles of wires: one snaked off to the left to control indicators and lights, one led to the right for stalk controls and the third bundle made its way into the steering column, where it controlled the ignition lock and switch assembly.

'Lovely, just the ticket,' said H as he separated the wires on the middle bundle. He pulled a knife from the holster on his leg and started cutting and connecting wires.

'This should do it,' he said as he made what he thought was the connection that would ignite the engine. Then the radio came on. 'Fuck it,' he said.

He spent some time thinking and tried again.

'Must be this fucker,' he said as he connected up more wires, and the engine burst into life. He surged up from under the dashboard, pleased with his work and ready to accept the admiration of the rest of the crew, and saw Marek Kucharski sitting with a big shit-eating grin at the wheel of a ten-year-old Volkswagen Golf, idling the engine and ready to go.

'Liven up, H,' shouted Yorkie Ted through a backseat window, 'it looks like it's getting ready to rain, and we've got a British monarch to save.'

96

Charles Mortimer-Dagwood, the Queen's private secretary and one of the closest people to her, sat in conference with her head of security, a smattering of lesser private secretaries and Peter Dimless, the Chief Constable of Police Scotland. Since the troubles had started the Queen had kept several appointments those responsible for her safety had wished she hadn't, and security levels at each event had been unprecedented.

Mortimer-Dagwood made a few minor adjustments to the knot in his sky-blue silk tie – not that any were necessary given he always looked immaculate – before re-iterating his point.

'My dear fellow,' he said to Dimless, with his characteristic sense of condescension, 'the Queen remains adamant she attends the service. This is non-negotiable, so please ensure you have fallen in line with Her Majesty's people and the security services and army, and that the entire area is fully locked down. After all the place is in the middle of nowhere, it shouldn't be too difficult.'

Dimless was not of the same opinion. 'Everything is under control, from very close to the ground to high in the sky – rest assured, nothing can get in or out without us knowing about it. But I don't like it. In these times the monarch should be kept secure. It's unwise to expose her during the current emergency, until we have more clarity about the threats we face.'

'My dear boy,' drawled the private secretary, 'we have never had, and will never have, full control of anywhere. There's always a threat to those in the public eye. If the country is to function, if people are going to get up and go to work and we are to prevent complete anarchy in the UK, it is imperative the masses see Her Majesty keeping to her routines, engaging in business as usual, and this they will be able to do tomorrow.'

Dimless knew the decision had already been taken by people way above his pay grade, but continued to express his concerns. He didn't have any news or intelligence of a likely assassination attempt, but having the Queen on public display on his patch made him anxious. He was a tetchy, jittery character, lacking in command presence at the best of times, and these were not the best of times. He wanted to distance Scotland from the troubles which had so far mostly been confined to England. He was also protecting his own backside, making sure his concerns were on record in case things went pear-shaped.

'Your concerns have been noted,' said Mortimor-Dagwood. 'I have every confidence you have the situation entirely under control.'

97

It happened just before they reached Ballater on the B976, a narrow country road H had chosen as he thought it would be better to keep off the main 'A' road. As soon as he heard the single shot his senses scanned the environment for the pattern of attack. Single sniper? A small guerrilla contingent? They were under attack and H's survival instincts were triggered in a heartbeat.

He suspected Kuba's driver, Marek, was dead when the car in front of them careered left and right before hitting the low stone wall that bordered the road on the driver's side, bounced off it, turned onto its roof and spun off the road on the passenger side, which in turn was bordered only by a fence of wire and wooden posts. H knew only an expert sniper could make a shot like that. Five hundred yards or so back from the wall, driver's side, was a thicket of woods from which H conjectured the shot must have come.

On the other side of the fence, passenger side, the land dipped about two feet below the road, and twenty or so yards further inland was a loch, after which there was a thicket of trees at the foot of the Cairngorms themselves.

H pulled the steering wheel left, smashed through the wire fence on the passenger side and barked his orders. 'Out, out.' He was out of the car while it was still in motion, faster than a rabbit down a burrow with a Lurcher on its tail. He was rolling – or more like spinning – across the cold wet ground as fast as he could when he heard the next shot. He figured it must have been meant for him when the bullet ripped through the driver's seat of the car he'd just abandoned.

Kuba and Yorkie Ted kicked their way out of the Golf and, along with Jarek, scrambled to the safety of the dip beside the road, which was where H ended his roll. He saw the three were OK before turning to check for the others. He could see blood flowing from Marek's head, and felt the usual pang of distress at the sight of another fallen comrade.

He took a deep breath and re-focused. Where was his boy, where was Zaida?

'Son…?'

'It's alright Pop, we're under the motor,' Little Ronnie shouted back,' don't much fancy being under here too long though, this shooter looks like he knows what he's doing.'

Relief flowed through every fibre in H's body.

'Hold tight son, I'm on it'.

H turned to Kuba, and said 'Analysis, mate. Now.'

'Based on the angle of the bullet that hit Marek the first shooter is somewhere over there,' said Kuba, pointing in the general direction of the woods but keeping his head below the dip.

'First?' said H

'Yes. As your car spun a second bullet hit it. Same general direction, different angle. So minimum of two, possibly more, spread out in a line. Waiting for us.'

H looked about – an unknown number of deadly snipers to the front of them; loch, trees and a mountain range behind them.

'Fuck it,' said H. 'this is really going to slow us down. We've got to get out of here, pronto.'

'Agreed,' said Kuba. 'Strategy?'

'No idea mate, no fucking idea whatsoever.'

98

H and his people were pinned down and keeping low. Behind them was a small loch that led into a small wood at the foot of the Cairngorm mountains. To his left were two cars looking oddly out of place in an otherwise calm Scottish countryside. Above them a Golden Eagle soared across the sky, it's all-seeing eye deciding that the humans far below were not of interest. H looked hard into the woods on the opposite side of the road – he saw nothing but knew for certain if any of his firm revealed themselves they would come under a deadly barrage.

They'd taken a quiet road, and in the thirty minutes they'd been tucked up only a single car had passed. H was relieved when it didn't stop – the driver's choice of ignoring the two abandoned cars was the right one. Stopping would only have led to the death of an innocent civilian.

'How's it looking, any plan yet Pop?' Little Ronnie shouted.

'Ain't got one yet son. They've absolutely got us by the bollocks here, any movement and we'll be lambs to the slaughter. Zaida, how are you holding up?'

'OK. Listen H, I've been thinking…'

'Glad to hear it. What about?'

'Can you swim?'

'Of course I can fucking swim. What do you…'

'It's just that you were flaying about so much in the dinghy I thought you might be scared of going under,' said Zaida.

'Make your point.'

'OK H, calm down, I was just checking. Let's get focused, we haven't got much time. How about we swim our way out of this?'

H had considered this as a last resort. Crawl to the other side of the bushes to the left of their position, slip to the loch, swim to the other side. That might put them beyond reach of the bullets as they zig-zagged their way into the woods. But that was not the main problem; the danger of hypothermia was. They could swim for maybe four or five minutes before losing the use of their muscles, before their bodies started to shut off blood flow to what it thought were non-essential extremities, like the arms and hands they needed to swim with. H estimated the extent of the loch and calculated the likelihood of getting across in the near-freezing conditions. He was a good swimmer, and he thought he could make it, as long as his body survived the initial cold shock response and he wasn't catapulted into cardiac arrest. And the rest of the crew were all fit – for their ages anyway.

'We might make it but then we'd be fucking freezing with no real way of warming up. And let's not forget we'll need to trek afterwards. How are we going to get across that mountain range and onto Crathie before the Queen shows herself?'

'We'd have to take our clothes off,' said Zaida.

H had enjoyed dreams featuring Zaida naked, but these tended to take place against a backdrop of balmy evenings in exotic locations, not on freezing Scottish winter mornings with snipers covering your every move.

'OK, go on, I'm listening,' said H.

'I noticed a big camping bag in the boot of the car – it's waterproof. We can put our clothes in it. If I can flip the boot open and get it, we crawl down to the water using the bush as cover, disrobe, swim and power over to the other side. They won't be expecting it.'

'Kuba,' said H, 'what d'you reckon? Fancy a swim?'

'No.'

313

'Any other ideas?'

'No.'

'Right you lot,' shouted H, 'start crawling. Me and Kuba will provide cover.'

They set up a mini bullet-storm in the general direction of the snipers as best they could while everybody else got going on the short crawl to the loch. It seemed in a way like a waste of good bullets, but H had been pondering the options whilst watching the seconds tick by. If they were to make a move it had to be now. There was no other choice. He waited until they all – Little Ronnie, Zaida, Yorkie Ted and Jarek – reached the loch side before following on with Kuba, crawling like a bull walrus sliding across a beach.

'No need to stand on ceremony,' said H as he took off his clothes and stuffed them into the bag on top of everybody else's.

'Well, I declare,' said Zaida, 'how dashing you do look, Mr Hawkins, stood there in your birthday suit like that.'

H pretended not to hear her; he heaved the bag up onto his back and put his arms through the straps, and shouted. 'Right, follow me kids, here we go. Swim as fast as you can. Keep your heads down. Don't look back.'

99

H plunged into the loch and led the way, powering through the freezing water hell-for-leather. He felt alive and exhilarated – for about ten seconds. Then he began to feel it: the searing pain in his lungs, the agony in his muscles, the swirling in his head. The anguish of understanding that the next couple of minutes, if he lived through them, were going to be hell on earth.

His will to live kicked in, and for a time he again surged through the icy water like a man possessed, spurred on by the sound of rifles. One by one his crew went past him: first Little Ronnie, then Kuba, then Jarek, then Zaida. H rolled over onto his back for a second or two, panicking as he fought to get air into his bursting lungs, fighting for composure. This he regained using his raw, mind-over-matter method for dealing with the agony that was now spreading to every part of his body. But he hadn't recovered from the beating he'd received at the hands of his Russian friend. It was taking its toll.

He was two minutes in, and surviving, getting there. But when he was taken over by Yorkie Ted – a man known by legend to have consumed twelve pints a day of Yorkshire Ale, when not on active duty – H knew he was in trouble. His mind was snapping, and he began to flail. His ability to move forward through the water had deserted him. He stopped dead and began to tread water; his mind was as frozen as his body, and he felt himself begin to go down.

He lost feeling in his arms – until he felt something gripping them under the shoulder, first left and then right, and bring him back to the surface, filling his head with light and his lungs with air. He had no power of his own but was borne forward by powerful forces, accompanying him on each side. He drifted into unconsciousness.

Little Ronnie and Kuba felt him get heavier, and now had to pull him on as a dead weight. They redoubled their efforts, moving through the water slowly, as they'd both been taught to as boys, many years apart, in training for their lifesaving medals. They turned the big man onto his back and brought him to shore, heaving with breathlessness and exertion but with the devotion of men who would take a bullet to their own heads before they would let their cargo slip from their grasp.

100

Andrew had been feeling severely put out since being locked out of what Amisha and Zaida were doing. He'd got a buzz out of being part of H's private army and felt more than a little deflated when Amisha told him to concentrate on the official cases they were supposed to be investigating. The top brass was piling the pressure on and they were desperate for a suspect on the Whitechapel killing. They needed a name, almost any name, they could feed to the media sharks.

But more than this he was troubled by the direction the investigation into the Wembley murders was taking. To start with, it didn't make sense – so much had happened since, so much murdering and fighting and rioting and chaos-making in general that one outrage bled into another; he couldn't really understand why so much emphasis was being placed on the Wembley case, or why the lead they had from Krakow wasn't being correctly progressed.

But that wasn't all. Working clandestinely with Amisha and Zaida meant that he now had a lot of knowledge that his colleagues at the Yard did not. He and Amisha had long since worked out that everything was most likely connected, one way or another, to some kind of Russian interests. They knew, at the very least, that large numbers of senior British figures had been bought and paid for with Oligarch money. He felt a growing sense of unreality, as the country's media continued to keep the focus on domestic terrorism. The picture presented to the public was at odds with what was happening, but there was nothing he could do about it. He was being made to investigate British extremist political organisations and other hooligan groups, and he was fed up with the insane work shifts and six am starts he was doing – that they were all doing.

So here he was back at work – having to bite his tongue, knowing too much, and not enough, and feeling deeper and deeper in his bones that he was being manipulated. He got up from his desk and went for coffee. What he got, instead, was Hilary Stone blocking his path to the machine – legs planted apart, hands on hips, wearing her hardest 'don't fuck with me' face.

'Andrew, I'd like a quick word. Have you heard at all from H? Got any idea what he's up to these days, how he's taking the meltdown? I'm asking off the record.'

Oh God, I'm in deep shit.

Hilary saw Andrew clam up and sensed his unease –it was obvious to her he knew something.

'Listen Andrew, I'm asking off the record. No comebacks. I just need to build up a picture of what he's been up to.'

'Er…well'

'Andrew, you know as well as I do how grave our situation is. We cannot afford for officers to open secret lines of enquiry of their own. It can only make matters worse. We have to stick together – pool our resources and keep focused, or we'll just drown under this wave of garbage. Now, I'll ask you again. What do you now about the lines of enquiry H, and maybe Amisha, have been unofficially exploring?'

Andrew was saved, temporarily, by Hilary's ringtone. She answered and received orders to attend, immediately, a meeting with the Commissioner, Deputy Commissioner and other luminaries. Andrew was trying to think of his appropriate answer while she spoke.

'Yes ma'am, on my way, I'll be there in five,' said Hilary.

She turned her attention to Andrew.

'I have to go to an emergency meeting. Be in my office in an hour. Think very deeply about how you answer my

318

questions – I've offered you an off-the-record chat. The offer runs out five minutes after you enter my office.'

101

Andrew's mood had changed after his confrontation with Hilary. From being aggrieved about missing out on the thrills and excitement of once again working, however distantly, for H, he now wondered what on earth he'd let himself get dragged into. He found a corner of the office and asked not to be disturbed while he thought about what he might say. But he found himself caught between thought and action, with his mind frozen, and sat for the best part of an hour pondering his fate before calling Amisha for advice.

'We had to tell Hilary, Andrew. We believe that there's a good chance an attempt will be made on the Queen's life tomorrow. We had to tell her. She has to take it upstairs. H has already spoken to her. I'm on my way back now, to back up what he said and try to convince her. I'll only be another few minutes.'

'Oh my God. And H?'

'He's in Scotland with a few of the others, trying to do what he can to prevent the assassination. It might be a wild goose chase but he really had no choice – he's convinced that the higher-ups won't take us seriously. He's not even sure Hilary will.'

'How did you find out about all this?'

'Some things are best not to know, Andrew.'

'Then what should I tell Hilary? That I was involved, up to a point? That I completely stepped over the line? That I've been withholding information pertinent to multiple ongoing investigations?'

'Yes, tell her. Tell her. Just keep her occupied until I get there. Anyway, our careers are not important. You must see the big picture. We have to get this message as far up the chain of command as possible. If she won't do it I'm going directly to the Commissioner myself, if he'll see me. When are you supposed to be meeting her?'

'Now, pretty much, I'm going to her office now.'

'OK. Just front it. I'll get there and follow you in as quickly as I can. We'll stick together.'

This did the trick. Andrew approached and knocked on Hilary's door feeling a little less afraid, a little less like the end of the world was coming.

There was no reply to his knock. He tried again...still no response.

Maybe she hasn't finished her previous meeting.

He couldn't just stand around. He had to be doing something. He took a deep breath and opened the door, to check she was not there. He made two steps in, and it hit him straight away – he felt the sickening realisation and emotional response before he understood mentally what was in front of him.

Chief Inspector Hilary Stone sat on her chair as still as a statue.

'Ma'am! Ma'am!' he shouted, rushing forward. Breathing heavily, and with his own dried-out tongue nearly choking him, he checked for a pulse. Nothing. Hilary Stone was dead.

102

H had been in a bad way when Little Ronnie and Kuba hauled him out of the loch, got him to his feet and zig-zagged as best they could to the tree line beyond the loch. But he'd rallied, and the ragged core of H's army was now on the verge of entering the Cairngorm National Park – shivering with cold, weary but unable to rest, given what was sure to be coming on behind them. They had been seriously side-tracked; the Queen's arrival at Crathie church was now three hours closer than it had been when the bullet went through Marek Kucharski's head on the road from Stonehaven, and now they were in the middle of the Cairngorms without transportation.

The Cairngorm mountains of Scotland are, in effect, Britain's arctic. During winter storm winds of over one hundred and seventy miles an hour can rasp relentlessly across their upper echelons. Avalanches scour the sides protected from the winds, making them rocky, harsh and unforgiving. H called them to a halt after half an hour's march from the loch, and they huddled around him to look at the map and hear his thoughts. They knew where they were and they knew where they had to get to, but the best route was another thing altogether.

'Right then kids, this is the situation,' H said as he contemplated the possibilities. 'How long it takes us to get there depends mostly on the weather. I reckon we've got just about enough time to make it, barring twisted ankles or getting caught up in freezing fog. But we've also got the problem of these bastards behind us, not to mention whatever manpower might lie up ahead, ours as well as theirs. Most of these mountain sides are open and we'll be in plain sight for long stretches.'

'We'll have to keep in front of the snipers Pop, keep the pace up,' said Little Ronnie.

'Maybe son, but I doubt we can outpace them. They'll likely be fit, fast and well equipped for the terrain.'

They discussed the best route further. If they went too high and mixed it with the snow-capped peaks it would get too cold – they'd have to take a circular route, use ravines to keep themselves out of sight as best they could, stay in the low-lying areas where the trees grew tall enough to hide them.

Zaida drew a big breath, stood up, moved away from the map and took in the panorama. 'It's so beautiful,' she said. For her, being in the great wild outdoors had always been a profoundly sensuous experience. H couldn't help but be swept up into her beauty, and her zen-like calmness in the face of adversity increased his admiration for her still further. He thought momentarily that he should tell her to get her shit together because they were in a bit of a jam, but he didn't. He smiled at her. She was right. H had been a city boy all his life and wasn't one for a lake and mountains holiday, he'd always been more of a beach and beer man. But now he looked to see what Zaida saw, and felt the sublime thrill of great natural beauty as he took a moment to look about. His eyes landed once again on Zaida, a stunning woman in a beautiful place, and he stood transfixed. He near forgot himself as he stared at the beauty before him; it was, for a moment, like something in a Hollywood film, where the hero embraces and kisses the heroine while pandemonium rages all around them.

Kuba killed the moment.

'H, we'll have to confront them, hand to hand,' he said, returning H to the here and now. 'It's the only way. They'll crucify us if we just keep marching on like this.'

103

'Go on mate,' said H, 'we're all ears.'

'It's the only option.'

'Why?'

'They will be properly dressed, with good footwear. They will move faster than us, they will catch us. They will be under orders to stop firing as they get closer to Crathie. They will track us, and deal with us hand-to-hand. If we build a barricade or dig in we could hold them off, but that would all take time we and the Queen don't have.'

Kuba's reasoning, as always, was spot on. H let him continue.

'We don't yet know their numbers. Maybe we split into two groups, one stands and fights, one moves on.'

This was where the thinking of H and Kuba diverged.

'You're half right,' said H, 'we have to make a stand, agreed. I should think there'll be half a dozen or so of them at least, so if we split there's a greater chance of losing the skirmish, and if we lose the skirmish the second group will soon be caught. We stand together.'

H also wanted to stay close to Zaida and Little Ronnie. The thought of them being in danger without him nearby curdled his blood. He wanted to keep them close, protect them. Zaida felt his reticence and understood the reasons. As usual she seemed to understand H, even before he uttered a word.

'I'm trained in hand-to-hand combat H, you don't have to worry about me. I can take care of myself,' she said. H smiled and turned to Kuba.

'We have one advantage then,' said Kuba. 'we choose where to fight.'

The group huddled again around the map, but now with a different purpose. H could read maps at lightning speed and get a mental image of the lie of the land based upon its contour lines.

'Here,' he said, pointing, 'we make sure they see us go into this wooded area. We'll lay low the other side of this ridge, but post a sentry at the top of one of these trees. When they reach here the sentry fires a shot at the moment they reach the ridge. They'll turn towards the gunfire, they won't be able to stop themselves. Then we pour over the ridge. We'll need to be on them double-quick, knives at the ready.'

'Who takes the tree?' said Kuba.

'Zaida,' said H, 'she'll keep calm until the moment comes.'

'When the moment comes,' Kuba advised, 'we all need to be quick, utterly ruthless, or we will lose.'

'Absolutely correct Kuba,' said H. He turned and took in the faces of Zaida, his boy, Yorkie Ted and Jarek Dydowicz, '…but have a look at this lot – you're preaching to the choir here son. Ruthless they know about.'

104

Aleksei Mikhailov always followed orders – to the letter. He'd come up the hard way in the Republic of Dagestan in the North Caucasus region of Russia, where poverty was a constant companion. Despite the end of communism and Russia's vast oil reserves the region had never experienced economic or financial stability. It did receive subsidies from the central government that made it just about possible to scrape by, but joining the army had been the obvious choice and Aleksei soon discovered that doing the bidding of his superiors with total conviction got him promoted, and promotions meant money, which meant food and medicines for his sick mother, who he loved unconditionally.

When he was posted to a covert operation in the middle of Scotland with orders to do nothing but keep out of sight until contacted, he obeyed without question. He and his ten men had been hiding out in the Scottish Highlands for several weeks without receiving any new orders. He'd started to enjoy it, living in the wild, taking down the odd deer to supplement their rations. Keeping their cars out of site, moving around at night to find a new bolt hole.

'You are there as insurance,' his commander told him, 'just in case we need you. Just don't be found – dig in deep, keep quiet and enjoy the hunting. That is all.'

When the command came in to find, intercept and eliminate a small group landing in a boat at Stonehaven he was happy to have something to do. Some of his men had been getting edgy and it was becoming harder to slap them down. A decent kill was just what they needed.

Mikhailov had been ordered to kill the whole group with extreme prejudice and dispose of the bodies in the mountains. When the lookout he'd sent to monitor their landing and subsequent actions called with details of the route they were taking everything fell into place. A long stretch of quiet road meant plenty of opportunities to take them out. They arrived early, fanned out and waited.

He'd been told to be careful, because the target group contained people who knew how to look after themselves. True, they'd been lucky and escaped across the loch, but all he'd really seen was an ill-disciplined, poorly equipped ragbag of fools who would offer little resistance when their time came. When he saw them emerge from the loch, like rabbits terrified by the howling of the wolf, he knew they were playing into his hands by heading for the mountains. Perfect. No need for any more rifle fire. They'd be able to get up nice and close, and finish the job.

'We will jog around loch, keep at constant speed, it will take us no more than an hour to catch them. Have your knives at the ready – we will take them at close quarters.'

105

It took thirty minutes to reach the spot where H had decided they would make their stand – a forested area of tall Scots pines ended abruptly as the land rose sharply to a high ridge. H pointed out the tree he wanted Zaida to climb; it was no easy task getting up it but her adrenalin helped pump her upwards, scampering from branch to branch until she reached the top.

The rest of H's army made their way to the top of the ridge and disappeared on the other side. They lay there, hearts pounding, waiting, not knowing who was coming or how many of them there would be. The men arranged themselves in a line, just below the crest of the ridge.

'Pop?' said Little Ronnie, lying next to his dad.

'Yes son?'

'If we don't make it, if we die here, I mean, er, I just wanted to say…'

'I know son, I know,' said H, 'no need to say it. At least we can go down together, fighting. I can think of worse things.'

H cleared his throat and gave his final orders.

'Right, from now on not a sound. No matter how long we have to wait here, no matter how much tension you feel, not another dickie bird until we hear Zaida's gun go pop. Then it's over the top faster than you've ever moved in your fucking lives, knives at the ready, screaming like banshees.'

***

Zaida had been on all types of training courses in her life and many had included field work, although this the first time she had really been out in the big wide world, with a gun in her hand and real men to kill. But her usual calmness prevailed as she waited high up in the tree, using her mindfulness techniques to sharpen her focus and prepare herself for their arrival.

She took one last deep breath and looked down with absolute focus at the ten men, quietly moving in single file, as they moved into and through her field of vision, led by a tracker following the clear trail of footprints H and co. had left behind. She identified their leader and made him her first target.

'Wait until they're at the top of the ridge,' H had told her. 'If you fire too early, we lose. Wait until they can almost see us, until they have as little reaction time as possible. Then treat whoever's in front to a bullet in the nut. One shot only, remember. Anyone who hears it might just think it's a hunter.'

The men themselves were moving like hunters, not wanting to make a sound. Zaida waited, and waited, and waited as they passed under her tree and came close – very close – to the top of the ridge, until the leader was close enough to plant his boot on its uppermost point, and could see over it. She watched him scour the land before him, as far as the horizon, with his binoculars.

Slowly the leader raised his second foot to align it with the first. Zaida fired, without qualms or doubt, straight down into the top of his head. Aleksei Mikhailov fell to the ground, forward over the ridge's top, and his men, as H predicted, turned instinctively to face the source of the gunshot.

106

H knew all there was to know about unarmed, close-quarters combat. From his young football hooligan years to his army experiences to the multitude of scraps he'd had as a police officer, he knew it was all about two things: speed of reaction and ruthless brutality. The trick was to get through whatever resistance your opponent might offer, get in close and crack on; focus on the body's weak points.

The first man to attain the ridge went down like a dead weight, Zaida's bullet gouging a chunk out of the crown of his head as he went. H surged over the ridge so quickly that the next nearest man barely had time to raise his knife before his arm had been broken and two seasoned fingers thrust under his right eyeball, instantly crushing the inner occipital cavity. H then ducked behind his newly-blinded man as another knife came at him and, with a hand-speed faster than a tired and wounded middle-aged grizzler should have been able to muster, he delivered a blow to the second assailant's throat with a devastating follow-through, crushing the windpipe. He snatched up the knife of the blinded man struggling to get himself upright and cut his throat with it from behind, and stabbed it hard though the skull of the voiceless man. The sight of H leading the charge like this exhilarated and emboldened his men, and they swarmed over their enemy in a frenzy of bloodlust.

The men they were fighting, well trained and hard as nails, rallied after the initial shock, but by the time they'd managed to get amongst their assailants they were seriously depleted with five of them lying dead or out of action, bleeding heavily into the cold Scottish earth.

It came down, for a time, to a series of intense one-to-one encounters, all surveyed from on high by Zaida. She was in the grip of mounting and conflicting emotions – horror at the animal rawness of the bloodletting, excitement triggered by the sight of H in full-on berserker mode. He was roaring, and moving, like a lion – here wrenching a knife from the hand of a man straddling a prone and injured Jarek and plunging it, sideways, through his neck – all the while scanning the scene for signs that his boy was OK. He needn't have worried; Zaida saw from her perch Little Ronnie lift a man clear above his head, turn quickly on his heels and drop his victim straight down onto the point of the ridge, breaking his back.

107

Zaida continued watching intently, closely. She wanted to help – to fire another shot, but the fighting was close-up and personal. She hesitated, the chances of hitting someone on the wrong side were too high. She watched on as a bayonet pierced Yorkie Ted's leg and he was smashed to the ground. His enemy, rifle raised and bayonet attached, was preparing a finishing thrust. Her choice was made.

She fired, and missed. The Yorkshireman's attacker spun around and released two shots up into the tree, in the general direction from which he'd heard the shots come. Ted was on him in a flash, kicking him over from behind, grabbing his rifle, and plunging the bayonet into his stomach with a twisting motion, ripping his guts to pieces. The man's death throes – the writhing, the kicking, the screams of agony – were terrible to witness, and it seemed like a long time for death to finally take him, his ancient Russian curses dying slowly in the wind.

Silence reigned. It was the deep silence of the cold winter north, and in it H and his people contemplated the scene: ten dead men, lying in various states of mangled disfigurement, blood pulsing or ebbing from their wounds. Jarek, injured; Yorkie Ted, injured; H, Kuba and Little Ronnie standing, breathing heavily, feeling the adrenalin and cortisone surge through their bodies, lost in the moment.

And then out of the blue the silence was broken, by a rustle and snapping of branches high up in one of the Scots pines, as of a heavy weight beginning to shift, and slide…and Zaida came crashing into view, slowly at first but then more quickly, as gravity took her and she cascaded down the side of the tree and hit the ground hard.

H ran and knelt beside her. She was not moving. Her eyes were wide open. There were small rivulets of blood seeping from her eyes and the corner of her mouth. H felt himself begin to shake, his chest begin to heave. Kuba joined him, kneeling gently on Zaida's other side and moving his hand over a bullet wound in her chest. He and H raised their heads simultaneously, looking into one another's eyes. H lowered his head again, and felt for a pulse at the neck, while Kuba did the same at the wrist.

They both came up empty. Zaida was dead.

108

They sat in silence, spread out in a wide semi-circle around the bodies of the men they had killed, as the afternoon darkened and the wind began to pick up. They were all lost in their thoughts, or attending to their wounds, and nobody spoke for five minutes.

H broke the silence.

'Alright then gentlemen,' he said calmly. 'Stock take. Injuries?'

'Stab wound on left thigh,' said Yorkie Ted. 'On the deep side but nothing to write home about. The tourniquet is holding. Found a medical kit in one of the Russians' backpacks, so I've dosed myself up with painkillers. I've sorted Jarek out as well, but I don't see either of us climbing many mountains for a day or two.'

'Jarek?' said H.

'Left leg calf muscle stabbed – could have been much worse, tendon is OK – and right upper arm. Broken nose, bruised rib and some smashed teeth. Pain OK, but trouble walking.'

'Right then,' said H, 'You two will have to head back to the cars – you're not up to what we've got ahead of us, and you'd slow us down too much. We've got to push on now. Little Ronnie will go with you and see you right.'

'But Pop, I…'

'No, son. Don't argue with me now. They won't make it without your help. You've seen what it's like up here, and it'll be getting dark soon. Equip yourselves with what you need from the Russians' supplies, and pile some rocks around Zaida's body so the critters can't get at her. We'll sort that out later.'

'No, we need to deal with her funeral now, H,' said Ted.

'Why?'

'Well, she was a Hindu. By birth, anyway. We need to send her off asap, they don't hang about. Should be done on the same day or the next, before dawn or dusk, whichever comes first.'

'It'll be dusk soon, by the look of it,' said Kuba.

'So what do we do?' said H.

'Well,' said Ted, 'far as I know we wash her, wrap her in some sort of shroud, put her on a funeral pyre and send her off.'

'Fuck me Ted, you sure about all this? How long's it all going to take? We've already lost the best part of a day and me and Kuba have got a tough night ahead of us. I…'

'No, Pop,' said Little Ronnie, 'Ted's right. We've got to do this properly.'

***

Kuba and Little Ronnie sorted everything out under Ted's supervision – H could hear them hustling and bustling about, but sat with his back to them, too choked to watch, or speak.

'Alright H, we're ready for her now mate,' he heard Ted say at length. 'She's all set. I can do the honours, but someone needs to say a few words. You knew her best.'

God give me strength.

'Pop,' he heard Little Ronnie say, quietly, after some time, into his ear. 'Come on Pop, everyone's waiting. We've got to get this sorted…come on, I'll help you up.'

H, feeling like he'd arrived at the most exhausted moment of his life, rose slowly to his feet with the help of his son and turned to face the pyre and the group of men around it. It was now almost dark, and bitterly cold. He staggered forward and took his place at the side of Zaida's covered body.

H looked at Ted, who gave him a wink and nod of encouragement.

But he could not find words inside him – not on the tip of his tongue, or the back of his mind, or anywhere else. Little Ronnie held his arm. H closed his eyes. The words came.

'Well,' he said, 'I didn't know you all that long, Zaida, or all that well. I'm not going to talk about how beautiful and lovely you were, it needs no comment. Everyone could see it, it just flowed out of you. But I will say this. You were the first one to understand the trouble we're all in, and…and you had more brains, and guts and conviction than anyone else I've ever known. You're worth a thousand of the people who killed you, and who killed Ronnie, and have attacked our country. Rest assured that we're going to stop them, and make them pay. For you, for Ronnie, for all of us. Off you go, my lovely, it was a privilege knowing you. I'll see you when I get up there. If the big man upstairs lets me in. Which I doubt. Anyway, rest easy.'

He finished speaking. All was quiet once again, except for the low sound of suppressed sobbing coming, it seemed, from one unidentifiable source. It spoke to, and for, all of them.

H gave them five minutes alone with their thoughts before moving them on.

'Alright boys, time to go. Son,' he said to Little Ronnie with a hug, 'you take good care of these two, they're the best of men. Keep going as you are, and one day you might be like them. And stay safe. Wait for us at the boat. Kuba, you and me had better get weaving.'

109

'She's dead,' Andrew said when Amisha entered the room five minutes after him.

'Dead? What do you mean, dead?'

'Well, I mean dead.'

'You just found her like this?'

'Yes, just a couple of minutes ago. I was all set for my grilling, but I got no answer when I knocked on the door, so I just walked in, and...'

'Anybody else know yet?'

'No. I've just been sitting here, waiting for you to arrive.'

Amisha got down to brass tacks

'OK. Initial observations or thoughts about cause of death?'

'None. No idea – no visible signs of anything untoward. Maybe all the stress got to her, heart attack perhaps? I know the Deputy Commissioner has really been on her case lately. I thought she looked the worse for wear when I saw her earlier, but then so does everyone else.'

'Cardiac event, eh? Well it's possible, I suppose,' said Amisha, 'but you know what H always says about coincidences. Think about it: she gets wind of an assassination plot to end all assassination plots, is begged to send it up the chain as a matter of urgency...and the next day just happens to drop dead in her office? No, Andrew, it's much more likely that this is evidence that we're right – that someone very senior in the COBRA system is a traitor.'

Amisha returned to her examination of the body. She checked the throat and neck, abdomen and back, arms and legs for cuts, abrasions, syringe holes, any breaking of the skin, but found nothing.

'Ingestion, then,' she said, turning to Andrew.

'You mean poison?'

'Yep.'

Amisha moved around the office fast, switched-on and scanning for clues.

'Andrew, coffee cup on the table – just a few dregs at the bottom, looks like she drank it not long ago. Here's what I want you to do: go and report Hilary's death. That'll cause a fuss like we've never seen here before. When the chaos starts you take this over to Toby in the lab, and tell him I need him to put it to the front of the queue and get these dregs analysed. Tell him me and H say it's the most important test he'll ever run. Do it without anyone noticing, and be mindful of fingerprint issues.'

'OK ma'am,' said Andrew, knowing there was no other choice.

110

Brad was hunkered down and happy. He felt alive, and free, and at one with the world, at peace with his impending death. He'd had his last drink of ice cold water from the stream just below his foxhole, and was working his way through the last meal of his life. It was not the feast fit for a king that he read they used to give the condemned the night before they were hung, back in the old days, but the last of his army ration supplies. It was industrial fodder, dried and compacted. But it tasted good; his senses were sharp, sharper than he could remember them being since his days in the Middle East; he was watching, listening, sensing atmospheres, and waiting, completely tuned into the present. Yes, the fodder tasted good, as the sound of the wind rustling through the pines sounded good, and the sight of the stars looked good. He was alive.

He heard sporadic shots in the far distance. He wasn't aware that people in these parts hunted at night – for sure they hunted, every chance they got, but at night? It seemed a little strange, but it was far away, back in the mountains.

Nothing could bother him now: not the sniffer dogs, who would be attracted away from his immediate vicinity by the vast number of squirrel corpses he'd carefully left rotting, and the liberal quantities of matured dog urine he'd left in the correct places; not by the police tramping through the area, who would not be able to follow his expertly concealed footprints; and not from the drones and helicopters buzzing overhead, which were easy to elude in forested areas if you knew what you were doing.

His world had shrunk now to the smallest, most concentrated point possible. To his foxhole, his own little world; to the sound of the rain, the calling of the night birds;

to the tree he would climb in the morning; and to the view of the carpark and pathway leading from it to Crathie church. These things were everything now, the last he would ever know. These, and the pain; a shockwave moved through his body, tearing at him, trying to bring him down. He took a deep breath and surfed the pain, going further into it, accepting it as a sensation, a sign of life.

The wind dropped, and the pain subsided. He was calm again. His mind was clear, his soul at rest. His last night on earth. He was pleased it would end this way, and glad the journey was finally almost over. Just one last thing to do.

111

'I tell you what, mate,' said H, 'this is worse than the fucking Falklands.'

'What is?' said Kuba. 'The howling winds? The freezing night fogs?'

H said nothing; he knew what was coming.

'You wouldn't last five minutes in a Polish winter. You English – obsessed with the weather, but unable to handle any. Don't make me laugh. Anyway, we need to find a place to rest up until it gets light – we're probably going around in circles.'

'Alright son, seconded. Do the honours will you, and find us a plot? I am absolutely knackered.'

***

H had known bad mornings before – a lifetime's worth of late nights and shocking hangovers had made him an authority on them.

His mind woke up before his body did, and he lay awake, thinking and trying to work out where he was and what should happen next, a long time before his limbs responded to the commands he was giving them. But before that came the pain. It was still everywhere – Agapov had dished out a proper beating, no doubt about that.

His limbs began to respond and he struggled, like a man heaving himself up the side of a steep mountain, up onto his knees. He was in the shadow of an enormous tree. The rain had stopped, and the fog had cleared, but God he was cold. Teeth-chattering cold. He became aware of a small fire nearby, and crawled around seeking its warmth.

'What time is it?' said H

'Just after seven. How are you? You look like Christ taken down from the cross.'

'What time is it?'

'Seven o'clock, I said it's seven o'clock. It's a good job we're on our fucking holidays.'

'How far out are we?'

Kuba already had the map spread out.

'Well, we're here,' he said. 'It's about five miles, as the crow flies, but you, my friend, are not a crow. Considering the condition you're in, and the two mountain passes we'll need to go through, I'd say we'll need a good three and a half hours.'

'Alright then son,' said H, 'let's crack on.'

He struggled to his feet, stretched as best he could, pulled on his pack and began to stride off in the direction Kuba had indicated. But Kuba did not follow.

'H,' he called, 'come back for a minute, we need to talk.'

'No, keep up with me mate – you can say what you need to say on the way.'

H marched on, slowly, trying to get himself going; Kuba was forced to raise his voice.'

'H…are you OK? Are you sure you're up for this? It's always been a long shot, but…'

'Of course I'm fucking alright. What are you talking about?' H shouted, over his shoulder.

'H, you need to get focused and have a proper look at yourself. You've had a hard time in all this – people close to you being killed, a beating that would have put another man in bed for weeks. You look like you're struggling, my friend, I just…'

'OK mate, got you. Thanks. You think I'm going to bits and you want to give me a little pep talk. Lovely. Understood. But, believe me, mate, I've been here before, and I'll either make it or I won't. The next few hours will tell.

342

But we haven't got time to stand about here having a therapy session. Let's get cracking.'

112

H and Kuba marched on, at H's pace, up onto a low but rocky mountain trail. A watery sun was climbing in the sky. After a windswept night on a wet ground in freezing fog the only way was up.

H's phone rang. Amisha.

Jesus wept…what am I going to say to her about Zaida?

H let the phone ring, making Amisha wait until he was ready, and answered.

'Blimey, you're up and about bright and early, Ames, it's only just gone half seven. Nice and eager – like it…what's happening down there?'

'It's Hilary.'

'What about her?'

'She's dead.'

'What?'

'She was found by Andrew, dead in her office. No autopsy yet and no physical signs of any attack. Some people are speculating a heart attack, all the pressure and stress taking its toll.'

'Not fucking likely,' said H, 'she promised to take all this upstairs and now she's dead, not fucking likely at all. What are your thoughts, Ames?'

'My working hypothesis is poison. There was an empty cup of coffee on her desk, I'm having it analysed.'

'Sounds plausible,' said H.

During normal times H and Amisha might have spent time talking about Hilary and lamenting her loss. But these were not normal times.

'Do we know who she spoke to?'

'I know she had a meeting with the Commissioner and Deputy Commissioner, but apparently there were representatives from the intelligence services and high ranking civil servants there as well – the usual COBRA crew. No minutes were kept – I'm asking around trying to find out if she raised it there, or with someone else earlier, off the record.'

'Find out the names of everyone there Ames. They are our chief suspects. Look into all of them, their backgrounds, sympathies, see if you can find anything. Drop everything else and scour the backgrounds of the top brass. This is top priority.'

'OK... one other thing, H.'

'What?'

'Well, the bad guys must know you're coming.'

'Yeah, we already met the welcoming party.'

'What happened? Is everyone OK?'

'Yeah, it's...OK. There was a bit of argy-bargy, but we're past it now. Most of them have gone back to the boat. Me and Kuba are pressing on. I'll brief you fully later. Thing for now is have they learnt that their men failed, and, if so, do they have other obstacles to put in our path? We're about three hours out from the spot Kuba likes the look of, and three and a half hours from the Queen showing herself at the church.'

'Jesus – that's cutting it fine, is there anything you can do to cut that down?'

'Well, Ames, you could fiddle about with your computer and see if you can get these fucking mountains out of the way.'

Amisha laughed, in the way only H could make her. 'Alright, guv, I'm on it,' she said.

'Good girl. Oh, and one other thing while you're at it – can you upload my brain into a new body or something? This one's just about reached its sell-by date.'

113

H and Kuba stopped for water at eight o'clock. Three hours to go. H was breathing heavily, and his legs and feet were killing him. The terrain they'd been struggling over would have suited a mountain goat better than it did him; steep gradients, followed by deep valleys with bitty rock underfoot, followed by slippery rain-soaked slopes.

'Kuba, what do you reckon, give it to me straight. Can we get there in time, at this rate?' said H through burning lungs.

'No, my friend, I could, but we can't. I think this is a bridge too far for you. You've almost used yourself up.'

H slumped to the ground and sat on his haunches.

'Alright son, you always were a straight talker. I'm tired, mate. Dead tired. I can't really think any more. Help me out, what happens next?'

Kuba got down next to him and spread out the map.

'Look,' he said, tracing his finger across it, 'if I power on I can reach this forested area where the shooter – if there is one – is most likely to be. Remember, it's more than half a mile outside the security perimeter. There shouldn't be too much activity on the ground, and with a bit of luck I can get in close and see what I can see. But…'

'But what mate? Spit it out, for fuck's sake.'

'It's a big ask – it always was. This guy will be world class, and completely dug in, and familiar with everything around him, and he will be very difficult to spot.'

'Go on.'

'Well, I may spot him, at some point he may reveal his position as he preps the shot, or goes up into a tree, and I may be able to take him with this rifle I took from one of the Russians, and…'

'OK mate, I get it – it's a bastard job. But let's get straight to the point, shall we? What is it you're really trying to say?'

'That we'd probably be better off creating a diversion, making a big show inside the perimeter, attracting the attention of the people on the ground before the Queen gets into the crosshairs. Get them to cancel the appearance.'

'Ah,' said H, 'you want me to get inside the perimeter, all guns blazing, make myself a sitting duck by putting on a show – and probably get myself shot at by the best marksmen in the country. Yes? In the hope that I can stay alive long enough to convince them I'm not some random nutter and they should listen to me. While you get in place unmolested and maybe have a crack at our man if all that fails? That is your plan?'

'Yes.'

H didn't think long about the new plan.

'OK. It increases our chances, and we have no choice. Pass me a few more of them pep pills from the Russians' medical kit, and I'll see you when I see you.'

114

Well-known to be an early riser, the Queen rested, breakfasted and ready to roll at nine o'clock, and though there were two hours to go before the service she indicated that she'd like to get going as soon as possible to maximise the time she could spend with the crowds.

There was a great buzz of anticipation in the area. As a rule the Queen holidayed at Balmoral in the high summer, not the winter. But she'd been persuaded that London was too dangerous and relocated to what was known to be her favourite place.

Mortimor-Dagwood summoned Chief Inspector Dimless and informed him that they would be setting off sooner than expected.

'Her Majesty,' he said, 'proposes the following revised itinerary. We leave now…'

'Now, at nine-fifteen, are you…?'

'We leave now,' said Mortimor-Dagwood, as if the policeman wasn't there, 'and make our way to the car park by the church. Her Majesty is in the mood for a lengthy walkabout, and the crowds are extensive, so let's say that takes us up to ten-thirty. This is when she would like to enter the church, as she wants to pray before the service.'

Dimless stood and took it, saying nothing, knowing he had no choice.

'All in all, the service will take about an hour, so at midday Her Majesty will leave the church and head back to her car, again via walkabout. All good?'

Dimless nodded his head, again said nothing, turned smartly on his heels, and marched out at speed to talk to his people.

***

Mortimer-Dagwood was in the second of the four-car convoy. Her Majesty was in the third with her Ladies-in-Waiting, smiling pleasantly and waving to the large crowd that had gathered to meet her. The convoy drew to a halt at the parking area, five hundred yards from the front of the church.

The crowd had been tightly managed. All of the members of it had been searched as they entered the one-and-a-half-mile security perimeter, and tightly controlled upon arrival at the viewing area. The crowd was supplemented by some of Mortimer-Dagwood's staff, who led the general cheering and flag-waving. The man himself checked the coverage on his tablet in the car. Everything was going swimmingly. He was thoroughly pleased with the spectacle and smiled broadly as he opened the Queen's door and held her hand as she made the effort to raise herself from the car seat.

'This way, your Majesty,' he said, steering her in the direction of the crowd. She received some flowers from a young child, smiling with her customary aplomb, before turning back to the church, accompanied by the watchful eye and presence of Dagwood-Mortimer, who was following her like a shadow. His tall, lean, angular frame loomed large above the Queen as she moved through the crowd, obscuring the view of many of them.

Over a mile and a half away, high up in his tree, Brad was also struggling to get a bead on her. As she approached the door of the church he knew exactly where she was but couldn't line up a clear shot with the tall guy in the way. He waited, and waited, and waited for his split-second opportunity, and she was gone. Inside. Out of harm's way, for now.

Goddammit.

He hadn't banked on this. It was not part of the plan. He closed his eyes and breathed deeply, waiting for another wave of excruciating pain to pass. He'd just have to get her on the way out, he thought, and risk a double-tap. It would be difficult, he'd need to re-adjust quickly and get the second shot off before her small army of security operatives launched themselves on top of her. But the elements were on his side – a cold clear day, no wind. He would bide his time.

OK, double-tap it is then. No problem.

115

Local weather patterns in the Cairngorms are legendary –
and H was in one. H marched on before deciding he'd have
to go up higher for a bit, as the mist was thickening.

*Whatever… I'm bursting through. Got to get there… I've got to get
there.*

He checked the map and figured he'd reach the boundary
of the perimeter in an hour or so. It was 9.30am.

*If I keep going as I am I'll get there around half-ten. That'll have to
do.*

He'd miscalculated the length of the upward slope he was
traversing. It seemed to go on forever, and before long the
localised area of thick cloud had enveloped him.

He realised he'd lost his way and stopped moving. The
time on his watch crept past ten o'clock, ten-fifteen…He
began to feel desperately anxious. Time was slipping away;
and he was up here, stuck in a cloud.

*Hold tight, son. Keep still and wait until the weather clears, or
you'll wind up running around in circles.*

He fished out his phone and called Amisha, wondering if
she couldn't get him some sort of weather update. She
answered from what seemed a world away, down in London
in the safe and warm.

'H, I was just about to call you. What the hell's going on
up there?'

'What do you mean?'

'The Queen is already inside the church. I'm watching it
now on the BBC – she's already inside, waiting for the
service to start. Have we got it all wrong? There's no word of
anyone trying to have a pop at her. Have we done all this for
nothing?'

'Steady Ames, steady. Firstly: no. Maybe he just missed her on the way in. Maybe he'll do the business when she comes out. He's there. I can feel it in my water. Secondly: why did she go in early? It's still nearly half an hour until eleven o'clock.'

'They say she wanted to spend more time than usual meeting the public. It's a PR thing I think – you know, reassurance in frightening times and all that.'

'I see. Well, maybe this turns out in our favour. The weather's bamboozled me though, I'm waiting for a big fuck-off mist to clear.'

'And how's Kuba? What's the plan?'

'He's gone on ahead, I'm not as young as I used to be, I was slowing him down. He should be just about in place now, setting himself up by that forested ridge.'

'And you?'

Just going full steam ahead, planning to get to the perimeter and cause enough fuss to get them to listen to me. Or get shot. One or the other.'

'So, basically, you want to cause enough drama to spook the authorities and let them know there's bad things happening.?'

'Yep. It might liven them up when it comes to getting her out of there. But I'm stuck halfway up a fucking mountain.'

'And the weather?'

'Thick cloud where I am.'

Amisha's end of the line went quiet for a spell, but H could almost hear the gears in her head moving.

He waited as long as he could.

'Speak to me Ames, speak to me.'

'Well, I think I might have a workaround for this H. I saw a thing in Brick Lane recently. If I can just hack into the wi-fi they're using up there…Listen H, I'll keep you posted. Stand by your phone.'

116

Kuba made good time across the lower path he'd taken; most of his journey was through a rock-strewn mountain pass that rose only gradually to a modest height which did not necessitate a trek through the clouds. Sure, the ground was crunchy and tricky underfoot, but Kuba was in tip-top shape for a man of his age and scrambled along just fine.

He reached the point he'd noted on the map – the trail ahead of him thinned out and began to rise much more steeply, and there were high hills banked up either side of him. All that was required was a scramble up the slope to his left and he'd emerge onto flat land with a view of the forested ridge above Crathie.

He slithered up, taking care to keep his head down as he neared the top of the slope, and bingo – there it all was, spread out before him just as he'd visualised it. The flat meadow half a mile before the trees began, the forest rising steeply in the distance, the bank of trees at the front of the ridge, higher than those around it, that he'd calculated to be the most likely spot for a shooter to choose. A high tree there, he knew, would have an absolutely commanding view of the village, and a direct line of sight to the front of the church.

It was 9.45am. He took a photo of the lie of the land with his phone and set off, keeping as low as he could – he knew the shooter would now be established, high in his tree, zoned in on the image of the church captured in his rifle's sight, but also that his man would survey his surroundings as a whole from time to time, on the lookout for any police and dogs that might have wandered out beyond the fringes of the security perimeter. The last thing Kuba needed was to be spotted on open ground by a Grade A marksman.

He reached the fringes of the forest, slowed to walking pace, got down lower still and began to make full use of his special operations training in Bieszczady. Anyone who could move, track and hunt through those parts on survival rations, avoiding the wolves and remaining undetected, was a force to be reckoned with. The further in he got the more Kuba felt a part of the forest, and the more he tuned into the memories from that earlier part of his life, when he'd been trained to defend the eastern fringes of his country from potential Russian incursion.

His blood was up – composed and focused as he was, inching carefully on in search of his prey, his every sense humming and buzzing.

117

The mist was beginning to clear, and H could see a little further into the distance. But he was still stuck, and still cold, and still running out of time – only faster now, it seemed – and still waiting for Amisha to get back to him. The pep pills had done their job but now he was coming down, having to work hard to control his agitation.

He needed to act, but felt suspended, held back, utterly stymied. He looked at his watch: 10.45am.

Christ, she'll be coming out of the church in not much more than an hour...

He sat down, out of steam, near the end of his tether, wondering if it was not time, finally, to give up hope and let fate take its course, like other people did.

Turn it in... I could just turn it in and give up. For once in my fucking life.

The phone rang.

'OK H, listen up, we can still crack this.'

'I'm all ears,' said H without much hope.

'Right, don't worry about trying to get into the perimeter and kicking off, I've figured out Plan B, and you don't need to be in Crathie for it to work. I won't go into details now, but I'm going to create pandemonium in the area in front of the church. The crowd will think the world is coming to an end and scream up a storm, but the authorities will understand themselves to be under attack and they'll go onto a war footing and get the Queen out of there. Trust me – this'll work.'

'Yes, but...'

'No buts, H. This will get the job done. Time is of the essence. This is the best we can do in the circumstances. The way forward now is for you to get over to where Kuba is and back him up, so we can give the situation a double-whammy. I've spoken to him – he has sight of the treeline he thinks the sniper is working from.'

'Are you having a laugh, Ames…how the fuck will I find him?'

'When we've ended the call, go back to the menu screen and go into messages. It's more or less like email. I've sent something to you. Open it. It'll activate a screen you haven't seen before, but don't panic. You'll see a green circle blinking and a directional path leading towards it. Follow the path. The curser is Kuba. He knows you're coming, and he's waiting for you.'

'How long'll it take me to get there?'

'About an hour, if you press on and just stick to the path. Don't worry about what's around you, just follow what's on the screen. It's just the same as the satnav in a car. It'll get you there.'

'Are you sure about all this Ames? I'm as fucked as a horse arrived at the knackers yard.'

'No you're not, H. You're Harry Hawkins – just sort yourself out and get rocking. And H, follow the screen, whatever you do just follow the screen.'

118

Kuba crept back and collected H as he entered the forest, panting like a dog and looking much the worse for wear, at 11.30am. There was no time for chit-chat.

'Take a minute to catch your breath and then fall in behind me,' Kuba whispered. 'We have a good position, well concealed, with a view of the church looking down and the shooter's treeline looking up. Make as little noise as possible, we'll be there in six or seven minutes…let's hope nothing happens before we get back. Stay low, be as quiet as you can.'

Complete silence reigned in the forest on the way back in, but a little further afield H could hear the hubbub of the crowd, no doubt building itself up for the Queen's re-emergence from the church and, a little closer, what sounded like the faint humming of a drone, or drones.

'Here,' said Kuba, 'down here. Sit down and collect yourself. Drink some water. He's up there, somewhere, I can smell him. Now we wait.'

***

H looked at his watch, again. 11.35am. He'd made it with minutes to spare and had now managed to calm his breathing, and collect his thoughts after his short but intense march through the mist. He was very still, lying on his stomach next to his friend, looking up and scanning the trees for any flicker or movement. There was nothing.

Everything in their line of sight, upon the forested ridge, was still. Ahead of them, all was quiet.

But something behind them, a little way back, was stirring. It began with a small buzzing, too low to be

357

registered by two eagle-eyed men waiting for the twitch of a branch, a momentary flash of a human form. But it was getting louder – little by little, it was getting louder.

'What the fuck is that?' said Kuba.

H turned around to have a look and saw two circular black drones buzzing haphazardly along the ridge, high up and just behind them. They put him in mind of old-school drunks, being asked to walk the line and ending up comically careering back and forth across it. He watched them for another minute – until Eleven fifty-eight, he noted – and was about to turn himself around again when their course, and their movement through the air, changed. The drunks had taken possession and control of themselves and were now moving swiftly and surely in a long wide arc above the valley, heading towards the church.

'Keep your eyes front mate,' he whispered, 'but be aware that something is about to happen behind us, near the church. A couple of drones are closing in on it. They don't look like they could do a lot of damage, but…'

'But what H, but what?'

The penny dropped with a clunking sound, deep inside H's head.

'But I think they're here to help – they're dive-bombing the crowd outside the church.'

'Dive-bombing the crowd? And this is helping us how exactly? H, did you find another stash of those Russian pep pills, or…'

'No, no…listen. Can you hear them all shouting and screaming? The drones are swooping and circling right above peoples' heads. Panic is breaking out, people trying to run out of the area, security people rushing in. It's Amisha. She's using them to create hysteria. The security people will read it as an attack. They'll treat the Queen's exit as an emergency evacuation now.'

'OK, but he's still up there. He has no way out now.'

'Yep, we've got him, one way or another. Watch the trees Kuba, keep watching them fucking trees. It's chaos down there. Amisha's flushing him out, he's going to have to show himself now.'

119

Brad watched in disbelief as the well-ordered crowd turned into a hysterical, rampaging mob, running in all directions, screaming in fear. It all seemed to him, at first, like a total over-reaction; but then he recalled that rumours were rife in the big cities that some of the drones circling the skies were carrying highly toxic chemical agents.

He snapped himself to attention and refocused – he was now in the business of trying to second-guess the security services' response. They would regard the drone activity as an act of war and deal with the Queen's evacuation accordingly.

There's no back way out. Nothing at the sides either. They've either got to spring her out of a window somewhere or bring her out through the front.

The drones were shot out of the sky. More police and security people appeared and started herding the remaining spectators out of the vicinity. The area immediately around the church was being made sterile. Marksmen fanned out around the church and grounds and hunkered down. A helicopter appeared and hovered directly above the small graveyard, bringing drama to the scene the way only a helicopter can. A line of vans filled with armed men parked up along the entire length of the front of the church, obstructing Brad's view of the door. Brad understood – they'd concluded the church itself might be a target. They were going to take her out.

There was nothing else for it: he would have to fire blind, and fire hard.

No product, no payment. That's the deal…that's always the deal.

He waited until he saw the church door open slightly. He knew there was no way his target would be among the first out, in the vanguard. She'd be kept back, way back from the door, until her car, or van, had been prepared. From a sniper's perspective it was wall-to-wall, high grade, bulletproof vehicle hell.

Wait...wait.

His finger caressed the trigger. He brought all his genius for concentration into the moment, fighting hard to resist the urge to just stand up and start blasting. It was late in the day now; his life was over. He wanted to forget all his caution, his calculations, his planning, his obsession with details, his dry intelligence, his self -control and cut loose, just stand up high, here in his tree – look ma, top of the world! Blam Blam Blam. A blaze of glory.

Wait...wait. She'll be out in the next group that comes. They always bring them out in the second wave.

The second wave of people exiting the church appeared; he saw the blur of the motion in little spots, between the vehicles, but when it came to framing a target he couldn't really see a damn thing.

God-fucking-dammit. Enough with this shit.

Without thinking he burst up, up from his prone position and onto his knees. He steadied himself on a branch and took aim.

Kuba reacted first, with a speed H had never seen before. He fired off two shots before H's brain had registered the movement he'd seen in the tree, and carried on firing until H sorted himself out and joined in the firing.

'Stay down,' said Kuba, 'stay down and just empty your weapon into that fucking tree. Give it all you've got.'

H did as Kuba suggested and together they threw everything they had at the man in the tree – or at least at his vicinity. The tree exploded in a maelstrom of flying branches, shattered fragments and dizzying noise. H watched in amazement as the tree was effectively cut in half a third of the way down. They continued firing until H realised something was wrong.

'Stop shooting!' he shouted to Kuba above the noise. Kuba gave him a quizzical look, but did as he was asked.

The shooting carried on – there was a massive barrage coming up from behind them, as an uncountable number of weapons blazed on, cutting the tree and the man in it to shreds.

'Fuck me mate, that's what you call backup,' said H, turning back to try and see what was what. He turned again quickly to face front when he realised the game was up, and saw that their man was done for and that his bloody, bullet-ridden remains were about to take the same long, strangely slow tumble down the side of the tree that Zaida had.

'Down, H, stay down,' said Kuba. 'Your people will be coming up behind us, and they won't ask questions before they shoot. We'll have to get our exit strategy right on this one.'

'Alright, alright – slow down K, I hear you. Here, listen mate, you still got them Russian smoke bombs in your pocket?'

***

H and Kuba emerged from the smoke into the reception party waiting below, stripped to the waist, arms raised and moving very, very slowly. The smoke cleared and they saw a group of paratroopers, eight-handed, awaiting them downslope, with their weapons raised and trained on them.

'Down, now – down on the ground! Hands behind your back! Now!' barked a chorus of voices.

They hit the deck as quick as they could, slithered onto their bellies, put their hands behind their backs and lay there, frozen and anxious, as heavy boots scrambled up the slope.

They were both subjected to silent below-the-belt searches where they lay, and then pulled up onto their knees without ceremony to face their captors.

They were led by a young sergeant, looking flushed and not a little twitchy. He opened his mouth as if to speak, but H got there first:

'Hello son, good shooting. I'm Harry Hawkins, formerly of New Scotland Yard and 19 Para. I think you'd better take us in for a debrief.'

EPILOGUE

1

One month later

Little Harry was becoming quite a handful. He'd thrown a wobbler, and his breakfast spoon, across the floor the moment he realised it wasn't one of the brands he liked, and stared Olivia in the face with a look that said, 'I will not budge.'

'You're as stubborn as your father,' she said as she picked up the breakfast and cleared the mess.

'He doesn't fancy that love,' said H, smiling broadly and dressed up to the nines in his new Marks and Spencer suit and tie. H had never been one to follow fashion. But he was in a terrific mood as he picked up his son and threw him into the air. Olivia winced as he came back down safely into his father's arms. H gave him a hug and a huge kiss before placing him back in his chair.

'They didn't have his usual brand, looks like I might have to go out and find it.'

H gave out a raucous laugh that seemed to bring sunshine into the house before sweeping Olivia off her feet and kissing her all over her face and head.

'Careful Tiger, remember your back.'

H laughed again, picked up his keys and headed for the door and his meeting with Amisha.

After he'd left and Little Harry had settled down for a nap Olivia did what she always did now, when she had a few moments. She sparked up her tablet and went directly to Joey Jupiter's Blog. Joey didn't blog as often as he used to, but today she was in luck and her eyes lit up when she saw a recently loaded post.

WHAT HAVE WE LEARNED

Well, boys, girls and others, here we are. We have been through the valley of death but now it seems we are coming out the other side. We have all learnt many lessons, and maybe this blogger more than most.

It's a month now since the attempted assassination of the Queen was foiled and our fortunes began to turn. Although much speculation and several conspiracy theories about the events of the last few months abound it is clear the authorities have started to get the situation under control, and many of the instigators of the trouble and their treacherous enablers have been rounded up. A semblance of normality is returning to our shores.

Though a full inquiry into the extent of foreign involvement in the attempt to destabilise the UK has yet to begin, we have learned a salutary lesson in how precariously balanced our democracy and our freedoms are. Freedoms that have taken thousands of years to come to fruition can be undone in the wink of an eye, so we must be forever on our guard. There is no golden rule that says democracy will replace dictatorships in this world. I have learnt that if we want to be free then we need to make a stand.

As I am sure you are aware I have been close to events at the heat of the troubles and even participated in activities that served to undermine our enemies. For obvious reasons, I cannot provide details or the names of the people I have met who have made such a difference these past few months.

But I digress. The purpose of this blog is not to brag about my exploits but to praise those who cannot be named. I have learned that in times of extreme crisis it is possible for a handful of people to turn the tide. The purpose of this blog is to thank them for their courage and for doing the right thing. You should believe me folks when I say it truly was a small group of resourceful people who turned the tide in our hour of need. If I had the gift of Churchillian rhetoric I might say something like 'Never, in the field of human endeavour...' – but I don't, so I won't. Suffice to say we should be forever grateful that such people exist and I extend them our eternal thanks.

You know who you are.

Olivia closed her laptop, walked over to the framed picture of her and H on their wedding day and kissed his image softly on the head.

2

Amisha insisted on it. H wasn't entirely sure why, but Amisha insisted on it. She was probably just using it as an opportunity for a proper talk. She hadn't seen him since his arrest in Crathie, what with his long period in detention and everything else, and there were things he still needed to know.

They arrived by car in front of the Redeemed Christian Church of Our Lord in Basildon, Deputy Chief Commissioner Jane McPherson's home town. Her funeral was classified as a Category II departmental funeral with some military-style honours. The type of funeral reserved for the non-traumatic death of distinguished high-ranking police. There'd be official police pallbearers, a guard of honour, a eulogy from the Commissioner and other members of the upper echelons of the police service, and a last radio call. It had taken a while to arrange, given all the troubles and the circumstances of her death.

'Not a lot of redemption to be found here, I shouldn't have thought,' said H as they walked inside. It was an austere place with little adornment, a small altar below a life-sized wooden crucifixion scene. They'd made it just in time. H nodded to faces he'd known for half a lifetime as they crept along the aisle and found space on the end of a pew near the front.

H sat stony-faced as the service got underway. The vicar's introductory sermon, a few hymns. H wasn't one to look at the songbook, let alone participate in the singing. Amisha turned to the pages instructed as the hymns rolled by, but couldn't bear to engage in a ritual of loving remembrance for the treacherous woman who'd murdered Hilary Stone.

370

The Commissioner was on next and gave a stirring speech about a wonderful woman and police officer who was taken too early, given she had so much left to offer. He was a fine orator and the congregation erupted into applause when his stint at the pulpit had ended – everyone, H observed, except Amisha, who was concentrating on an older couple at the front, sobbing deeply at the loss of their loving daughter. She didn't know them, but it was partly for them that Amisha had made the choices that had led them all here.

The service came to an end and the grieving family filed out of the church followed by the congregation. Amisha said her goodbyes to colleagues and went to join H, who had eschewed all the post service social stuff and gone straight to his car.

'Jump in Ames,' he said, "we need to talk.'

3

'OK , Ames, talk me through it. Why am I here? What's so important about McPherson? I never even met her.'

'OK, let's get one thing straight. I don't want to talk about Zaida, at all. I'll put you in the picture on McPherson, and Lambert and the rest of it. But not…'

Tears began to cascade down Amisha's cheeks. It looked to H like the dam was about to burst, and he got ready for it. But she took a long, deep breath, wiped her face and sat upright. He put his arm around her shoulder and gently kissed the top of her head. She took another big breath, and began.

'OK. She was in it H, up to her neck. McPherson. She didn't appear on Zaida's list – or hit list, as we should call it – because she was better than the others at covering her tracks. But she slipped up in the end, as the pressure built.'

'How?'

'Well, as I told you, Andrew and I got to Hilary's body first. I sent Andrew to Toby with a coffee cup I found on Hilary's desk. Off the radar.'

'And?'

'The obvious. Cyanide.'

'What about the report, Toby's report said natural causes?'

'I got him to doctor it.'

'He's a stickler for the rules. What did you say to him?'

'I persuaded him.'

'How?'

'I persuaded him.'

'And he's secure? On board?'

'Don't worry. He'll tell nobody. I told him some of our story. I turned him round, and got him to check the cup for prints and DNA.'

'OK…go on.'

'Well, I'd had my suspicions about McPherson for a while. The way she kept pushing for us to investigate the internal political extremist angle, parroting the stuff people like Lambert were coming out with.'

'Trying to keep everyone off the scent. Supporting fake news with fake policing.'

'Exactly, but it wasn't only that. I had a gut instinct about her, like something about her was off, didn't add up. I did a bit more digging around in her past and found something that really rang alarm bells…'

'Come on Ames, spit it out.'

'She was connected to Lambert. They went way back, he endorsed her and supported her when she was spotted, earlier in her career, and selected for the female leaders fast-track programme. It turned out they'd been lovers, on and off, for years…She also spent a couple of years in Russia when she was younger, studying. I couldn't link her to him directly on that, but their spells there did overlap, and…'

'Too much of a coincidence. Let me guess – you got hold of her dabs and DNA and they fitted the coffee cup?'

'Yes, I broke into her office and collected samples.'

'Fuck me Ames, you've come on a bundle. You broke into the Deputy Commissioner's office? Tasty, very tasty. You'll be telling me next it was you who topped her off,' he said with a grin.

Amisha looked him hard in the eye and said, 'Well H, the thing is…'

4

The area around the church was deserted now, and the late afternoon was degenerating into sleet-drenched darkness. H had a body-memory of his time in the Cairngorms – the cold, the wet, the never-ending discomfort. But this was somehow worse; this empty, small town bleakness in filthy weather. The perfect setting.

Amisha, the sweet, bright-eyed kid he'd taken under his wing not so long ago, was now about to take him into her heart of darkness. He felt for her, for what he and the world had done to her, and he knew what was coming before he heard it.

'How did she die, Ames?'

'I gave her a choice.'

'What kind of choice?'

'A choice of ways to die. I went to her flat with a syringe filled with a substance that would cause cardiac arrest and told her she could inject it. It would look like a heart attack, there'd be no questions asked. All that stress. I'd keep what she'd done quiet, she'd have an honourable ceremony.'

'Or.'

'Or I'd blow her brains out and fake a home invasion, and expose her after her death. I knew she'd take me up on the former option.'

'How?'

'I figured her out. She loved her parents, she was the apple of their eye. She would have wanted them to remember her sweetly, and not heap shame on them. At the end of the day, that would override everything.'

'What was in the syringe?'

'Potassium chloride.'

'So you were judge, jury and executioner?'

'I had a good teacher. We were in a crisis. She had to be stopped.'

H started up the motor and flicked on the wipers to clear away the sleet. He turned to look at Amisha and held her stare for several moments. The history of their partnership flashed once again across his memory. He wondered whether he'd made her like this, that the years of their partnership had made her a different person, or whether it was always there, lying latent. His steely stare was returned with interest, daring him to judge her. He surmised it was probably the latter.

'Fucking hell, Ames,' he said.

'Well, it's off my chest now, dear confessor. What I need now is a drink. Fancy it?'

'Yeah, but we'll have to make it a quick one. I'm getting up early to take Ronnie back to Winson Green. He's negotiated his return. The nicks are filling up again – at least with the non-desperate cases. I think it's a good policy.'

'That's funny,' said Amisha.'

'Well, I wouldn't say that. The authorities are getting things under control, which is good. Not a lot funny about it.'

'No,' said Amisha, 'I'm talking about Ronnie…you called him Ronnie.'

'That's his name.'

'H, you've only ever referred to him as Little Ronnie. That's his name, always has been.'

'Well, he's not a boy anymore, Ames, and Big Ronnie's dead. Now he's Ronnie. That's who he is – Ronnie Hawkins.'

5

'It's so depressing, Pop,' said Ronnie as H eased the car onto the M1 through banked grey clouds and driving rain.

'Nah, you'll only finish up with a little stretch. You can do that standing on your head son. No danger.'

'No, I don't mean that.'

'What then?'

'I mean…it all seems so random, so pointless. All that madness, all that violence and blood and guts everywhere. What was it all for?'

'Hard to say son, to be honest.'

'But you must understand it, you must know what it's all about? If you don't, then…'

'Well, how can I put it? The world's a mad place, and getting madder – that is for certain. And there are a lot of evil bastards about, I don't need to tell you that, but then there always have been. So…'

'So what Pop, you're just telling me the world's a shithole?'

'No, I'm telling you that the world's a hard place, but there's good in it, and that's what we fight for.'

'Why?'

'To protect the good, to help people who need it, to get in between them and the evil bastards.'

'Oh that sounds like a standard speech, another fucking pep talk.'

Ronnie saw his father's hands take a tighter grip on the wheel, his arms straighten out, the muscles in his face tighten and his jaw start to work. Not good.

They rode on in silence for a full minute.

'Listen, you don't talk to your father like that…If I'd ever spoken to my old man like that he'd have knocked me over and given me the full treatment with his belt.'

'What, at twenty-three?'

'Listen, what I'm telling you is this: the country's nearly been brought to its knees, and we've personally lost your uncle Ronnie, and Zaida, and a lot of other good people have been killed or badly hurt. People who should still be here and living their lives…'

Ronnie bit his lip and stared hard ahead into the cold, grey English morning.

'…and you just want to mope about and feel sorry for yourself? I want you to have a good, hard look at yourself while you're up here, think about what sort of man you want to be, how you can live a good life and not just waste your time.'

Ronnie sighed, sunk his head, bit his lip and smiled to himself.

'And anyway, Ron, if you do manage to get a grip on yourself I might have a proposition for you when they let you out…how does *Hawkins and Hawkins*, Private Investigators sound?'

#####

Did You Enjoy this Book?

Thank you for reading our book. If you enjoyed it, won't you please consider leaving us a short Amazon review. Reader reviews are extremely important for independent authors.

Thanks!

Garry and Roy Robson

Other Titles in this Series

London Large: Blood on the Streets

A corrupt system. A city in meltdown. A rogue cop, bent on revenge.

Who will deliver justice?

Blood on the Streets is the first in the London Large crime thriller series, featuring the exploits of Detective Inspector Harry 'H' Hawkins, an old-school London copper with over thirty years of besting villains under his belt. When a bloody international gang war threatens to rip the metropolis apart, 'London's top copper' finds himself under siege as never before.

Haunted by flashbacks of the horrors he experienced in the Falklands War, held accountable for the unstoppable wave of violent chaos that is turning the streets of his city red with blood, hounded and ridiculed by a media he cannot understand and continually thwarted by an establishment cover up of he knows not what, the big man is bang in trouble.

As the chaos in London reaches boiling point can H, against all the odds, bring the streets under control, see through the fog of a high-level conspiracy and rescue his partner Amisha before she is killed by her ruthless kidnappers? And will he himself be forced to step outside the law to do so?

If you like the hard-boiled, gritty and action-packed novels of Martina Cole, Stephen Leather and Andy McNab you'll love Blood on the Streets – let it take you through a thrilling rollercoaster ride through the dark underbelly of criminal London.

This title is free

To load down your **FREE** copy of Blood on the Streets go to www.londonlarge.com

London Large: Bound by Blood

Mass murder stalks the land. A damaged, hurting cop at war with his son.
One last shot at redemption.

Bound by Blood is the second book in the London Large crime thriller series, featuring the exploits of Detective Inspector Harry 'H' Hawkins, an old-school London copper in a new world. H is only just back at work after a mental and physical breakdown when pop superstar Bazza Wishbone is murdered in the dead of night in a top London hotel. As the whole world looks on in horror H investigates the crime in the only way he knows how; he embarks on a full-blooded, uncompromising search for the truth.

But the truth can be brutal. As the investigation gathers pace H discovers that his own neglected son has been sucked into the international crime ring responsible for one of the worst mass murders in British history, and has been turned against his father.

H's mission is now no longer merely a search for a killer but also a quest to save his boy and deal with the man who has corrupted him. As events move towards their climax H is faced with a trio of extraordinary challenges: can he find the killer of Bazza Wishbone, get to the truth about the twenty bodies discovered in a mass grave in Kent, and find and reconnect with his son before he is spirited out of the country – or worse?

If you like the hard-boiled, gritty and action packed novels of Martina Cole, Stephen Leather and Andy McNab you'll love Bound by Blood – let it take you through a thrilling, rollercoaster ride through the dark underbelly of criminal London.

###

Bound by Blood is now available on Amazon

Bound by Blood: Chapter 1

This was his time. At this moment in his life he could have anything he wanted; women, yachts, a mansion with a swimming pool in deepest Surrey. It was the women he wanted more than anything now – now he'd made it. After a short lifetime of dreaming and praying for success here he was, on the top floor of The Ritz, overlooking the London skyline. He felt like London was all his – like he really owned it. A world of endless possibilities lay before him.

'Sort another line out will you babes?' he said to his latest impossibly sleek, skinny and beautiful supermodel girlfriend. Jacynta Packington nodded yes and carried on getting set for another night of fun and games in the marbled bathroom. That was where Bazza liked to go large. They'd met a few months before, at a celebrity bash to celebrate another number one single. Their whirlwind romance was near perfect for the times, a celebrity journalist's ideal story delivering a stormy on/off affair of two beautiful young stars at the top of their game. Since they'd met the tabloids had been filled with lurid tales of the affair, of the arguments and bust-ups and reconciliations, of the sex and the drugs, of their infidelities.

Kicking back, he recalled the previous week's centre spread in one of the red tops that gorge on celebrity relationships like vultures on the corpse of a slaughtered animal, and a wry smile spread across his face: 'Bazza Beds a Brace of Bouncing Beauties.' Sex God, he thought, No. 1 Party Animal. His world was moving faster than a tornado tearing up a row of houses, and it was a world full of low-hanging fruit – he hadn't even bothered to ask the names of the bouncing brace of beauties but had just picked them out of the scrum that had been lying in wait for him as exited the back entrance of another gig in another provincial town, a town he'd forgotten about as soon as he'd left it.

He hadn't yet reached the point where all the media hype annoyed him. In fact he loved it. He craved the attention that he felt was his due, now that he was one of the world's most marketable superstars. Jacynta had read the article of course, like she'd read all the others since they'd hooked up. But she had a career to build and being associated with the new Prince of Pop was doing it no harm at all. So she kept quiet – she'd take what she could before the relationship blew up once and for all. Faithfulness was most definitely not on the agenda.

Bazza had never been the sharpest tool in the box, and had dropped out of school at 16 after failing his exams. But he was an angular, blonde and blue-eyed boy with a finely chiselled face, had a passable voice after auto-tuning and just the right amount of late-adolescent arrogance to make him irresistible to the kiddies. And his backstory was spot on: raised in an utter dump by a single mum after his father overdosed on barbiturates, in and out of trouble with the police as a boy, a proper little tearaway. Redeemed by his love of music. The British public ate it all up and begged for more, voting for him in their millions as he romped home as the winner of Britain Blazes Bright, the most watched talent show on T.V., the show that had propelled him to global stardom.

Within the space of a year Bazza Wishbone had gone from wannabe nobody to one of the biggest pop stars on the planet. He didn't know how long it would last but one thing was for sure – while it lasted he was going to gorge on success like a hungry wolf. He was going to gorge until he could gorge no more.

'Come on then babes, I'm ready for you,' he heard Jacynta call from the bathroom. The marbled bathroom. He bounded in to find her dressed in high heels, a dirty look and not much else. She bent down to get at the marching powder set out by the sink; Bazza followed suit.

The charlie hit the spot, and as the drug surged through his body he stretched out on the cool floor in a state of euphoria and thought again of just how lucky he was. When Jacynta eased herself down to join him – lower, lower, as if in slow motion – he wondered if it was all a dream. Could he really be here, top of the charts, top floor of the Ritz, with one of the world's top supermodels getting on top of him? Her silky-smooth blonde hair caressed his face; her lithely perfect body joined itself with his. His pulse raced, and as the blood pumped around his body he embraced her and proceeded to make the most of his good fortune. Yes, he could take whatever he wanted now – every minute of every day belonged to him, up here on top of the world

Much later, when they had finished, he curled up on the floor and Jacynta brought him a pillow and cover from the bedroom. He was tired now. 'If this is a dream I hope I never wake up,' he thought, as he closed his eyes in the hope that sleep would take him.

Bound by Blood: Chapter 2

Outside the Ritz the killer stood behind a street light, head down low. It was cold and raining so he didn't look out of place wrapped up in his long trench coat, collar up, ensuring the hoodie he wore beneath his coat covered his face. He looked up at the top floor and considered his course of action. He knew without doubt his prey was in there. He wasn't sure of the room number, but he soon would be.

He'd been outside now for some time and had seen Bazza and Jacynta pull up in a limo, witnessed the army of photographers descend on him like a pack of braying hyenas, watched as the army of fans, all young girls, screamed with uncontrollable hysteria, with unquenchable desire. He wondered jealously what it was that fed such unthinking adoration. He watched as the celebrity boy-god of the moment, shielded by an phalanx of heavies, pushed his way through the crowd to the front of the hotel, stopped for a brief moment to wave and soak up the adoration and disappeared into a world of opulence the likes of which his adoring army would never see or know.

The killer decided to go for a walk, to let things settle down a bit. He set off up Piccadilly, took a stroll around Leicester Square and found one of the many pubs that adorned the side streets of London's West End, all the time keeping his head down low, hoodie on, shades pushed up on to the bridge of his nose. He ordered a pint of London Ale and supped slowly as he reflected on the task at hand.

He was a small fish, and felt the resentment that small fish feel when they spend most of their time swerving from the path of big fish. Tonight, however, would be different; tonight he was going to take down a big fish, and to hell with the consequences.

If Bazza wants to play in the big pond he better watch out for the fucking sharks.

Ping! He read the text that came through on his mobile and replied. The meet was on. The landlord called last orders so he went to the bar for a second pint. Just enough to steel his nerves but not too much to make him sloppy. He sat over it until the girl he'd been waiting for entered the pub. Svitlana Kovalenko caught his eye and moved across the room; she looked tired and drawn but was pretty with light auburn hair and a winning smile. She sat down next to him.

'Hello,' she said in one of those east European accents that had become so much a feature of the metropolis in recent years.

'Have you got it?'

'Yes,' she replied.

Svitlana worked on the desk at the Ritz. Like all the central London hotels it could only function now with employees from the far flung corners of the world. So many employees started and finished their stint in the great global village each month that it was almost impossible for anyone in authority to keep up with the constant flux.

Finding a chancer who was just passing through to describe the layout and confirm Bazza's room had been easy. She had already provided the killer with a plan of the top floor suites. Two grand and a glass of wine was a small price to pay for the information he was about to receive. He had given her to believe he was a thief who'd like a chance to root about in some of the pricier rooms. What difference did it make to Svitlana? Where she came from, money talked. In any case she'd be heading home soon to take care of her ailing mother. She passed him an electronic key and a piece of paper with the name of a suite on it and walked her 'thief' through the plan. She would text when the coast was clear. In through the tradesmen's entrance, through the kitchen

388

and up the lift reserved for staff. Turn left, 3rd door on the right, a quiet entry: game on.

He knew Bazza had the girl in tow, the one he'd seen him with in the papers. He didn't have a plan for her. He'd cross that bridge when he came to it. Then the retreat, back down in the same lift, lower ground floor, stroll out through the car park and melt into the London night. Head down, hoodie up, shades on tight. He knew he'd be on every CCTV in London, then on the TV and in the grainy pictures in every paper. He also knew the images would be useless as long as he kept his face under wraps.

Svitlana herself had no idea who he was. He looked at her with a mixture of desire and contempt, contempt for the unsuspecting, the weak and naive. She was pretty, no doubt about that, and in different circumstances he'd be all over her whether she liked it or not. But as the pretty girl left to return to her late-night duties he had no regrets that the only thing he would be giving her tonight was an appointment with the grim reaper.

Time for the kill.

####

London Large: Tipping Point

A father and son standing together. A brutal political conflict. Can they, and their bond, survive?

Tipping Point, set against the backdrop of the dark days of the 1974 three-day-week crisis and wildcat strikes, follows the fifteen-year-old Harry Hawkins through a crucial, formative week in his life. When his father persuades him to get involved in his strike-breaking activities Harry is launched onto a steep learning curve that will test both his ability to hold his own in a violent street-level struggle and his allegiance to his father.

Can, and should, the strike be broken? Will the son live up to the expectations of the father? Will they get out of the conflict in one piece?

This short story is free

To load down your **FREE** copy of Tipping Point please go to www.londonlarge.com

London Large: Lockdown

Book four of the London Large series has a working title of "Lockdown" and will be published in 2018. Details to be announced on the London Large website at http://www.londonlarge.com

If you wish to be kept informed of the release date, please subscribe to the website.

London Large: Sharp Shorts

A collection of short stories detailing events from Harry Hawkins' earlier life will be released in 2017. Details to be announced on the London Large website at http://www.londonlarge.com

If you wish to be kept informed of the release date, please subscribe to the website.

About The Authors

Roy and Garry Robson are, unsurprisingly, brothers from the Elephant and Castle, south east London.

Their father (variously a pig farmer, cab driver, haulage contractor and general ducker and diver) and mother (homemaker, cook and doctor's receptionist with a well timed left hook) raised them and their siblings with some old fashioned south London working class values. These included hard work, respect for their elders and a willingness to duck and dive when required.

One day, whilst enjoying a beer or two, they decided to write a Crime Thriller Series. They awoke the next day and were surprised to discover that they meant it.

Roy lives in Bromley and works as a Service Delivery Manager for an International IT Consultancy. Garry lives in Krakow and is now, of all things, a sociology professor. Both career choices served as a source of confusion and humour to their parents, who were born and raised in the days before computers and sociology professors existed.

Harry 'H' Hawkins, the protagonist of the London Large novels, is not based upon Garry or Roy, neither of whom would survive the first chapter of a Harry Hawkins novel.

Website http://www.londonlarge.com
Twitter https://twitter.com/londonlarge
@londonlarge
Facebook https://www.facebook.com/LDNLarge
Email: mailto:info@londonlarge.com

Printed in Great Britain
by Amazon

65691563R00226